M000076912

What people are saying about ...

The Ultimate Gift

"I love this book. I see this book becoming one of the great and inspiring movies of all time [2001]. It touches my heart and soul deeply, profoundly, and permanently, and will yours too. Happy reading of *The Ultimate Gift*."

Mark Victor Hansen, cocreator, #1 New York Times best-selling series Chicken Soup for the Soul

"*The Ultimate Gift* provides us all with a marvelous glimpse of life as it is and as it can be when we change our attitudes. Jim Stovall delivers an important message of hope and possibility."

Dr. Robert Schuller, senior pastor, speaker, and author

"*The Ultimate Gift* was fabulous! Margie and I just loved it. This is going to make a major difference in our company."

Ken Blanchard, coauthor, *The One Minute Manager*

"A wonderful story. Needed wisdom for young and old alike. Written by one of the most extraordinary men of our era."

Steve Forbes, president, CEO, and editor-in-chief, *Forbes* magazine

What people are saying about ...

The Ultimate Life

"Ultimate wisdom periodically endows our rebellious planet with a fresh young keeper of the flame. Jim Stovall from his demi-darkness has illuminated ultimate truth—that to do unto others is all we know and all we need to know."

Paul Harvey, ABC News

"What a treat! After reading *The Ultimate Gift*, it was truly a joy to read the follow-up. The message in each book is certain to provide food for thought. You will find it difficult to put either one down once you have started until you have read it through."

John Wooden, Basketball Hall of Fame player and coach

"I told you and many others you could never write another book to equal *The Ultimate Gift*. Last night I had the joy of reading *The Ultimate Life*. I was wrong. I hung on every word. I laughed and was wonderfully blessed and deeply moved as I reread the lessons in a more vivid setting.... Thank you for helping change the world one book at a time."

Charlie "Tremendous" Jones, founder
and president, Executive Books

"Nothing is more powerful than a story, and no one tells better stories than Jim Stovall. Like *The Ultimate Gift* before it, *The Ultimate Life* touches the reader in places we desperately need to be touched."

Richard Exley, author, *Witness the
Passion* and *The Alabaster Cross*

Look into the depths

OF ANOTHER'S SOUL
AND LISTEN,

not only with our ears,

BUT WITH OUR HEARTS
AND IMAGINATION,

and our silent love.

—Joye Kanelakos

The Ultimate Gift

BY
JIM STOVALL

David C Cook

transforming lives together

THE ULTIMATE GIFT AND THE ULTIMATE LIFE
Published by David C. Cook
4050 Lee Vance View
Colorado Springs, CO 80918 U.S.A.

David C. Cook Distribution Canada
55 Woodslee Avenue, Paris, Ontario, Canada N3L 3E5

David C. Cook U.K., Kingsway Communications
Eastbourne, East Sussex BN23 6NT, England

David C. Cook and the graphic circle C logo
are registered trademarks of Cook Communications Ministries.

All rights reserved. Except for brief excerpts for review purposes,
no part of this book may be reproduced or used in any form
without written permission from the publisher.

The Web site addresses recommended throughout this book
are offered as a resource to you. These Web sites are not
intended in any way to be or imply an endorsement on the
part of David C. Cook, nor do we vouch for their content.

This story is a work of fiction. All characters and events are
the product of the author's imagination. Any resemblance
to any person, living or dead, is coincidental.

Mass Market ISBN 978-1-4347-6445-4

© 2001, 2007 Jim Stovall

Printed in the United States of America
First Edition 2009

1 2 3 4 5 6 7 8 9 10

040309

Introduction

You and I are preparing to take a journey together within the pages of this book that you hold in your hands. I want to thank you for the investment you have made and will be making in our journey.

I believe that when you read the last page of *The Ultimate Gift*, you will be a different person than you are at this moment. At that point, our journey together will have ended, but your journey into the fullness of your destiny will be just beginning.

Like any other journey or trip you have ever taken, it becomes more meaningful based upon the special people in your life who share this trip with you. I am sure you can remember wonderful trips or vacations that you have been on in the past. As those pleasant memories of your travels come back to you, they are filled not only with your destination, but the special people and loved ones who shared the journey with you.

When you have concluded reading *The Ultimate Gift* and have begun in earnest your life's journey, my fervent hope is that you will share *The Ultimate Gift* with friends, family, and the special people in your world who make your life's journey priceless.

Thank you for sharing this part of my life's journey and for allowing me and the *The Ultimate Gift* to travel with you on part of your life's journey.

Respectfully,
Jim Stovall

Table of Contents

One

In the Beginning

*A journey may be long or short,
but it must start at the very spot
one finds oneself.*

I t was in my fifty-third year of practicing law, and my eightieth year of life here on this earth, that I was to undertake an odyssey that would change my life forever.

I was seated behind my mahogany monstrosity of a desk in my top-floor, corner office of an imposing building in the most prominent section of Boston. In the marble foyer, the antique brass plate on the outer door reads Hamilton, Hamilton, & Hamilton. Of the aforementioned, I am the first Hamilton—Theodore J. Hamilton, to be accurate. My son and grandson account for the remainder of the Hamiltons in the firm.

I would not say that we are the most prestigious law

firm in all of Boston, because that would not be totally circumspect. However, if someone else were to say that, I would not go out of my way to disagree.

As I was simply drinking in the ambiance in my antiquated but palatial office, I was thinking how far I had come since the lean days in law school. I enjoyed gazing upon my wall of fame, which includes photographs taken of me with the last five presidents of the United States, among other significant persons.

I glanced at the familiar sight of floor-to-ceiling shelves of leather-bound books, the massive oriental rug, and the classic leather furniture, all of which predate me. My enjoyment in simply experiencing the familiar environment was interrupted when the telephone on my desk buzzed. I heard the reliable and familiar voice of Margaret Hastings. "Sir," she said, "may I step in and have a word with you?"

As we had been working together for more than forty years, I knew that tone was reserved for the most serious and somber of circumstances.

"Come in, please," I replied immediately.

Miss Hastings entered promptly, securing the door behind her, and sat across the desk from me. She had not brought her calendar, her correspondence, or documents of any type. I was trying to remember the last time Margaret had entered my inner sanctum without some baggage, when she said without preamble or delay, "Mr. Hamilton, Red Stevens just died."

When you get to be an octogenarian, you grow as accustomed as one can to losing friends and family. But some of the losses hit you harder than others. This one shook me to my core. Amid all of the emotions and memories that flooded over me, I realized that I would have to do what Red would expect of me, which was simply to do my job.

I shifted into my lawyer mode and told Miss Hastings, "We will need to contact all of the family members, the various corporate boards and business interests, and be ready to control the media circus that will begin any minute."

Miss Hastings stood up and said, "I'll handle everything." She quickly walked to the door and then hesitated a moment. After an uncomfortable pause, during which I realized Margaret Hastings and I were crossing that line that divides professional and personal, she said quietly, "Mr. Hamilton, I am sorry for your loss."

Miss Hastings closed the door and left me alone with my thoughts.

Two weeks later, I found myself at the head of our massive conference table with all of Red Stevens' various relatives gathered around. The feeling of anticipation—bordering on greed—was almost a physical presence in the room.

Knowing Red's feelings toward the majority of his relatives, I knew he would want me to prolong their misery as long as possible. Therefore, I had Margaret offer everyone coffee, tea, or soft drinks along with anything else she could think of. I scanned and rescanned the voluminous documents before me and cleared my throat multiple times. Finally, realizing that I was stretching the bounds of propriety, I rose to my feet and addressed the motley assemblage.

"Ladies and gentlemen, as you know, we are here to read the last will and testament of Howard 'Red' Stevens. I realize that this is a difficult time for all of us and that our personal losses individually far outweigh any legal or financial concerns we might have this morning."

I knew that wherever he was, Red would enjoy the irony.

"I will dispense with the preliminaries, the boilerplate, and the legalese, and will go directly to the issues at hand. Red Stevens was a very successful man in every sense of that word. His bequests are much as Red was himself—very simple and straightforward.

"I drew up this revised will for Mr. Stevens just over a year ago on his seventy-fifth birthday. I know from our subsequent conversations that this document does, indeed, reflect his final wishes. I will read directly from his will, and you will realize as I read that while this document is totally legal and binding, some of the passages are in Red's own words.

"To my eldest son, Jack Stevens, I leave my first company, Panhandle Oil and Gas. At the writing of this will, Panhandle's worth is somewhere in the neighborhood of $600 million."

Several gasps could be heard from around the table along with one prolonged, audible squeal of glee. I set the document down on the edge of the table and looked over the top of my reading glasses with my most intimidating courtroom stare. After a significant pause, I picked up the will and continued.

"Although Jack will be the sole owner of the company, its management and operations will be left in the hands of Panhandle's board of directors, which has served me so well over so many years. Jack, I want you to know that since you didn't have any interest in the company when I was living, I figured you wouldn't have any interest now that I'm gone. And letting you control something like Panhandle would be like giving a three-year-old a loaded gun. I want you to know that I have instructed Mr. Hamilton to write this will in such a way that if you fight for control or hinder the board or even complain about the nature of my bequest to you, the entire ownership of Panhandle Oil and Gas will immediately go to charity."

I looked up from the will and stared at Jack Stevens. The entire range of possible emotions was displayed on his face. Jack Stevens was a fifty-seven-year-old playboy who had never known the privilege of earning a day's wages. He had no idea of the favor his father had done for him by taking the control of Panhandle Oil and Gas out of his hands. I knew he was feeling that this was just one more time when he failed to live up to his illustrious father's expectations.

I actually felt some pity for Jack as I explained, "Mr. Stevens, the will does direct that each bequest be read in order and that the parties be dismissed after the portion of the document pertaining to them has been read."

He looked at me with a confused expression on his countenance and said, "What?"

At that point, always vigilant Miss Hastings took his arm and said, "Mr. Stevens, I'll escort you to the door."

When everyone had settled back into their chairs, and the level of anticipation had again risen to a fever pitch, I continued.

"To my only daughter, Ruth, I leave the family home and ranch in Austin, Texas, along with all working cattle operations."

Ruth was seated at the far end of the table with her dubious husband and offspring. Even at that distance, the sound of her hands slapping together and greedily rubbing back and forth could be heard. She and her family were so self-absorbed that I do not believe they understood the fact that the entire operation would be managed for them and that they would be kept at arm's length where they could not hurt themselves or anyone else. Miss Hastings promptly showed them from the room.

I cleared my throat and continued. "To my youngest son, and only other remaining child, Bill, I leave the entire holdings of my stock, bond, and investment portfolio. However, Bill, this portfolio will be left in the hands of Mr. Hamilton and his firm to be managed in trust for you and your heirs so that there will be something left to divide when somebody is reading your will someday."

The room continued to clear as each of the more distant relatives received their eagerly awaited windfall. Finally, there was but one, lone occupant of the room remaining with Miss Hastings and me.

I looked down the table at young Jason Stevens, the twenty-four-year-old great-nephew of my longtime friend, Red Stevens. He glared back at me with a look of rage, defiance, and disrespect that only someone who has made a lifelong practice of selfish anger can muster.

He slammed his hand on the table and yelled at me, "I knew that mean old man wouldn't leave anything for me. He always hated me." He stood and began to stomp out of the room.

"Not so fast," I called to him. "You are, indeed, mentioned here in the will."

He slid back into his chair and stared toward me, stone-faced, not wanting to signal the hope he felt.

I returned his cold stare, determined not to speak until he did. Patience comes easily to those of us who have seen eighty birthdays. Finally, when he could stand it no longer, he said, "Okay, what did the old goat give me?"

As I sat down and reached for the document, I heard young Jason Stevens mutter, "I bet it's nothing."

I sat back in my chair and smiled at him as I said, "Young man, it is, indeed, nothing and everything—both at the same time."

Two

A Voice from the Past

*In the end, a person is only known
by the impact he or she has on others.*

Jason Stevens and I sat in silence as Miss Hastings left the room and quickly returned with a large cardboard box. She set the box next to me at the end of the table and took her customary place on my right.

I turned to Jason and said, "Young man, this box was given to me by your great-uncle, Red Stevens, on the day he prepared his last will and testament. The box was sealed at that time and has been kept in our vault per Mr. Stevens' instructions until today. As you can plainly see, the seal is still intact. There are very specific and detailed instructions as to how I am to administer this gift to you."

I broke open the seal, reached inside the box, and took out a videotape. I handed it to Miss Hastings, and she put the tape in the video player contained in the built-in console at the end of the conference room. She sat down next to me holding the remote control.

Jason Stevens blurted out, "What's going on here? Everyone else walks out with millions of dollars, and I get some kind of home movie."

I tried to ignore his smug attitude and replied, "I think it will all become clear to you shortly."

I nodded to Miss Hastings. She dimmed the lights and started the video. After some brief static, the image of seventy-five-year-old Red Stevens appeared on the screen. Red Stevens was a big man in every sense of that word. He had come to Texas out of the swamps of Louisiana with nothing but determination, strength, and the clothes on his back, and during the Depression and war years, had built an oil and cattle empire that rivaled any in the world. He was the kind of man who dominated every situation in which he was involved. Even now, with just his video image on the large screen at the end of the conference room, I could feel the energy level in the room climbing.

Red Stevens cleared his throat and began to speak. "Well, Jason, since you're watching this videotape, we will assume that I have kicked the bucket, bit the dust, bought the farm, and gone on to my just rewards. I know that my instructions have been followed to the letter, so you are viewing this video with my oldest and dearest friend, Theodore Hamilton, and his trusted associate, Margaret Hastings. Son, you don't know enough to realize it, but these are two of the finest people to ever walk God's green earth."

Red paused for a minute and then spoke directly to Margaret and me using a derivative of my name that only Red Stevens was allowed to use.

"Ted, I want to thank both you and Margaret for dealing with all of my in-laws, outlaws, and assorted misfit relatives earlier today. I know that none of them will win any prizes. I also want to apologize to both of you for the sorry attitude that I'm sure Jason has already displayed during these proceedings."

Red paused for another brief moment, cleared his throat, and began again. "Jason, I lived my life in a big way. I had a lot of big accomplishments, and I made a lot of big mistakes. One of the biggest mistakes I ever made was when I gave everyone in our family everything that they thought they ever wanted. It took me many years to figure out that everything we ever do or know or have in this life is a gift from the good Lord. He has a special plan for each of us, and He has provided everything we need to fulfill that plan. I spent many years trying to achieve happiness or buy it for friends and family. Only as an old man did I come to learn that all happiness comes from the gifts that God has given us. Unfortunately, the money and possessions I spread around didn't help people to understand the gifts that have been provided for us. In trying to make up for all the times I wasn't there, I gave them all material things. In doing so, I robbed them of everything that makes life wonderful.

"Gratefully, I also discovered God is merciful, and I believe I've made peace within regarding my shortcomings. However, I think my family members are all permanently ruined. It's like when a horse goes bad. You simply have to take him out and shoot him. Unfortunately, as my lawyer Mr. Hamilton advised me, shooting our entire family would be frowned upon. He also rightly reminded me that God never gives up on people. Therefore, I leave my family in God's hands, and I have taken steps in my will to provide a living for all of these relatives even if they will never experience life.

"You, on the other hand, Jason, may be the last great vestige of hope in our family. Although your life to date seems to be a sorry excuse for anything I would call promising, there does seem to be some spark of something in you I am hoping we can capture and fan into a flame. For that reason, I am not making you an instant millionaire for the rest of your life."

Jason slammed his open palm onto the conference table and began to speak, but was interrupted by Red Stevens' words from the videotape. "Now, Jason, before you mouth off and embarrass both you and me in front of these fine people, let me explain the ground rules here.

"On the first of each month for the next year, you will meet with Mr. Hamilton and Miss Hastings and be given one element of what I call the ultimate gift.

"If you stay the course over the next year, and embrace each element, at that point you will be the recipient of the most significant bequest I can leave you through my will. But understand, if at any time you do not perform as indicated, or if you give Mr. Hamilton or Miss Hastings an undue amount of difficulty, I have instructed Mr. Hamilton, through my will, to stop the process and leave you with nothing."

I heard a deep sigh and exhalation of breath from the direction of Jason Stevens.

Red continued. "Now, don't forget, boy. If you turn out to be more trouble than you're worth—which is not difficult for you—Mr. Hamilton will simply cut you off without another word.

"And, finally, to you, Theodore J. Hamilton," Red

chuckled and continued. "I bet you didn't think I remembered your real name, Ted. I want to thank you for undertaking this little salvage operation on my behalf with Jason. And I also want to thank you for being the best friend that any man ever had. I accumulated a lot of things in my life, but I would trade them all in an instant for the privilege I have of sitting here, right now, and being able to say that Theodore J. Hamilton was my friend."

At that point, the video ended, and we all sat in silence. Finally, Jason turned to me and, in a belligerent tone, said, "That old man was crazy."

I sighed and replied, "Well, young man, it is certain that someone is crazy, and I think this little project is going to give us all the opportunity to find out who that someone may be."

I stood and offered my hand to Jason as I moved toward the door. He ignored my outstretched hand and said, "Wait a minute. What's the deal here? Why don't you just tell me what's going on, and what I get?"

"All in good time, young man," I said to him over my shoulder as I walked out of the room.

I could hear Jason's angry voice as I retreated down the hall. "Why couldn't he just leave me money like everybody else?"

I could hear the calm voice of Miss Hastings reply, "He loved you too much to do that."

Three

The Gift of Work

He who loves his work never labors.

I must say I was rather anxious during the ensuing weeks and very relieved when the first day of the next month rolled around. I was sitting in my office working on other matters trying to keep my mind occupied and off of the fact that Jason Stevens would be arriving shortly.

Finally, the buzzer on my telephone sounded, and Miss Hastings informed me that young Jason Stevens had arrived and was waiting in the conference room. I collected the appropriate files while Miss Hastings retrieved Red Stevens' box from the vault. When we entered the conference room, we found Jason slumped back in a chair with his feet up on the conference table. I strode across the room and slid the box that Margaret had handed me onto the table in such a way as to knock Jason's feet off of it.

"Good morning, Jason," I said. "I'm glad that you found

a chair and are making yourself comfortable. Some people never have learned the proper use of furniture."

Jason dismissed my comment with a bored wave and replied, "Can we just get on with it here? I've got things to do and people to see."

I laughed aloud as I sat down and said, "Young man, I do anticipate you will have things to do and people to see, but it may not be exactly as you think."

I took another videotape from the box and handed it to Margaret. She placed it in the video player and, in a few moments, Red Stevens appeared on the large screen. He said, "Good morning, Ted, and to you, Miss Hastings. Once again, I want to thank you for undertaking this little chore. And, Jason, I want to remind you of the rules. If at any time during the next twelve months you do not perform as called for, or if Mr. Hamilton does not approve of your attitude and demeanor, he will simply stop the process and cut you off from my ultimate gift to you.

"I will warn you about Mr. Hamilton. He may appear very patient and long-suffering, but, young man, if you push him too far, you will find that you have let an angry tiger out of its cage."

Jason looked at me with a bewildered expression on his face. I simply stared back at him.

Red paused and seemed to be remembering days gone by. "Jason, when I was much younger than you are now," he continued, "I learned the satisfaction that comes from a simple four-letter word: work. One of the things my wealth has robbed from you and the entire family is the privilege and satisfaction that comes from doing an honest day's work."

I could see Jason rolling his eyes as he let out a deep sigh.

"Now, before you go off the deep end and reject everything I'm going to tell you," Red continued, "I want you to realize that work has brought me everything I have and everything that you have. I regret that I have taken from you the joy of knowing that what you have is what you've earned.

"My earliest memories in the swamps of Louisiana are of work—hard, backbreaking labor that as a young man I resented greatly. My parents had too many mouths to feed and not enough food, so if we wanted to eat, we worked. Later, when I was on my own and came to Texas, I realized that hard work had become a habit for me, and it has served as a true joy all the rest of my life.

"Jason, you have enjoyed the best things that this world has to offer. You have been everywhere, seen everything, and done everything. What you don't understand is how much pleasure these things can bring you when you have earned them yourself, when leisure becomes a reward for hard work instead of a way to avoid work.

"Tomorrow morning, you are going to take a little trip with Mr. Hamilton and Miss Hastings. You will be going to meet an old friend of mine on a ranch outside of Alpine, Texas. When I was young and struggling to stay alive during the Depression, I met Gus Caldwell. We learned the power of hard work then, and today there's no one better to teach you this lesson than Gus.

"I have already prepared a letter outlining this entire situation to be sent to Gus Caldwell. Mr. Hamilton has forwarded that letter to Alpine, Texas, and Gus Caldwell will be expecting you.

"Please remember, if at any time you do not complete the activities outlined in my will, or if Mr. Hamilton is not pleased with your attitude, this endeavor will simply end, and you will forego the ultimate gift."

The screen went black.

"This is ridiculous," Jason shot at me angrily.

I smiled and replied, "Yes, dealing with you can be trying, but there are some things you just do for friends like Red Stevens. I will see you at the airport at 6:45 in the morning."

Jason looked at me as if he were addressing an imbecile. "Didn't they have any flights later in the day?" he asked.

I replied with more patience than I felt, "Yes, but Mr. Caldwell—I think you will find—is not one who wants to waste any time. See you tomorrow."

Jason left our office, and Miss Hastings made all of the necessary arrangements.

The next morning, just as the airline attendant was preparing to close the door, a bleary-eyed Jason Stevens came running down the concourse. Miss Hastings handed the attendant the tickets for the three of us, and we boarded the plane.

Miss Hastings and I took our assigned seats, which were the first two on the right side of the aircraft in the first-class section. Jason stood there with a confused expression on his face as there were no more seats in the first-class cabin.

He turned to me and asked, "Where's my seat?"

Miss Hastings responded to his question using her most efficient tone, but I knew she was enjoying every moment of it when she said, "Oh, Mr. Stevens, you have been assigned seat 23F."

She handed Jason his ticket stub, and he stomped down the aisle toward the coach seating.

When we got off the plane at the Midland-Odessa

airport, Gus Caldwell was there to meet us. I had known Gus for years as a friend and associate of Red Stevens. We shared a mutual love of our lifetime friend. Gus shook my hand warmly with the callused grip of a man of thirty-five instead of what I knew must be his real age of seventy-five. He greeted Miss Hastings politely but was somewhat gruff with Jason.

He said to him, "Red Stevens was one of the best men I ever met. I don't see how you're going to live up to that."

As Jason was preparing to protest this cold greeting, Gus shot back at him, "Son, why don't you go downstairs and see if you can find the luggage. Make yourself useful."

A few moments later, we were downstairs in the airport, and Jason had, indeed, located all of the luggage. Gus pulled around the parking lot to pick us up at the door in his deluxe pickup truck—a vehicle we rarely see in Boston. Gus held the door for Miss Hastings and me and said to Jason, "Well, don't just stand there, boy. Get these bags in the truck."

Jason loaded all of the luggage in the bed of the pickup truck and then asked sheepishly, "Where am I supposed to sit?"

"You can ride in the back or walk," Gus said. "It's all the same to me."

Gus got in and began to pull away just as Jason scrambled into the bed of the pickup truck. I glanced back and saw him sprawled out among the luggage, rolling from side to side, as Gus summarily ignored all of the speed limit signs as we left the airport complex.

During the ride out to Gus' sprawling ranch, with Jason out of earshot, we discussed memories of Red and our desire to help Red redeem Jason Stevens. We agreed that

Gus would spend the next four weeks communicating his version of the work ethic to Jason while Miss Hastings and I would leave the following day and spend several weeks in Austin, where I was to do some legislative work for another client.

After traversing what seemed to be an endless gravel road, we turned into a driveway that led off into the distance. A sign read: Gus Caldwell Ranch. Friends are welcome. Trespassers will be shot.

After another ten-minute drive, we arrived at a huge ranch house where we were greeted by Gus' extended family, several of his workers, and a number of dogs. Gus led Miss Hastings and me into his comfortable home and yelled back at Jason, "Don't just lie there in the truck, boy. Get the bags."

Gus had informed Miss Hastings and me that the next day would start early at the Caldwell ranch. He decided to let Jason find out the hard way.

The next morning, Miss Hastings and I, and all of the Caldwell family, enjoyed a huge breakfast of monumental cholesterol before 6:00 a.m. As we were enjoying our second cups of coffee, Gus said, "Well, I better go get Sleeping Beauty. This is going to be an interesting day. Real educational, if you know what I mean."

We could hear Gus climbing the stairs and banging open the door to Jason's room. He called out in a thunderous voice, "Boy, are you alive? You're sleeping through the whole day, here. Get dressed and get downstairs."

Gus rejoined us as we chatted amiably over the strong coffee, and a few minutes later, a disheveled, sleepy-eyed Jason joined us. He sat down at the table. No sooner was he seated than Gus rose and said, "Well, that was a good breakfast. Time to get to work."

Jason glared at him and said belligerently, "Can I have some breakfast, please?"

Gus smiled and said, "Yes, sir. First thing tomorrow morning. Nobody ever leaves Gus Caldwell's home hungry. But there's not much I can do if people are going to sleep all day."

Jason looked out the window and exclaimed, "It's not even daylight yet."

Gus chuckled and replied, "That's very observant, son. I thought I was going to have to teach you everything. Now get out to the bunkhouse and see if you can find some work clothes. That's about the most worthless get-up you have on there I've ever seen. We'll be leaving in about five minutes."

Gus agreed to take Miss Hastings and me out to where Jason would be working to see him get started before we left for Austin. We were seated in the truck when Jason stumbled out of the bunkhouse and dutifully climbed into the back of the pickup truck. Before he was seated, Gus shot out across the yard and drove through a gate, bouncing out across an immense field.

Just as the sun was rising, Gus stopped at a remote corner of the ranch where a huge pile of fence posts lay on the ground. Gus jumped out of the truck and yelled, "Boy, would you get out of that pickup bed. I've never seen one for lyin' around like you."

Miss Hastings and I followed Gus and Jason to the last fence post standing in a long line that stretched out of sight. "Welcome to Fence Post 101," Gus proclaimed proudly. He quickly showed Jason how to dig a post hole, set the post, and string the wire in a straight line. Even at seventy-five, Gus Caldwell showed immense strength and incredible stamina. He made everything look easy.

He turned to Jason and said, "Now, you try." And Gus joined Miss Hastings and me near the truck.

Jason stumbled through the process almost comically, and Gus called out, "Well, hopefully you'll get the hang of it before you beat yourself to death. Somebody will come by to pick you up for the noon meal."

Jason seemed alarmed and called out, "How far is this fence supposed to go?"

As Gus helped Miss Hastings and me into the truck, Gus laughed and said, "No more than a mile, and then we'll turn and go the other way. Don't worry. We won't run out of things for you to do. I wish I had a dollar for every post hole good old Red Stevens and I dug all across Texas."

We left Jason there to his labors.

⁓⁓⁓

Almost four weeks later, Miss Hastings and I returned from a successful trip to the Texas state capitol in Austin. Gus, once again, picked us up at the airport, and as we were driving to his ranch, I couldn't help but ask, "Well, how is young Jason getting along?"

Gus chuckled and said, "I wasn't sure he was going to make it. Between the sunburn, blisters, and heat exhaustion, it was a close thing, but I think you are in for a pleasant surprise."

When we reached the ranch, Gus drove us directly to the field where Jason had been working the first day. I noticed that the fence extended far beyond its original point, and Jason was nowhere in sight. Gus drove on a distance, and once we crested a short rise, I spotted Jason in the distance.

An amazing transformation had taken place. Jason

was browned by the sun, lean from his physical labor, and working steadily as we arrived. He waved to us and walked over to join us as we got out of the truck.

"Jason, did you dig all of those post holes and set all of those posts yourself?" I asked.

He seemed to have a gleam in his eye as he answered, "Yes, sir. Every one of them. And they're straight, too."

Gus put his arm around Jason's shoulder and said, "Son, I wasn't sure you were going to make it, but you turned into a really good hand. Your great-uncle, Red, and I discovered nearly sixty years ago that if you can do this kind of work with pride and quality, then you can do anything. I think you've learned your lesson. Now it's time to get you back to Boston."

I was shocked when Jason replied, "I only have a few more to finish up this section. Why don't we leave in the morning?"

The next day, after breakfast, Gus volunteered to drive us to the airport. Jason dutifully carried the bags out onto the porch, but instead of the pickup truck, Gus was driving a new Cadillac.

Jason laughed and asked, "Where's your truck, Mr. Caldwell?"

Gus smiled and replied, "I can't have one of my best hands rolling around in the back of the truck with the luggage. Now let's get you to the airport."

As we flew 30,000 feet above middle America, I couldn't help but think of Red Stevens and the lesson on work he had taught Jason. I hoped the lesson meant as much to Jason as it did to me.

FOUR

The Gift of Money

Money is nothing more than a tool.
It can be a force for good,
a force for evil, or simply be idle.

There are certain times in this life that you find yourself pursuing a course that you are not certain will prove to be fruitful. Then, all of a sudden, out of nowhere, miraculously you receive the smallest sign or indication that you're on the right track. Just such a moment occurred when Jason Stevens came in for our second monthly meeting.

Jason and I were seated in our customary spots in the conference room discussing his work experience in Alpine, Texas. Miss Hastings returned from the vault carrying Red Stevens' box. With no prompting or forewarning, Jason got out of his chair and helped Miss Hastings by taking the box from her and carrying it to the end of the table.

To most people, this, in and of itself, would seem like nothing—or at most an extremely small thing. However, I recognized how Jason had been raised and that he had always taken such minor courtesies for granted. I chose to look upon this incident, even if small, as a positive sign.

Red Stevens stared back at us from the large screen. He had a bit of a mischievous grin on his face which I suspect came from his private thoughts about Jason's work experience on Gus Caldwell's ranch.

His voice boomed out, "Well, Jason, welcome back from the Garden of Eden—better known as Texas. Since I am talking to you now, I will assume you survived a month with Gus Caldwell. I always found that soaking blistered hands helped."

I actually heard Jason let out what might be described as a brief chuckle.

Red continued. "Today, we are going to talk about what may, indeed, be the most misunderstood commodity in the world. That is, money. There is absolutely nothing that can replace money in the things that money does, but regarding the rest of the things in the world, money is absolutely useless.

"For example, all the money in the world won't buy you one more day of life. That's why you're watching this videotape right now. And it's important to realize that money will not make you happy. I hasten to add that poverty will not make you happy either. I have been rich, and I have been poor—and all other things being equal—rich is better."

At that, we all laughed.

Red took on a more serious expression and continued. "Jason, you have no idea or concept of the value of money.

That is not your fault. That is my fault. But I am hoping in the next thirty days, you can begin to understand what money means in the lives of real people in the real world. More of the violence, anxiety, divorce, and mistrust in the world is caused by misunderstanding money than any other factor. These are concepts that are foreign to you because money to you has always seemed like the air you breathe. There's always more. All you have to do is take the next breath.

"I know that you have always flashed around a lot of money and spent it frivolously. I take the responsibility for this situation because I deprived you of the privilege of understanding the fair exchange between work and money.

"Last month, you began to get just an inkling of the pride and satisfaction that can come from doing a good job even at the most menial task. Since money is the result of most people's labor, I think you need to begin to understand it.

"If Gus Caldwell had paid you for the work you performed last month, you would have earned approximately $1,500. I know that it seems like almost nothing to you, but I can assure you it is the going rate.

"When you leave today, Mr. Hamilton will hand you an envelope that is inside the box. The envelope contains $1,500. During the next month, I want you to go out and find five different people who are in situations where a portion of that $1,500 can make a real difference in their lives. I want you to notice how anxiety caused by a lack of money is affecting them in real ways, and how once you give them the money, they can focus on real and important issues in their world.

"I realize that in the past you have probably blown

$1,500 in a few hours with some of your so-called friends. Now it's time to begin understanding what $1,500 can do if it's put in the right place.

"By the end of this month, you will report five such instances to Mr. Hamilton, describing each situation and what you did about it. If Mr. Hamilton feels you have learned the lesson of the gift of money, I will talk with you next month."

Red's image faded from the video screen, and we sat in silence for a few moments.

Jason turned to me and said, "I'm not sure I understand what it is I'm supposed to do. Where do I find these people, and how much—"

I interrupted him by explaining, "Young man, you heard your instructions just as I did. I am not authorized to give you any additional information or assistance. This lesson, like all of the others your great-uncle is trying to teach you, is one you must learn primarily yourself. I can assure you that Red Stevens was a thorough man, and he has given you everything you need to succeed."

I reached into the box and took out a small envelope just as Red had described. I handed the envelope to Jason and said, "We will look forward to hearing from you on or before the end of the month."

Jason rose slowly with a bewildered expression on his face. He turned and slowly retreated to the door. Miss Hastings and I remained in the conference room for several minutes. Finally, she broke the silence. "I don't think he has any concept of what to do with that envelope full of money."

I thought for a moment and then replied, "Most of us have learned about money over a number of years. Jason has been absent from school, and he has a lot of catching up to do."

~~~~~~

It was the next to the last day of the month before we heard from Jason, and I will admit to being a bit anxious about his progress. Jason arranged an appointment for the next morning. At the appointed hour, Miss Hastings ushered him into my office, and he and Miss Hastings sat in the two leather chairs in front of my desk.

Jason seemed a bit nervous and uncertain of himself. I paused for a few moments, thinking about what I might have done had I been given one month to find five people whose lives I could affect with money. I resigned myself to performing my tasks as Red Stevens' attorney and the executor of his estate. I knew that if Jason had not lived up to the letter of the agreement, I would have to end the journey at that point. That was a prospect that did not appeal to me for Jason's sake and, I must admit, for my own as well.

Finally, I turned to Jason and asked, "Well, young man, are you prepared to present your report?"

Jason nodded and drew a piece of crumpled paper from his inside jacket pocket. He cleared his throat and began to speak slowly. "Well, I'm not quite sure if this is right, but here goes.

"First, I was driving late one evening and passed one of those fund-raising car washes people hold in parking lots. It was nearly dark, so I knew they were about done for the day. I asked the man in charge what group this was and how they were doing. He told me that it was a group of inner-city Boy Scouts who were trying to raise the money to go to their Jamboree the following week. He went on to explain that it had been a bit disappointing because this was their last effort, and since they were a bit short, at least one or two of the boys were not going to be able to go. I asked him how much they needed to reach their goal. He seemed discouraged when he replied that they were almost $200 short, and they were going to have to clear the lot within ten minutes. I pulled my car into the space designated and told the boys to do their best job. When they were done, I handed one of the boys $200 and drove away."

Jason looked up at me seeking approval. I merely nodded for him to continue. Although he was still shaky, he seemed to be gaining momentum as he consulted his sheet.

"Next, I found myself at the mall looking for a parking space. I spotted a young woman holding a baby, standing in front of an old car, and shouting at a guy driving a tow truck parked behind her. The two seemed to be really arguing, and since they had one of the best parking spaces, I stopped and asked what the trouble was. The guy told me he worked for ABC Used Cars and that the girl had missed her last two payments. He told me that the payments were only $100 a month on an old junker like that. The girl began crying and said that her baby had been sick, and if she lost her car, she wouldn't be able to keep her job, and then she didn't know what would happen. I asked the tow truck driver how much the balance was on her car loan. He told me it was four more payments of $100 each. I gave him $400 and got a paid-in-full receipt for the young mother. Here's a copy."

Jason dropped a soiled and creased receipt on the edge of my desk, and then he pressed on. "While I was in the mall, I discovered a young husband and wife with two small children shopping in a toy store. Each of the children repeatedly asked for various toys, but their parents regrettably told them that Santa Claus probably wouldn't come this year since their father had lost his job. While the children were at the end of another aisle looking at some stuffed animals, I handed the mother $300 and asked her to be sure that Santa made it to their house this year.

"As I was leaving the mall, I noticed an old woman sitting on a bench. As I passed, she dropped her purse, and when I picked it up to hand it back to her, I noticed that she had been crying. When I asked her what the problem was, she told me that her husband, Harold, and she had been married fifty-seven years and, for the first time in their lives, they just couldn't make it. His heart pills cost over $60 a month, and the pharmacy in the mall wouldn't take her food stamps for the medicine. I spent $200 buying a three-month supply of Harold's heart medication and leaving her $20 to take him out for his favorite lunch."

Jason looked at me expectantly, and I smiled at him and said, "It sounds good so far, but you were instructed to find five examples."

Jason appeared more nervous than ever as he explained, "While driving one day, I discovered a car broken down at the side of the road. I got out and met a young man named Brian. He's about my age, and we found we have a lot in common. I used my cell phone to call a tow truck, and they towed him into a garage. The mechanic said the engine in the car was really shot and needed to be replaced.

"Brian was totally panicked because he needed the car to get back and forth to school and work. The mechanic said it would cost $700. Brian nearly went into shock because he didn't have any money, so I gave him the $700 he needed to get a new engine."

Ever efficient Miss Hastings seemed to have an emotional quiver in her voice as she said, "Sir, that seems to add up to $1,800. I believe the original document called for only $1,500."

Jason seemed alarmed as he leaned forward in his chair and said, "Well, I put in $300 of my own money. Is that okay?"

Miss Hastings beat me to the punch and replied, "Of course, it's okay. Mr. Hamilton is a fair and reasonable man."

She glared at me and said, "Aren't you, Mr. Hamilton?"

I assured both Jason and the indomitable Miss Hastings that I was fair and reasonable, and Jason had learned an important lesson in the value of money. I hoped he would never forget his lesson. I knew I never would.

Five

The Gift of Friends

It is a wealthy person, indeed,
who calculates riches
not in gold but in friends.

T he next morning, Miss Hastings let me know that Jason Stevens had arrived and would be waiting in the conference room. After his successful journey into the realm of work and money, I had hoped that his sullen attitude would have improved; however, upon entering the conference room, I rapidly discovered this was not the case. Before I could even sit down, he started in on me.

"Look. Why do I have to go through all this stuff? This is ridiculous. You have a copy of the will. You must know what it is that I'm going to inherit. Why don't we just cut through all the garbage and get down to the bottom line?"

I smiled at him and said, "Good morning, Jason. It's

nice to see you, too. I had hoped after your great-uncle's lesson in money, you would be more understanding of this process."

I rose to my feet slowly—which is not unusual when you're eighty years old. I gave him a stare that I had used successfully during my years as a judge. "Young man," I said, "you have two—and only two—options. You can go through this process the way Red Stevens laid it out for you, or you can quit right now; but I will tell you one thing, your attitude is putting you dangerously close to losing the ultimate gift that your great-uncle planned for you."

Jason leaned back in his chair and sighed. "Okay, let's get on with it," he said. "What's next?"

Miss Hastings brought in the box and set it on the table next to me. I took out the next videotape, and Miss Hastings started the VCR. Once again Red Stevens appeared and began to speak.

"Jason, as you heard me tell Mr. Hamilton at your first meeting, he is quite simply my best friend. *Friend* is a word that is thrown around far too easily by people who don't know the meaning of it. Today, people call everyone they know their friend. Young man, you're lucky if you live as long as I have and can count your real friends on the fingers of both hands.

"I am now going to share a story with you, Jason, that I promised I would never tell as long as I lived. Since you are watching this after my death, and in the presence of the one whom I promised, I feel comfortable sharing it. As you know, I lived past my seventy-fifth birthday and enjoyed what to most people was a long and healthy life. But this was not always a sure thing.

"I remember when I had just turned thirty-eight

years old and was hospitalized with an extreme fever. The doctors weren't sure what was wrong with me, so they brought in every specialist from across the country. Finally, I was diagnosed as having a rare kidney disease which was incurable. The only hope they gave me was a new procedure called a kidney transplant.

"You've got to realize that this was unheard of at that time, and donors were not readily available as they are today. I called Mr. Hamilton, who has always acted as my attorney, and told him we would need to start a nationwide search to find me a kidney. I was very frightened because the specialist had told me that without the transplant I might not have more than a few weeks. You can imagine my relief when Mr. Hamilton called me two days later and told me he had located a kidney on the East Coast.

"Well, as I'm sure you can guess, the operation was a success and gave me back over half of my adult life. What I'm sure you couldn't guess, and what no one has known until now, is that the kidney that Mr. Hamilton found was his own."

Red paused on the videotape to take a drink of water, and young Jason Stevens stared at me in disbelief. On the big screen, Red continued. "There's only one way in the world to explain something like that, and it's called friendship. Now, Jason, I know you think you have a lot of friends. But the reality is, you have a lot of people who simply want your money or the things it will buy. Except for your time with Gus Caldwell, you've never worked a day in your life nor done anything I would call productive. But you have been the life of the party and an easy touch for a lot of weak hangers-on you casually call friends.

"During the next thirty days, I want you to spend a lot

of time thinking and observing. I want you to find what you feel to be the principles that underlie true friendship, and I want you to be able to report to Mr. Hamilton an example of true friendship that demonstrates your principles. Jason, you will never do anything in your life that will bring more quality to your existence than growing to understand and nurture friendship."

The videotape ended, and Jason seemed to be deep in thought. Finally, he blurted out, "I don't understand. I mean—"

I interrupted him. "I know you don't understand. That's the whole point. I only hope that you will remember your great-uncle's words and, for your sake, by the end of the month you are at least beginning to understand. I will look forward to your report."

I walked out of the conference room, leaving young Jason Stevens to his assignment.

On the last day of the month, Miss Hastings called into my office to let me know that Jason had set up an appointment and would be arriving within the hour. I sat back and thought about my lifelong friend, Red Stevens. I wasn't sure how you could teach someone the depth to which a friendship could grow, especially if the person had never experienced it himself. I will admit to feeling a great sense of doubt and foreboding as I considered Jason's prospects of succeeding in the task Red Stevens had given him.

As we gathered around the conference table, Miss Hastings and I were quiet. Both of us were observing Jason's expression and manner. He seemed to have a lot on his mind. He gave us each a perfunctory greeting and muttered, "I hope that . . . well, I mean . . . I just don't—"

Miss Hastings stopped him by saying, "I believe our agenda today involved your report to Mr. Hamilton on your progress with respect to understanding friendship."

Jason looked at me doubtfully, and I nodded and gave him a brief smile of encouragement.

He began. "I thought a lot about friendship this month, and I tried to come up with the principles that define friendship. The best I can do is to say that friendship involves loyalty, commitment, and a process that includes sharing another person's life. It even goes deeper than that, but it's hard to put into words.

"The best example of friendship I can give to demonstrate my principles is a story that Gus Caldwell told me when I was working for him in Texas. He explained that when he and Uncle Red got started in the cattle business, they had ranches several miles apart, but they and several other ranchers all shared the same range. Each spring, all the ranchers would have what they call a roundup, which apparently involved collecting and branding all of the new calves, called yearlings, which had been born since the last roundup.

"As Mr. Caldwell explained it to me, the young calves simply follow their mothers wherever they go, so as the cattle are collected, representatives from each ranch are present to brand each new calf with the same brand as its mother's.

"Well, it seems that early on, Mr. Caldwell was very concerned that Uncle Red wasn't going to make it as a rancher. So, during the roundup one year, Gus simply branded a number of calves that should have been his own with Uncle Red's brand. He told me that he figured that he had been able to give over thirty calves to Uncle Red through that process.

"But at the end of the roundup, when Gus performed what is called a tally, which is simply counting all the cattle with his brand, he found that instead of being thirty calves short as he thought he should, he actually had almost fifty more than he started with.

"He was confused about that incident for many years until, while Mr. Caldwell and Uncle Red were on a fishing trip, Uncle Red told Gus that when they first got started, he had been worried about Gus making it in the business. Since he didn't want to lose his best friend and neighbor, he had actually branded a bunch of his calves with Gus Caldwell's brand."

Jason paused and glanced at both Miss Hastings and me for any sign of approval. He continued. "That story that Mr. Caldwell told me about my Uncle Red best describes how I understand each of the elements of friendship. I know it takes many years to build a friendship like that, but I think somehow it must be worth it.

"As you know, last month I met Brian when his car broke down at the side of the road. I helped him get a new engine for it, and since then we have done several things together, and I hope that someday we can be friends like Gus Caldwell and my Uncle Red."

Jason looked directly into my eyes and said, "And I hope I can be as good a friend as you were to Red Stevens."

I smiled at him and said, "In my best judgment, you have begun your lifetime lesson in friendship. The only thing I can tell you is that any effort you put into a friendship is always returned manyfold."

I thanked Jason for sharing the story about Red Stevens

and Gus Caldwell. I had known for half a century that they were both great men and great friends. Jason's story, passed to him by Gus Caldwell, was just one more example of great friendship.

Miss Hastings walked Jason out of the conference room, leaving me alone with my memories.

As I sat back in my chair and remembered my lifelong friend, Red Stevens, I reflected that our friendship had begun simply and without either of us understanding what our relationship would grow to be. Jason had learned the beginnings of how to be a friend, and I hoped that his new friendship would blossom into a lifelong treasure giving him as much pleasure as Red Stevens and I had enjoyed.

SIX

The Gift of Learning

*Education is a lifelong journey
whose destination expands
as you travel.*

R ed Stevens' bequest to his great-nephew, Jason, represented the most unusual and, potentially, the most important matter I had ever handled for a client or a friend. As we entered the fourth month of our one-year journey with Jason, I wasn't sure how much progress we were making. He had shown many signs of improvement, but his belligerent, arrogant, and selfish attitude—borne of a life of idle privilege—still showed through from time to time.

As we began our monthly ritual around the conference room table, he interrupted the proceedings before Miss Hastings could even start the videotape.

"Look, I have done everything you have said up to this

point, and this has all been well and good, but I need to have some idea of where we are going here and what I get at the end of all of this. I can't just waste a year out of my life."

I stared at Jason for several moments and tried to think of what Red would want me to say. Finally, I responded. "Jason, it seems to me that your entire life to date has been a series of wasted years. I don't see how this one-year acquiescence to your great-uncle's will could do anything but improve your track record; however, you do have the option to stop this process at any point in time."

He fired back at me, "Can't you just give me some idea of what I am going to get out of this so I can decide if it's all worth it?"

I gave him my courtroom stare and stated, "Young man, I am bound by honor, duty, and friendship to perform each step of this process as directed by Red Stevens. I have no option in the matter. You, indeed, do have an option. Either you play or you don't play, but if you're going to play, you're going to play by the rules. Is there any part of that you don't understand?"

Jason and I locked eyes, and we were in a staring contest that represented a test of wills. Unfortunately for him, my will had been tested many, many times over eighty years, and his was only just now being tested due to the love and concern of Red Stevens.

He finally looked away and mumbled, "Okay, let's play the video."

Red Stevens appeared on the screen and seemed to display a bit more intensity than before. It seemed that as we cleared each hurdle, the one before us seemed to take on more importance and significance.

Red began. "Jason, the next element of the gift I am trying to leave to you encompasses knowledge and learning. As you know, I never had the benefit of a formal education, and I realize that you have some kind of degree from that high-toned college we sent you to that is little more than a playground for the idle rich."

Jason leaned back in his chair, slammed his fist onto the table, and blew out a long stream of air.

Red continued. "Now, before you get your feelings all hurt, I want you to realize that I respect universities as well as any type of formal education. It just wasn't a part of my life. What was a part of my life was a constant curiosity and desire to learn everything I could about the people and world around me. I wasn't able to go to school very long after I learned to read, but the ability to read, think, and observe made me a relatively well-educated man.

"But learning is a process. You can't simply sit in a classroom and someday walk offstage with a sheepskin and call yourself educated. I believe the reason a graduation ceremony is called a commencement is because the process of learning begins—or commences—at that point. The schooling that went before simply provided the tools and the framework for the real lessons to come.

"In the final analysis, Jason, life—when lived on your own terms—is the ultimate teacher. My wealth and success have robbed you of that, and this is my best effort to repair the damage."

Red paused for a few seconds, collected his thoughts, and continued. "Jason, you are going to be going on a little trip. Mr. Hamilton and Miss Hastings will be accompanying you. Your destination will be the greatest source of learning I ever discovered. If you will keep an open mind, you will find the key to the gift of learning that will serve you all the days of your life.

"After one month in this great place of learning, you must be able to explain to Mr. Hamilton—to his satisfaction—the fundamental key to all learning, education, and knowledge. Mr. Hamilton has all of the details and will give them to you as you need them. I wish you well."

Miss Hastings got up to retrieve the videotape as Jason asked in a bored but resigned tone, "Where do we have to go, and what do we have to do?"

As I stood and started walking out of the room, I said, "Jason, we don't have to go anywhere or do anything. We can stop this process right now, but if you want to continue, be at the airport, Gate 27, at seven in the morning. Bring your passport, some summer clothes, and a good attitude."

The next morning, we actually met Jason—luggage in hand—crossing the long-term parking lot outside of the airport. I called to him, "Jason—good morning. I'm surprised to see you here a half-hour before the plane leaves."

He laughed and said, "I thought I'd try to catch one without running a hundred-yard dash and squeezing in as they close the door."

Miss Hastings took my arm as we crossed the driveway toward the terminal. She whispered to me, "It may be small and slow, but it does seem to be progress, indeed."

Jason caught up with us and asked, "So, where are we going?"

I smiled at him and replied, "South America."

Jason stopped in his tracks and asked, "What university or graduate school is located in South America?"

Miss Hastings responded to his question cheerily, "I'm quite certain you have never heard of it."

———

Three flights later, we found ourselves in a rickety taxi, winding along a dirt road with dense jungle on either side. Eventually, we arrived at a dusty village with dirt streets and a few dilapidated buildings running along the edge of the jungle.

The taxi stopped in front of the largest building on the street, and we got out and retrieved our luggage. As the taxi drove off in a cloud of dust, Jason asked incredulously, "Are you sure we're in the right place?"

I laughed and replied, "Education and learning are where you find them."

We got settled into our three rooms in the modest but surprisingly comfortable hotel and agreed to meet in the lobby for breakfast the next day. I was very tired and fended off each of Jason's queries by simply telling him that the lesson would begin in the morning.

With the hectic day of travel behind me, I slept well and met Miss Hastings in the lobby, where she had already procured a table for us at the edge of what passed for a dining room. Several moments later, Jason arrived, and we ate a quick and simple breakfast.

As I got up from the table, I said, "Jason, we're going to walk down to the end of this street. There's a building there where your education will begin."

Jason stood and sighed, saying, "I've come this far. I may as well see what my crazy great-uncle had in mind."

As we walked along the dusty street, the three of us must have made quite a conspicuous sight, as many of the local residents came out to look at us. There were many simple wood and sheet-metal structures, and as we got to the end of the street, the last building on the left was slightly larger and more modern than the rest. A sign over the door in both Spanish and English read, Howard "Red" Stevens Library.

When Jason spotted the name, he began to laugh and asked, "What is going on?"

As I climbed the three steps and opened the door, I said, "I think you'll find out what you need to know inside."

We entered the library and were greeted by a pleasant young woman at the counter. She spoke English very well as she greeted us and said, "I assume you are Mr. Hamilton and Miss Hastings."

I nodded yes, and her eyes brightened as she looked at Jason and exclaimed, "You must be Jason Stevens. We are very proud to have you here. Señor Red Stevens was a great man who helped all the people in our village."

I cleared my throat and said, "Jason, for the next four weeks, you will be assisting the librarian in her duties. You will have everything you need here to learn the lesson that your great-uncle wants you to learn."

Jason raised his voice louder than necessary and stated, "I may not have done well in school or learned much in college, but I can't believe that there is anything to be learned in this tiny place that I haven't had access to before."

Jason turned a complete circle as he surveyed the one-room library.

"This place is made up mostly of empty shelves. There's only a handful of books here," he observed.

The librarian smiled and explained, "All of the books are being read by people in our village and for miles around.

Your great-uncle told us when he gave us this library that books don't do any good sitting on the shelf."

I told Jason that Miss Hastings and I would be leaving him to his work, but we would be checking in on him daily.

Over the next four weeks, I slipped into the pleasant lifestyle of the village. Miss Hastings and I took several side trips and had ample opportunities for sightseeing and the collection of native artwork. The people were all friendly and pleasant, especially as they learned that I represented their late, great benefactor Red Stevens.

As we checked on Jason each day, we discovered he was actually going about his task with more energy and diligence than I had expected. He became proficient at getting the books checked in and checked out rapidly, and he would often converse with the library patrons about the books that they had read.

As the last day of our scheduled trip arrived, I almost hated to leave the pleasant village. Everyone came onto the street to wish us well, and we departed in what seemed to be the same cab in which we had arrived.

After a hard day of traveling, we found ourselves back at the Boston airport, where we collected our luggage and walked toward the parking lot.

Jason hurried a few steps in front of us, turned to block our path, and said, "Hold it right here. I did everything that you said, I worked hard in the library, and I looked at every book they had in that dinky little place. There was nothing new to be learned there. The only thing that I found out is that there are good and simple people who will get up hours before daylight and will walk many miles along mountain trails to get a tattered old copy of a book. The only thing I can honestly say I know now that I didn't know when we left here four weeks ago is that the desire and hunger for education is the key to real learning."

As Miss Hastings and I stepped around either side of Jason and moved toward the car, I called over my shoulder, "Congratulations, young man. I will see you in the office on Monday, and we will discover where we go from here."

Miss Hastings and I got our luggage into the trunk of the car, and as we drove through the exit of the airport parking lot, I could still see Jason rooted in the same place—no doubt thinking about the lesson we had all learned.

Seven

The Gift of Problems

Problems can only be avoided
by exercising good judgment.
Good judgment can only be gained
by experiencing life's problems.

I will admit to having a sense of anticipation the following Monday as I contemplated the possible direction of the next act in Jason Stevens' life drama. I marveled at how my oldest and dearest friend, Red Stevens, could reach out from beyond the grave to impact a young life.

At the appointed hour, Miss Hastings ushered Jason into the conference room and summoned me to our monthly encounter with destiny. Jason seemed to be more mature and confident than he had been just four short months earlier. He actually greeted both Miss Hastings and me as we began the next phase of our odyssey.

The image of Red Stevens materialized onto the large screen. He gave Jason his customary congratulatory salute for passing the gift of learning milestone.

Red began in earnest. "Jason, life is full of many contradictions. In fact, the longer you live, the more the reality of life will seem like one great paradox. But if you live long enough and search hard enough, you will find a miraculous order to the confusion.

"All of the lessons I am trying to teach you as a part of the ultimate gift I am leaving you through my will are generally learned as people go through their lives facing struggles and problems. Any challenge that does not defeat us ultimately strengthens us.

"One of the great errors in my life was sheltering so many people—including you—from life's problems. Out of a misguided sense of concern for your well-being, I actually took away your ability to handle life's problems by removing them from your environment.

"Unfortunately, human beings cannot live in a vacuum forever. A bird must struggle in order to emerge from the eggshell. A well-meaning person might crack open the egg, releasing the baby bird. This person might walk away feeling as though he has done the bird a wonderful service when, in fact, he has left the bird in a weakened condition and unable to deal with its environment. Instead of helping the bird, the person has, in fact, destroyed it. It is only a matter of time until something in the bird's environment attacks it, and the bird has no ability to deal with what otherwise would be a manageable problem.

"If we are not allowed to deal with small problems, we will be destroyed by slightly larger ones. When we come to understand this fact, we live our lives not avoiding problems, but welcoming them as challenges that will strengthen us so that we can be victorious in the future."

Red Stevens paused and stared directly into the camera in a way that let us all know his conviction was borne through a life of experience in dealing with problems.

Red continued. "Jason, I cannot turn back the clock and allow you to deal with each of the problems in the past that I eliminated from your life when I should have given you the opportunity to deal with them yourself. If I could take us both back in time, I would, but now I am left with trying to teach you the value of problems, struggles, and obstacles.

"Since you have not had any experience in this area, you will have to learn quickly. There are problems heading your way that you are not prepared for. During the next thirty days, you will begin the preparation.

"This month, I want you to go out and find people with problems in each stage of life. I want you to find a child, a young adult, a full-grown adult, and an older person—each of whom is experiencing a profound problem. Not only are you to find these four individuals, but you must be able to describe to Mr. Hamilton the benefit or the lesson that is derived from each specific situation.

"When we can learn from our own problems, we begin to deal with life. When we can learn from other people's problems, we begin to master life.

"I wish you well, and I hope to talk with you again next month."

Even though the video had ended, Jason continued staring at the blank screen. He rose slowly and walked toward the door. As he opened it, he paused, turned back toward Miss Hastings and me, and said, "I will do my best and call you later."

Then he closed the door behind him.

Miss Hastings turned to me and said, "The process seems to be beginning to work. I am detecting a shift in his attitude. What do you think?"

"I hope you're right," I responded, "because I have a feeling the road gets steeper the farther we go."

~~~~~~~

Once again I found myself waiting for Jason's call and hoping he was faring well. I felt the same way I did the first day I sent my son off to kindergarten. With three days left in the month, Jason finally called and set up an appointment with Miss Hastings for the following morning. Miss Hastings told me he had sounded very worried and unsure of himself. All I could do was hope for the best.

The following morning at the appointed hour, Miss Hastings ushered Jason into my office, got him seated, and pulled up a chair for herself. Jason sat silently, and as I looked at him, I had to admit he did seem very quiet and a bit apprehensive.

Finally, I said, "Well, Jason, it's good to see you again. I assume you have a report on your progress."

Jason glanced up at me and said, "I think I do."

He stared down at his hands, which were folded in his lap, and after a long pause, he slowly began. "Well, I knew I had to find people with problems from the four age groups. So I started by looking for a child. After almost two weeks—during which I was unable to find anything—I was so frustrated one afternoon, I just went for a walk in the park.

"I was feeling sorry for myself and considering that after all this work I was going to lose my inheritance and whatever this ultimate gift is that my Uncle Red has for me.

"Finally, I sat at the end of a bench, and I noticed at the other end of the bench there was a young woman watching a little girl playing on the swing. The woman told me she thought the little girl was really amazing, and in my depressed condition, I was not as kind with her as I should have been because I told her that I didn't see anything amazing about her six- or seven-year-old daughter playing on a swing set.

"She told me, 'First of all, I'm not her mother, although I wish I were. Second, she's probably the most amazing person I have ever seen in my life. I am a volunteer at St. Catherine's Hospital. I work in a program where we try to grant special wishes for terminal patients. Emily has a rare form of cancer. She has been through countless operations and has spent probably half her life in hospitals dealing with great pain. When we told her that we could try to make a special wish of hers come true, she said she would like a fun day in the park. We told her that many kids went to Disney World or ball games or the beach, but she just smiled and said, 'That's very nice, but I'd just like to have a fun day in the park.''

"This woman went on to tell me that Emily had touched everyone in the hospital and had made a real difference in everyone's life. About that time, Emily stopped swinging and slowly walked across the grass and sat between the two of us on the bench. She turned to me with a smile I'll never forget and told me that her name was Emily and that this was her special day in the park. She asked me if this was my special day in the park too. I told her that I didn't think it was, and she laughed and told me that I could share hers with her.

"So, Mr. Hamilton, I spent the rest of the day in the

playground with Emily. I realized that she has more courage and joy in her little seven-year-old body than any normal human being could possibly have.

"At the end of the day, she was very tired, and the young lady from the hospital had to take her away in a wheelchair. But, before Emily left, she told me that when she got back to the hospital, she would talk to the nurses and see if they could arrange for me to have a special day in the park too."

Jason paused and looked directly at me. He had a tear in his eye, and I must admit I was fighting to control my composure as well. Miss Hastings retrieved a box of tissues and said something about her seasonal allergies. We all sat in silence and thought about a young girl whose problem could affect us so profoundly.

Finally, Jason cleared his throat, wiped his eye, and continued. "Later that week, I found a middle-aged man walking down the sidewalk in front of my house. He spotted me getting into my car, so he smiled and walked directly over to me. He stuck out his hand and told me his name was Bill Johnson and that my car was one of the most beautiful cars he had ever seen. He told me that he was in the neighborhood doing odd jobs for people and that it would be a privilege to wash a car like mine.

"I asked him why he was out doing odd jobs, and he told me that through a series of corporate cutbacks, both he and his wife had lost their jobs and that they had three young children at home. Both he and his wife were doing anything they could to make ends meet. Apparently, they had gone through their savings, and they were making it just day to day on what they could pick up doing these jobs. I asked him what would happen if he didn't get enough money, and he just smiled and told me that there was always enough, and that the problem had created some interesting situations for their family. They were spending more time together than they had before, and their children had learned the value of money and work.

"He chuckled as he recounted an incident the previous week when they had no food other than a little oatmeal. He said he was just about to give up when he heard his wife explaining to their children that many of the pioneers in the Old West went for days at a time eating nothing but oatmeal. He told me that their two youngest boys would probably want to eat only oatmeal from now on, no matter how much money they ever had."

Jason paused for several moments, searching for the right words, and then he continued, "He went on to tell me about all the wonderful things that he and his wife and family were learning and doing together. He washed my car, and I paid him what he asked. I tried to give him more, but he wouldn't take it.

"Before he left, I told him that I was sorry for his situation. He just laughed that amazing laugh of his and told me that he felt like he was the luckiest man on earth—that in the whole world, he couldn't think of anyone he would want to trade places with."

Jason seemed deep in thought and finally said, "You know what's funny, Mr. Hamilton? As he was telling me that there was no one in the world he would trade places with, I was thinking to myself that in a lot of ways I would love to trade places with him."

Miss Hastings supplied the three of us with glasses of water. Jason took a sip of his and resumed his report.

"The next day, I was driving past the entrance to a cemetery, and I noticed the largest funeral procession I had ever seen. I didn't think anything of it, and later that day I was passing back the same way, and out of curiosity, I thought I would drive through and ask one of the workers if it had been a celebrity or something. I drove through the cemetery, and the only person I could see was one very old man standing alone by a grave. Since the funeral procession I had seen had been several hours before, I assumed he was there on his own.

"I got out of my car and approached the old gentleman. When he heard me walking up behind him, he turned in my direction. I told him I was sorry for interrupting him, but that earlier in the day when I was driving by, I had seen the largest funeral procession I had ever witnessed. I told him I was just wondering if he might have known if it was a celebrity or superstar or something.

"He laughed softly and told me it had, indeed, been a celebrity and a superstar. He told me he knew that for a fact because he had lived with her for almost sixty years. Apparently, his wife had been a schoolteacher for forty years and had influenced so many of her students that literally hundreds of them had come in from all parts of the country for her funeral. So, he felt that made her a celebrity and a superstar, both.

"I told him I was sorry for disturbing him on what must be the worst day of his life. He just laughed that quiet laugh again and told me that his life would be different, but that no one who lived sixty years with his Dorothy could ever have a bad day. 'I was just standing here thanking Dorothy for everything she had done, and I had just promised her I wouldn't let her down.'"

Jason took another sip of his water, looked at both Miss Hastings and me, and continued. "That old man put his arm around my shoulder, and we walked out of the cemetery together. As I was getting in my car, he told me that if there was ever anything he could do for me that I was to call on him. I just sat in my car and watched him slowly drive away."

Jason seemed to have concluded his report at that point. I waited, but he did not continue, so I finally said, "Jason, you found a child who is living through one of the most difficult problems anyone could face with a joy that it is hard for me to understand. You found a middle-aged man and his family who are dealing with financial crisis while maintaining their sense of family and dignity. You found an older man who has taken a tragedy of death and turned it into a celebration of life. But, Jason, you were to have also found a young person with a problem."

Jason cleared his throat and finally resumed speaking. "Well, Mr. Hamilton, I know I was supposed to find a young person, and during the month I found several possible candidates, but I have to admit to you today that I couldn't find any young person who has learned as much from their problem as I have from mine. I have lived my whole life in a selfish and self-centered fashion. I never realized that real people have real problems. It always seemed that problems happened to people on the news or in the movies or something.

"But, thanks to you and my Uncle Red, I finally realized that I have been sheltered from problems, and that I have never learned the wonderful lessons that the people I met this month are learning. I finally know that joy does not come from avoiding a problem or having someone else deal with it for you. Joy comes from overcoming a problem or simply learning to live with it while being joyful."

Miss Hastings' allergies seemed to be acting up again at that moment, as she was dabbing at her eyes and nose.

Finally, Jason asked, "Do you think it will be okay if I serve as one of the four people I was supposed to learn from this month?"

I assured Jason that it met both the spirit and the letter of Red Stevens' final will and testament.

Jason glanced at his watch and said, "If that's all, I need to hurry to be at another appointment on time."

I told him that would be fine, and as Miss Hastings was showing him to the door, she asked, "Where are you rushing off to, Jason?"

He said, "I have to meet a special friend in front of the swing set at the park. I will see you both tomorrow."

EIGHT

The Gift of Family

*Some people are born
into wonderful families.
Others have to find or create them.
Being a member of a family
is a priceless privilege
which costs nothing but love.*

T he following day, Jason Stevens, Miss Hastings,
and I gathered in the conference room for our
monthly meeting which was becoming a welcomed
ritual for me. We sat in our established places. I was lost
in thoughts of what the next month might bring as Miss
Hastings started the videotape.

Red Stevens greeted Jason warmly. "Hello, and
congratulations on learning to value the gift of problems.
That lesson will serve you well all the days of your life. You
are now entering the sixth month of our one-year remedial

lesson in life. This month, you will begin to understand and respect the gift of family.

"Now, Jason, I realize that our family is about as messed up as a family can be, and I accept my full share of responsibility for that. However, the best or the worst family situation can teach us a lesson. We either learn what we want or, unfortunately, we learn what we don't want in life from our families. Out of all the young men in the world, I have selected you. I have asked Mr. Hamilton to undertake this monumental task on my behalf for you because you are my great-nephew. It's hard to understand why that means something, but I want you to know that it does.

"Families give us our roots, our heritage, and our past. They also give us the springboard to our future. Nothing in this world is stronger than the bond that can be formed by a family. That is a bond of pure love that will withstand any pressure as long as the love is kept in the forefront.

"It's important for you to realize that families come in all shapes and sizes. Some very blessed people are able to live their whole lives as part of the families they were born into. Other people, like you, Jason—through a set of circumstances—are left without family other than in name. Those people have to go out and create family.

"I know this seems odd to you, but by the end of this month, I believe you will begin to understand what I am trying to tell you. This month, you, Mr. Hamilton, and Miss Hastings will be going on another trip. You will be meeting people who seem to have no family, and in this way I am hoping you will learn the value that a family can provide.

"At the end of this month, I will ask you to demonstrate to Mr. Hamilton that you know and understand what the gift of family means.

"Mr. Hamilton has all the details for your trip, and assuming you accomplish this objective, I will talk to you next month."

Jason turned to me and said, "I don't suppose you're going to tell me where we're going, what we're going to do, or whom we're going to meet, are you?"

I smiled and said, "All in good time, young man. I have been instructed to tell you only what you need to know and only when you need to know it."

Miss Hastings interrupted. "I believe we have made arrangements to pick you up at your home at 7:30 in the morning. We will be traveling several hours by automobile. Please be prepared to stay one month in a climate similar to the one which we are enjoying here in Boston."

The next morning, Miss Hastings and I were comfortably installed in the back of a long, black limousine driven by a very large gentleman selected especially for this mission. We pulled up in front of Jason's palatial home, which his great-uncle had purchased for him via a trust fund.

Our driver got out and went to the front door to collect Jason and his luggage. A few moments later, I saw the chauffeur—easily carrying both of Jason's suitcases in one hand—leading Jason toward the car. Jason seemed a bit timid around the giant, and when the back door was opened to let Jason in, he appeared relieved to be in the company of Miss Hastings and me.

"Who in the world is that huge guy?" asked Jason.

Miss Hastings replied cheerily, "Oh, you mean Nathan? He is a very nice young man selected especially for this trip."

"What does that mean?" Jason asked.

Miss Hastings just smiled and sipped on a cup of coffee.

I turned and shook hands with Jason, greeting him. "Good morning, Jason. All will become clear at the appropriate time. For now, I suggest you sit back and relax, and I will tell you some' of the details as we approach our destination."

We enjoyed a beautiful drive out of Boston, across eastern Massachusetts, and into New Hampshire. As we turned north along the coast, I began to explain our trip to Jason.

"Before too long, we will be entering the state of Maine. We will travel several miles into a private forest, and we will arrive at the Red Stevens Home for Boys, where you will be a substitute houseparent for the next month. This will give the resident houseparent an opportunity for a well-deserved vacation and will give you an opportunity to get very well acquainted with thirty-six boys ranging in age from six to sixteen."

Jason stared at me dubiously and said, "I thought I was supposed to be learning about family. How in the world did that old man think I would learn about family from a bunch of orphans?"

"*That old man*, as you so eloquently put it, started this place over thirty years ago and has funded it ever since," I responded. "He knew it inside and out, and I am sure the lesson he has planned for you can be found there. I just hope for your sake you can keep an open mind and find it."

"Well, it doesn't make any sense to me," Jason mumbled.

"Nevertheless, you're in for a unique month, to say the least," I said. "As your great-uncle made me the chairman of the board of this institution upon his death, Miss Hastings and I will spend the month working in the office, dealing with some of the donors, and seeing to next year's budget."

A few moments later, we drove off of the main highway and onto a gravel side road. We passed a rustic sign reading, *Red Stevens Home for Boys*. Several moments later, our excellent driver, Nathan, guided the limousine to a stop in the middle of a courtyard surrounded by several buildings, including a dining commons, a dormitory, a classroom building, a gymnasium, and an administration building.

Nathan got out of the limousine and opened the rear door for the three of us to get out. As he was getting the luggage out of the trunk, the door to the dormitory burst open, and an entire herd of young boys rushed to Nathan and began to mob him. He picked several of them up in the air, hugged several more, and slapped hands with still others. They were all calling his name and seemed to be terribly excited to see him.

Finally, the enthusiastic greeting seemed to be over when Nathan said in a tone that would be hard to ignore, "Now, men, let's get into our dormitory and make sure everything is squared away, because we have a new houseparent here for the month."

The boys responded immediately and rushed back into their dormitory. Nathan, somehow carrying all the luggage at once without seeming to be burdened down, led us into the dormitory. There were two rows of bunks lining each wall with lockers in between.

Nathan dropped Jason's luggage onto the first bunk and said, "Welcome home. This will be your palace for the next thirty days. Mr. Hamilton and Miss Hastings will be staying in the private apartments connected to the administration building."

Nathan turned back to Jason and said, "I would suggest you get unpacked and settled in. You have a lot of catching up to do."

We all agreed to meet in the dining room in approximately twenty minutes. Nathan showed Miss Hastings and me to the two comfortable apartments adjoining the administration building.

At the agreed upon time, we were all seated at the end of a long table in the dining room. Several dozen boys streamed in and sat at what appeared to be assigned places. They were talking excitedly and seemed to be curious about us as a group of outsiders gathered at the end of their table.

After several moments, Nathan stood to his full height, which was, indeed, impressive. I estimated at least 6 feet, 8 inches. At that point, the boys went silent, and Nathan spoke.

"Boys, as you know, your regular houseparent, Brad, will be on vacation for the next month. Jason Stevens will be filling in for him."

Nathan turned to Jason and said, "Stand up, Jason."

Jason stood slowly, and a chorus of young boys called out in ragged unison, "Hi, Jason."

Jason cleared his throat and stammered, "Hi." Jason sat back down quickly.

Nathan resumed his address to the young boys. "Also, Mr. Hamilton and Miss Hastings will be with us for the next month as well. Some of you will remember them being here during our board of director visits with Mr. Stevens. They are very fine people that we are lucky to have here."

Then Nathan bowed his head and gave thanks for the food. All of the boys followed suit and were polite and respectful throughout the meal.

As we enjoyed our lunch, Jason asked Nathan, "Have you been here before?"

Nathan laughed and responded, "You better believe it. The first time I came here, I was smaller than the smallest kid at this table. I was in and out of a few foster homes, but when I think of the good things from my childhood, they all happened here."

"Do you work here now or something?" Jason asked.

Nathan laughed, which sounded like a low rumble of thunder. "Yes and no," he said. "I guess people would think of my main job as being the tight end for the New England Patriots, but as soon as the season's over, I do whatever I can to be useful around here."

Jason seemed shocked and said, "I'm sorry. I thought you were just a limo driver."

"Well, today I am, and proud to do it," Nathan responded. "Tomorrow I may be the head maintenance man or disciplinarian here. One of the things we learned from Red Stevens when I was growing up is that we all do what needs to be done because it's the right thing to do."

"Well, what am I supposed to do here?" Jason asked.

"I believe Mr. Stevens' instructions through Mr. Hamilton were to let the boys help you figure out what you're supposed to do here," Nathan answered. "So, if they're done eating, I will take Mr. Hamilton and Miss Hastings to the administration building to discuss next year's budget and let your lessons begin."

Nathan slapped Jason on the back with a giant hand and led Miss Hastings and me from the dining room building. As we were passing through the door, I heard Jason calling to us, "Look, I don't have a clue here. I've never been around any kids."

The young boys around the table all erupted into laughter which could be heard as we walked across the courtyard and into the administration building.

For the next month, Miss Hastings and I did all of the legal and budgetary work required for the coming year. We did have several opportunities each day to look in on Jason, and Nathan told us he would keep us informed.

For the first several days, Jason seemed like a stranger. But, eventually he settled into his duties as father, brother, teacher, and friend to three dozen boys. On the last day, as Nathan was loading our luggage into the limousine, each of the boys came out, one at a time, to tell Jason good-bye. Hugs were exchanged, a few tears were shed, and Jason received a number of gifts which would be considered exceedingly valuable to young boys. I noticed several oddly shaped rocks, a four-leaf clover, and an arrowhead, among other heartfelt offerings.

As Nathan drove us out of the courtyard along the gravel driveway, Jason was turned in the seat waving to the boys until they were out of sight. We sat in silence until we were well along the highway back to Boston.

Finally, Jason spoke. "You know what's amazing? Not one of those boys has a family, but each of them knew more about a family than I did. I think family is not as much about being related by blood as it is about relating through love."

The limousine horn honked, and Nathan let out a blood-curdling yell which I am sure serves him well on the football field. "You finally got it!" he shouted. "I thought you were pretty useless when you got here, but I knew that if you were related to Red Stevens, we had a chance. You see, you come from a great family, and so do I."

Nine

The Gift of Laughter

*Laughter is good medicine for the soul.
Our world is desperately in need
of more such medicine.*

W hen you become an octogenarian, you find
yourself dealing with your memories and your
mortality. I was sitting in my office thinking
of all the wonderful memories I carried with me, and my
mind drifted back to Red Stevens.

I had just gotten out of law school and opened my
office. The sign on the door read, Hamilton and Associates.
The Associates part was more of a wish than a reality, as I
spent the majority of each day by myself.

One day, I heard the bell on the outer door ring. I knew
that my part-time secretary had already left for the day, so
I got up and rushed out to see who it was. There stood a
formidable man I later learned was Red Stevens. He told

me that he was going to be the biggest oil man and the biggest cattleman in Texas, and he was looking for a good lawyer. He said that he had called the best law school in America and learned that I had graduated first in my class the previous spring.

He just smiled that huge smile I came to know and love, and boomed, "So I thought the best lawyer in the world and the best oil man and cattleman in the world ought to get together."

It didn't seem to bother either of us that I was a lawyer fresh out of law school with no clients, and he was an oil man and a cattleman without any oil or cattle. It began that simply and grew into a longtime professional and personal relationship.

My thoughts of Red were interrupted when Miss Hastings stuck her head into my office and said that Jason Stevens was waiting for us in the conference room.

———

Red appeared on the video screen and said, "Well, Jason, you've made it through six months of this twelve-month project. I want to remind you that you've come a long way, but you have a long way to go, and if at any point your attitude or your conduct does not meet Mr. Hamilton's expectations, we will end this journey immediately, and you will not receive the ultimate gift, which is the bequest I have left to you in my will.

"This month, you are going to learn about the gift of laughter. The gift of laughter I want you to learn about is not a comedian in a nightclub or a funny movie. It is the ability to look at yourself, your problems, and life in general, and just laugh. Many people live unhappy lives because they take things too seriously. I hope you have learned in the last six months that there are things in life to be serious about and to treasure, but life without laughter is not worth living.

"This month, I want you to go out and find one example of a person who is experiencing difficulties or challenges in his or her life but who maintains the ability to laugh. If a person can laugh in the face of adversity, that individual will be happy throughout life.

"At the end of the month, you will report to Mr. Hamilton and Miss Hastings about the individual you have found and what you have learned from him or her about the gift of laughter."

Red Stevens began laughing and said, "Someday, Jason, you will have to ask Ted to tell you about some of the laughable situations we got ourselves into in the olden days." As Red continued laughing to himself, the screen went black.

Jason asked, "What is he talking about, Mr. Hamilton?"

I smiled and replied, "That would, indeed, be for another time and another place, but for now, young man, it is time for you to get serious about the gift of laughter."

At that, Miss Hastings walked Jason out of the office.

Our firm's private investigator, Reggie Turner, discreetly followed Jason throughout the month. Reggie reported that Jason seemed to be going about his normal routine and did not appear to be showing any outward signs of exploring the gift of laughter.

On the last day of the month, Miss Hastings buzzed me to say that Jason had called and asked if he could stop by in the afternoon. I told her that would be fine, and she let me know that Jason had informed her he would be bringing someone with him.

At the appointed hour, Miss Hastings escorted Jason into my office along with another young man who was obviously blind. He wore dark glasses and carried a white cane. Miss Hastings seemed uncomfortable as she watched the blind man walk across the office, and I must admit to feeling a bit of apprehension myself.

"Mr. Hamilton and Miss Hastings," Jason said, "I'd like you to meet David Reese."

Mr. Reese held his hand out and said, "Long time, no see."

It took me a moment to overcome my anxiety and to be able to enjoy his humor. I shook his hand, and we all sat down.

"I met David on a commuter train last week," Jason explained. "We talked during the train trip and several times since, over the phone. He is simply the best example I can imagine of the gift of laughter."

David Reese blurted out, "Yeah, David told me that you guys needed a few laughs around here, so he dragged me in."

David turned his head to the right and said, "Boy, this is really a beautiful office."

"Thank you," I said and was about to tell him about my furnishings when I realized he had been pulling my leg. We all laughed.

I asked Jason, "What was it about this young man that made you believe he had the gift of laughter when you first met him on the train?"

David Reese cut in and answered, "It was my magazine trick, sir."

I smiled and asked, "Okay, what's the magazine trick?"

David Reese explained. "Some of the commuter trains are not as clean as they should be, so whenever the seats are dusty, people often sit on magazines. Since I can't tell when they're clean and when they're not, I always sit on a magazine. While Jason and I were getting acquainted on the train, a gentleman behind me, as people often do when they're looking for something to read on the train, asked me if I was reading the magazine."

At that point, Jason began laughing out loud and interrupted. "Right after the guy asked David, 'Are you reading that magazine?' David stood up, turned the page, sat back down, and said, 'Yes, sir, but I'll be done before long.'"

When our laughter died down, I asked David how and when he developed the gift of laughter. He explained that he lost his sight early in life and had dealt with many struggles and challenges, not the least of which being people treating him poorly.

"Mr. Hamilton, sometimes in life, either you laugh or you cry," he said. "And I prefer to laugh."

I thought about David Reese and what a wonderful outlook he had on life. His gift of laughter had not only benefited him, but everyone around him, including me. I told Jason that he had certainly fulfilled the assignment for this month.

As Jason walked with David Reese out of the office, David stopped, turned, and said, "Mr. Hamilton, I wanted to tell you before I left—I think that's a beautiful tie you have on."

I was halfway through thanking him for the compliment

when I realized he had done it to me again. He and Jason could be heard laughing all the way down the hall to the elevator. Miss Hastings was laughing softly as well.

"So, what are you laughing about?" I finally asked her.

"Well, it is a nice tie," she replied.

Ten

The Gift of Dreams

*Faith is all that dreamers need
to see into the future.*

There are days when you can just feel in your bones that something extraordinary is going to happen. There are other days when the extraordinary things in life surprise you.

As I was waiting for Jason Stevens to arrive for his scheduled appointment, which would begin another month of discovery for both of us, I was standing at my window looking over the Boston skyline and thinking about Red Stevens. It is hard to feel the loss of someone you love when so much of that person remains with you all the time. There are people who have such a huge impact in our lives that they become almost a part of us. Red Stevens had that effect on me, and I know he had the same effect on many others.

There were, indeed, many days I wanted to pick up the phone and hear that gravelly voice with the West Texas accent boom back at me. But, somehow, I knew that I would never be without the good things that Red Stevens had brought into my life.

Red Stevens appeared before us on the large video screen at the end of the conference room. He was, indeed, a great man, and his greatness had manifested itself in every area of his life. Now he was attempting to pass that greatness on to his great-nephew.

"Jason, while you're sitting there, I want to take just a minute to thank Mr. Hamilton and Miss Hastings for agreeing to take on this yearlong project. I hope you'll remember that when you receive the ultimate gift that I have planned for you as my final bequest, the delivery of that gift will be due in large measure to the efforts of my dear friends Theodore Hamilton and Margaret Hastings."

Red seemed so lifelike on the big screen that I wanted to tell him that I was more than glad to do this for him, but I knew it wouldn't do any good to speak those words. Somehow I felt—in my own way—that he would know I was pleased that he had selected me to accompany Jason along this journey.

"Jason, this month you're going to learn about a gift that belongs to all great men and women—the gift of dreams. Dreams are the essence of life—not as it is, but as it can be. Dreams are born in the hearts and minds of very special people, but the fruit of those dreams becomes reality and is enjoyed by the whole world.

"You may not know it, but Theodore Hamilton is known far and wide as the best lawyer in the country. I know that performing at that level was a dream of his when I met him, and he has been living that dream for over fifty years. The dream came true in his heart and mind before it came true in reality.

"I can remember wandering through the swamps of Louisiana, dreaming about becoming the greatest oil and cattle baron in Texas. That dream became such a part of me that when I achieved my goals, it was like going home to a place I had never been before.

"I have been trying to decide, as I have been formulating this ultimate gift for you, which of the gifts is the greatest. If I had to pick one, I think I would pick the gift of dreams because dreams allow us to see life as it can be, not as it is. In that way, the gift of dreams allows us to go out and get any other gift we want out of this life."

Red paused for several moments and seemed to be collecting his thoughts. Then he continued. "Jason, the best way to introduce you to dreams is to acquaint you with some dreamers. I knew many throughout my life. I always considered my friendship with the dreamers to be a treasure.

"One of the first truly great dreamers I ever met in my life had a passion to create places and things that would touch the imagination of people. This passion was with him all the days of his life. He had his share of setbacks and failures as well as many detractors. I never saw him or talked to him at a time when he didn't want to share his latest project with me. He was in the habit of creating huge dream boards that he would hang on the wall and draw out the plans for each of his projects on.

"I remember that when he was on his deathbed, he had arranged to tack the plans for his newest project onto the ceiling of his hospital room. That way, he could continue to look at his dream as he constructed it in his mind.

"A reporter came to visit him while he was in the hospital, and my friend was so weak he could barely talk. So, he actually moved over and asked the reporter to lie on his bed with him so the two of them could look at the plans on the ceiling while my friend shared his dream.

"The reporter was so moved that a person would have that much passion while dealing with a serious illness in the hospital. The reporter concluded his interview, said good-bye to my friend, and left the hospital.

"My friend died later that day.

"Please do not miss the point. A person who can live his entire life with a burning passion for his dream to the extent that he shares it on his deathbed—that is a fortunate person. My friend had his dream with him all the days of his life. It continued to grow and expand. When he would reach one milestone of his dream, another greater and grander one would appear.

"In a real way, my friend taught a lot of people how to dream and imagine a better world. His name was Walt Disney.

"But let me warn you. Your dreams for your life must be yours. They cannot belong to someone else, and they must continue to grow and expand.

"I had another friend whose name you would not know. He said it was his dream to work hard and retire at age fifty. He did, indeed, work hard and achieve a degree of success in his business. He held on to that dream of retiring, but he had no passion beyond that.

"On his fiftieth birthday, a number of us gathered to celebrate both his birthday and his retirement. This should have been one of the happiest days of his life—if his dream had been properly aligned. Unfortunately, his entire adult life had been spent in his profession. That is where he had gained a lot of his pride and self-esteem. When he found himself as a relatively young man without his profession to guide him, he faced the uncertainty of retirement. It was something he thought he had always wanted, but he discovered quickly it created no life-sustaining passion for him.

"A month later, my second friend committed suicide.

"The difference between one dreamer who was still energized by his lifelong passion while on his deathbed and another dreamer whose goal was so ill-fitting for his personality that he committed suicide should be apparent to you.

"Jason, it is important that your dream belong to you. It is not a one-size-fits-all proposition. Your dream should be a custom-fit for your personality, one that grows and develops as you do. The only person who needs to be passionate about your dream is you."

Red Stevens paused, cleared his throat, and seemed to mentally shift gears. He finally continued. "Jason, this month, I want you to begin experiencing the gift of dreams. Assume everything is possible. Make a list of all the things you would like to do and be and have in your life. Then begin to prioritize that list as you discover the ones that generate the most passion in your soul.

"At the end of the month, I want you to share a handful of those dreams with Mr. Hamilton. There are no right or wrong answers, and keep in mind your dreams will grow and develop through the years. What is more important than the dreams, themselves, is the process of becoming a dreamer.

"I wish you a life of pleasant dreams."

Red Stevens' image faded, and for a moment Jason stared down at his hands, which were folded on the conference room table. Finally he spoke. "I have never thought about what I wanted to do with my life. I guess I always felt that just existing and drifting through day to day was enough."

I stood up and began walking toward the door as I said, "Jason, this would be a good time to start dreaming, and there is no one better to learn the process from than Red Stevens. I look forward to your report at the end of the month."

I walked out of the conference room and left Jason there with his thoughts and—I hoped—his dreams.

⁓⁓⁓

I will never forget the day, more than three weeks later, that I sat across my desk from Jason Stevens as he shared the beginnings of his lifelong dreams. He began slowly, but gained momentum as he spoke.

"Well, in the beginning I had a huge list of things I thought I wanted to do or be or have. But I realized these weren't really dreams—they were things I could do now if I wanted to. I just hadn't taken the time or energy to do them yet. But when I thought about Walt Disney, several things came to me."

Jason paused for a moment. He looked from Miss Hastings to me and back again. I felt he was seeking encouragement. Miss Hastings smiled and nodded at him, and Jason seemed to gain confidence as he continued.

"Somehow, some way, I would like to be able to help deprived young people live a good life. I don't really mean poor young people. I mean young people who have not learned the power and the passion and the values they can have that will make their lives worth living. Somehow I am going to do for other young people what my Uncle Red is doing for me."

Miss Hastings clapped her hands and replied enthusiastically, "Jason, that's exciting. I can't think of anything better you or anyone else could do with their life."

Jason looked toward me and asked, "Well, does that sound okay to you?"

I smiled and replied, "Jason, after forty years of working with Miss Hastings, I have learned one principle of survival. That is simply to always agree with her. And I do, indeed, agree with her. You have established a most worthwhile dream and goal for your life. Just be sure to remember both of your great-uncle's friends whose stories he shared with you, and keep your dream alive as long as you stay alive."

Miss Hastings walked Jason to the elevator, leaving me alone at my desk. I thought about my dreams and how they were still alive in my eightieth year, although I did vow at that moment to make sure all of my dreams stayed alive and continued to grow.

Eleven

The Gift of Giving

*The only way you can truly get
more out of life for yourself
is to give part of yourself away.*

I was amazed at the progress young Jason Stevens was making as we traveled through our yearlong lesson in life together. He still had a long way to go, but there was definitely a light appearing at the end of the proverbial tunnel.

As we sat at the conference table to begin our ninth month of this journey together, I noticed an amazing change in Jason's countenance, attitude, and demeanor. I felt that he was actually looking forward to whatever Red Stevens had in store for him this month. I knew that I was.

Miss Hastings pressed the appropriate button on the remote control, and Red Stevens appeared once again on the video screen.

"Jason, I want to congratulate you on passing your test as a dreamer. Don't ever think that you have this skill mastered. Your ability to dream and turn those dreams into reality will grow as long as you grow as a person.

"This month, I want you to learn about the gift of giving. This is another one of those paradoxical principles like we talked about several months ago. Conventional wisdom would say that the less you give, the more you have. The converse is true. The more you give, the more you have. Abundance creates the ability to give; giving creates more abundance. I don't mean this simply in financial terms. This principle is true in every area of your life.

"It is important to be a giver and a receiver. Jason, financially, I have given you everything that you have in this world. But, I violated the principle involved in the gift of giving. I gave you money and things out of a sense of obligation, not a true spirit of giving. You received those things with an attitude of entitlement and privilege instead of gratitude. Our attitudes have robbed us both of the joy involved in the gift of giving.

"It is important when you give something to someone that it be given with the right spirit, not out of a sense of obligation. I learned to give to people my whole life. I cannot imagine being deprived of the privilege of giving things and part of myself to other people.

"One of the key principles in giving, however, is that the gift must be yours to give—either something you earned or created or maybe, simply, part of yourself.

"This month, I want you to experience the gift of giving, but if you simply give away the money that I gave you or the things it will buy, we will have once again violated the principle. Therefore, every day for the next thirty days, I want you to give something to someone else that is a gift from you."

"I don't have anything," Jason mumbled.

Red's voice interrupted him. "Now, I know you're probably trying to figure out what in the world you have to give that really came from you. Discovering the things that you already have to give to others will unlock the gift of giving and let you enter into a joyous realm you have never known before. If you are to continue along the path to receiving the ultimate gift I have left you in my will, at the end of this month you will return and report to Mr. Hamilton a gift that you have given each day of this month. As always, I wish you well."

"How in the world am I going to come up with something to give away every day that didn't come from my Uncle Red?" Jason exploded as the video ended. "Everything I have came from him."

I thought for a minute and then replied, "I knew Red Stevens for more than half a century. He was a tough man but a fair man. He would never demand anything of you that you didn't have the capacity to accomplish."

As Jason slowly walked out of the conference room, I thought about how far he had come, and I hoped the journey would not end at that point.

Throughout that month, I tried to think of things that someone who had been given all his worldly possessions could give away that could actually be called his own. I will admit to having a struggle coming up with a handful of them, and I hoped Jason was doing well on his own. I knew my sense of duty and loyalty to my oldest and dearest friend would oblige me to judge the process fairly.

When Jason returned on the last day of the month, he and Miss Hastings sat across my desk from me. After we had exchanged brief greetings, Jason said, "Look, I want you to know that I did my best, and I'm not sure all of my gifts will fit into whatever Uncle Red had in mind. This wasn't easy."

I smiled and replied, "No lesson worth learning is ever easy."

Jason unfolded a piece of paper and began his report. "It was really tough to come up with thirty things I could give to someone that I didn't get from my great-uncle. But here goes.

"On the first day, I stopped at a shopping center and found a parking space on the first row. As I was getting out of my car, I noticed an elderly couple looking for a space. I backed out and allowed them to park in my space, and I parked in the back of the lot."

Jason looked at me for approval. I simply nodded and said, "Go on."

"On the second day, I got caught downtown in a thunderstorm. I shared my umbrella with a young lady who didn't have one. On the third day, I went to the hospital and donated a pint of blood. On day four, I called a man in my neighborhood who had told me he needed to buy new tires to tell him there was a really good sale going on across town. On day five, I helped an elderly woman carry her packages to her car. On day six, I agreed to watch a neighbor's children for her while she went out with some friends. On day seven, I went to the Center for the Blind and read articles to visually impaired students. On day eight, I served lunch at the soup kitchen, and on day nine I wrote a note and sent a poem to a friend.

"On day ten, I agreed to take my neighbor's kids to school. On day eleven, I helped box and move donated items for the Salvation Army. On days twelve and thirteen, I let some visiting foreign exchange students stay in my home. On day fourteen, I helped a local Scout troop with their weekly meeting. On day fifteen, I found a man with a dead battery and jump-started his car. On day sixteen, I wrote letters for several people who were in the hospital. On day seventeen, I went to the local animal shelter and walked several of their dogs in the park. On day eighteen, I gave the frequent flyer miles I had earned with an airline to a high school band group planning a trip to a parade in California. Day nineteen, I worked with a local service organization and delivered meals to disabled and elderly people.

"Days twenty, twenty-one, twenty-two, and twenty-three, I took a group of inner-city kids who had never been camping and fishing on a trip with the Scout troop. I had never been camping or fishing either. On day twenty-four, I helped a local church with their rummage sale. Days twenty-five and twenty-six, I worked with a crew on a Habitat for Humanity house. Day twenty-seven, I let a local charity group use my home for a reception. Day twenty-eight, I helped one of my neighbors rake the leaves out of his yard. Day twenty-nine, believe it or not, I helped to bake cookies for the elementary school's bake sale."

Jason stopped his report at that point. I couldn't imagine he had gone through twenty-nine days of giving only to fail on the thirtieth day. Finally, feeling alarmed, I asked, "And what about day thirty, Jason?"

Jason laughed and said, "Today is day thirty, and I would like both you and Miss Hastings to have some of my homemade cookies from the bake sale."

Jason reached into a bag I had not noticed at his feet and gave us each some of the cookies.

I felt a sense of relief that Jason had completed his task for the month. I took a bite of one of his cookies and responded, "Not too bad, but I'm glad that your dream does not involve a lot of baking."

We all laughed, and Jason talked well into the afternoon about all the people he had met and given part of himself to throughout the month. I was reminded of how a small gift when it is given can be a magnificent gift as it is received.

Twelve

The Gift of Gratitude

*In those times when we yearn
to have more in our lives,
we should dwell on the things
we already have. In doing so,
we will often find that our lives
are already full to overflowing.*

As Jason arrived for our tenth monthly meeting together, I was still marveling at how he had found enough gifts within himself to give away something every day of the previous month. I thought of all the lessons we had learned, and I was reminded of the fact that we just had a few months to go to complete Red Stevens' ultimate gift to Jason.

I had the feeling that is described by baseball pitchers who are close to completing a no-hit game: You realize that one minor mistake at any point can ruin the entire effort.

As Jason completed each monthly task, I think we both felt a sense of accomplishment but, at the same time, a realization that we had more to lose than ever before.

As Miss Hastings, Jason, and I gathered in the conference room, I think we were all anxious to find out what Red Stevens had in store for us. Miss Hastings started the video, and the familiar image of Red Stevens appeared before us.

"Greetings to you all, and my congratulations to Jason, and thanks to Mr. Hamilton and Miss Hastings."

Red Stevens then winked his right eye, which was a gesture I had enjoyed for over five decades. That wink could speak a myriad of emotions, and I never thought I would see it again after attending his funeral.

"When you prepare your will and a video like this, you automatically have to think about your entire life," he continued. "I have been so many places and experienced so many things, it is hard to remember that I have only lived one lifetime.

"I remember as a young man, being so poor that I had to do day labor for food to eat, and had to sleep along the side of the road. I also remember being in the company of kings and presidents and knowing all of the material things this life has to offer. As I look back, I am thankful for it all.

"During what, at the time, I considered to be some of my worst experiences, I gained my fondest memories."

Red paused, collected his thoughts, and pressed on. "Jason, this month, you are going to learn a lesson that encompasses something that has been totally lacking in your life. That is gratitude.

"I have always found it ironic that the people in this world who have the most to be thankful for are often the least thankful, and somehow the people who have virtually nothing, many times live lives full of gratitude.

"While still in my youth, shortly after going out on my own to conquer the world, I met an elderly gentleman who today would be described as homeless. Back then, there were a lot of people who rode the rails, traveling throughout the country doing just a little bit of work here and there in order to get by. It was during the Depression, and some of these so-called hobos or tramps were well educated and had lives full of rich experiences.

"Josh and I traveled together for almost a year. He seemed very old at that time, but since I was still in my teens, I may have had a faulty perspective. He is one of the only people I ever met of whom I could honestly say, 'He never had a bad day.' Or if he did, there was certainly no outward sign of it. Traveling about as we did, we often found ourselves wet, cold, and hungry. But Josh never had anything but the best to say to everyone we met.

"Finally, when I decided to settle down in Texas and seek my fortune there, Josh and I parted company. Settling down was simply not a priority in his life. When we parted, I asked him why he was always in such good spirits. He told me that one of the great lessons his mother had left him was the legacy of the Golden List.

"He explained to me that every morning before he got up, he would lie in bed—or wherever he had been sleeping—and visualize a golden tablet on which was written ten things in his life he was especially thankful for. He told me that his mother had done that all the days of her life, and that he had never missed a day since she shared the Golden List with him.

"Well, as I stand here today, I am proud to say I haven't

missed a day since Josh shared the process with me almost
sixty years ago. Some days, I am thankful for the most
trivial things, and other days I feel a deep sense of gratitude
for my life and everything surrounding me."

Red cleared his throat, took a sip of water, gathered
himself, and continued. "Jason, today, I am passing the
legacy of the Golden List on to you. I know that it has
survived well over one hundred years simply being passed
from Josh's mother through Josh to me, and now to you. I
don't know how Josh's mother discovered the process, so its
origins may go back much further than I know.

"In any event, I am passing it on to you, and if you
will be diligent in the beginning, before long it will simply
become a natural part of your life, like breathing.

"This month, I want you to think about all of the
things you have to be thankful for. And when you return at
the end of the month, you are to share your version of the
Golden List with Mr. Hamilton. I hope you will continue
the process for the rest of your life, and someday you will
have the privilege—as I now have—of sharing the legacy
again."

Red's image faded away, leaving the screen blank.

The next morning, as is my usual habit, I woke up
precisely at 5:00 a.m. I have done this for years without
the aid of an alarm clock. I lay there thinking about the
Golden List that Red had shared with Jason, and I began to
construct my own list in my mind before I got out of bed.

As an eighty-year-old, it takes me more time to get out
of bed than it used to, so I knew from that point on, I would
have plenty of time each day for Red Stevens' exercise in
gratitude.

As the end of the month approached, my thoughts were drawn to Jason Stevens. I hoped he was progressing with the Golden List each day as I was. I was concerned because he had spent his whole life taking everything for granted.

Jason arrived a bit early on the last day of the month, and he had a gleam in his eye and a spring in his step. My concerns began to fade just a bit. Jason and I shook hands, and he greeted Miss Hastings. I sat behind my desk, and Jason helped Miss Hastings with her chair and then dropped into the vacant one beside her.

"Well, you seem to be in a good mood today, Jason," I observed.

He laughed aloud and responded, "I have more reasons than I ever imagined to be in a good mood."

Then he began to share his Golden List.

"Each day this month, I have been thinking about things I am grateful for. I never would have imagined that there are so many.

"First, I am thankful for my health. I have always had my health, and over the last ten months, through the directives of Uncle Red's will, I have met several people who have physical problems. So I will always be grateful for my good health.

"Second, I am thankful for my youth. I have learned that I have missed many of the important things in life thus far; however, I feel that youth can overcome any obstacle.

"Third, I am thankful for my home. It's a wonderful home, made possible through my Uncle Red's generosity. I never really appreciated it as I should, but through this ultimate gift from the will, I have been able to share my home with other people and have come to appreciate it myself.

"Fourth, I am thankful for my friends." He looked toward Miss Hastings and me, then continued. "Including both of you, Brian, Gus Caldwell, the boys at the Red Stevens Home, and—in a special way that is hard to explain—my Uncle Red.

"Fifth, I am thankful for my education. Although I did not apply myself well during college, it did give me the tools I need to go out and make education and learning a real part of my life.

"Sixth, I am thankful for all of the places I have been able to travel to and experience throughout the years thanks to my Uncle Red.

"Seventh, I am thankful for my car. It is fun as well as dependable and reliable. I learned from my friend Brian that everyone isn't as lucky as I am.

"Eighth, I am thankful for my family. Although I have not always appreciated them throughout the years, I have learned enough about families to know that, in the future, I can get along better with the family I have and at the same time create family relationships with new people.

"Number nine, I am grateful for the money that my Uncle Red has made possible over the years. But even more than that, I am grateful for the fact that, through my Uncle Red's efforts, I have learned the value and use of money. I look forward to learning more about the subject in the future and handling the money I have more wisely.

"And finally, number ten, I am thankful for each of the steps leading up to the ultimate gift. I am thankful to my Uncle Red for thinking of me as he went to the trouble of putting it together, and I am grateful to both of you for carrying out his wishes."

Miss Hastings broke in and said, "Jason, that is a marvelous list. I think you have done very well in understanding the Golden List and the gift of gratitude."

Jason smiled and remarked, "What's really amazing, Miss Hastings, is that I could go on and on. There are so many things that each of us has to be grateful for, it is hard to limit it to only ten."

I congratulated Jason, and we all shook hands as he parted. I reminded myself to be sure that Red Stevens and Jason were both on my Golden List the next morning as I thought of all the things for which I was grateful.

Thirteen

The Gift of a Day

*Life at its essence boils down
to one day at a time.
Today is the day!*

As we entered the eleventh month of Jason Stevens' pursuit of the ultimate gift, I realized that during this month we would pass the one-year anniversary of Red Stevens' death. My thoughts were often of my longtime friend and companion.

Red Stevens and I had come from two totally different worlds, and outwardly we had seemed to have very little in common. But somewhere, we had found a point of common ground between us that enabled us both to develop and nurture a friendship through five decades.

I will always remember Red Stevens as being bigger than life. While I felt comfortable in the confines of my office in Back Bay Boston, Red Stevens always seemed at home in Texas. Somehow, it seemed to fit him. It takes a place like Texas to build men like Red Stevens.

I had heard it said before that no one is ever alone if he or she has just one friend. I came to believe that no one could be alone if he or she ever had a friend like Red Stevens. I knew he would always be with me. I felt pride and responsibility that he had selected me to accompany Jason through each step of the journey toward the ultimate gift Red had planned for him.

These thoughts were in my mind when Jason Stevens arrived, and we settled into those familiar places in our law firm's conference room. Right on cue, Red Stevens came to us once again via the videotape and the large screen at the end of the room.

He smiled and boomed, "Congratulations, Jason. Since I am talking to you today, I know that Mr. Hamilton approved of your handling of the gift of gratitude last month.

"Jason, I want you to know that as I was contemplating the ultimate gift I wanted to present you through my will, I spent a lot of time thinking about you. I think you gained a permanent place in my Golden List each morning. I am thankful that you and I share a family heritage, and I sense a spark in you that I have always felt in myself. We are somehow kindred spirits beyond just our family ties."

Out of the corner of my eye, I could see Jason nodding his head as Red spoke.

Red continued. "As I have been going through the process of creating my will and thinking about my life and my death, I have considered all of the elements in my life that have made it special. I have reviewed many memories, and I carry them with me like a treasure.

"When you face your own mortality, you contemplate how much of life you have lived versus how much you have left. It is like the sand slipping through an hourglass. I know that at some point I will live the last day of my life. I have been thinking about how I would want to live that day or what I would do if I had just one day left to live. I have come to realize that if I can get that picture in my mind of maximizing one day, I will have mastered the essence of living, because life is nothing more than a series of days. If we can learn how to live one day to its fullest, our lives will be rich and meaningful.

"Jason, during the next thirty days, I want you to plan how you would live the last day of your life. And at the end of the month, I want you to give the details to Mr. Hamilton. I think you will discover how much life can be packed into one simple day, and then I hope you will discover the same thing I have discovered. Why should we wait until the last day of our lives to begin living the maximum day?

"You have all of the tools and elements you will need to design this last day for yourself. I wish you well today and every day of the rest of your life."

Red Stevens vanished from the screen.

Jason let out a deep sigh and said, "You know, I've never really thought about dying or the last day of my life."

I smiled and responded, "When I was your age, I didn't think about it much, either, but I think what your great-uncle is trying to teach you is that there is a lot to be gained by thinking through the process; and I believe the younger you are when you learn this lesson, the more quality you will have in your life."

Jason and I rose and shook hands, and he left to go about his month of discovery in the realm of the gift of a day.

Unlike Jason, I had, indeed, thought quite a bit about how I might spend the last day of my life, and all of the things I would want to pack into that one twenty-four-hour period. These thoughts were much on my mind throughout the entire month.

～～～～～

At the end of the month, Jason Stevens entered my office with the demeanor and carriage of a man on a mission. He sat down in one of my client chairs, and Miss Hastings took the other.

"Jason, it is wonderful to see you again," I said, "and I hope the month has been fruitful for you."

"It has been great," Jason blurted out excitedly, "but I'm not sure a day is long enough to cram in all the things I would want to do before I die. What I found to be amazing is the fact that the things I would most want to accomplish on the last day of my life are really simple and ordinary things.

"When I first started thinking about the process, I thought I would want to climb a great mountain or create some wonderful art or something. But after much thought, I have come to realize that my perfect day would be filled with the best of simple things."

Jason paused and looked at both Miss Hastings and me. He reached into his jacket pocket and drew out a single sheet of paper. He glanced at his notes and began again.

"Well, on the last day of my life, I would like to wake up early in the morning—there is certainly no time to waste. Before even getting out of bed, I would go through all of the things I am grateful for and create my mental Golden List. But unlike the list we talked about last month with ten things, I think on the last day of my life I would have to add many more things to the list for which I am thankful.

"I would like to have an early breakfast outdoors on a patio or balcony with a group of very special friends. I would tell them how much they mean to me, and I would want to give them each a gift that would be the recipe for getting the most out of their days and, therefore, their entire lives.

"After breakfast, I would want to call a number of people who have been special to me—people like Gus Caldwell in Texas, the people at the Red Stevens Library in South America, all of the boys at the home up in Maine, and many others. I would also want to call all of my relatives and other people with whom I have not had a good relationship. I would want to tell each of them I am sorry for whatever has gone wrong between us, and I would want to ask them to do what I am doing, which is simply hold on to all the good memories and release all the bad ones.

"For lunch, I would like to take my friend Brian to his favorite restaurant and buy him anything he wanted. I would ask him to share with me the dreams he has for his life.

"During the afternoon, I would like to enjoy some of the simple pleasures, including a walk in the park—hopefully with the little girl named Emily I met earlier this year—followed by a trip to the art museum and a brief outing on a sailboat around Boston Harbor.

"Then, in the evening, I would like to have a special banquet for all of my friends and their friends, and I certainly would want both of you there. At the end of the banquet, I would like to step up on a platform and share with everyone the gifts that my great-uncle, Red Stevens, left to me. I would want to have it videotaped so that my dream of sharing this wonderful gift with other young people like me could go on after I died."

Jason glanced up at Miss Hastings and me, and then back down to his sheet of paper. After several moments, he folded the paper and put it back into his jacket pocket. "Well, there are many other things I thought of to do, and they're all good," he said, "but those are the ones I thought I could fit into my last day."

I smiled and responded, "Jason, I can't think of any better way to spend one's last day. I think we can all agree that you have come to a wonderful understanding of what your Uncle Red had in mind in the gift of a day."

Jason stood and shook my hand warmly and actually gave Miss Hastings a brief hug. As she escorted him to the elevator, I couldn't help but remember the sullen, angry young man who had come into my office just one year earlier. I knew that Red Stevens was smiling down on us.

FOURTEEN

The Gift of Love

Love is a treasure
for which we can never pay.
The only way we keep it
is to give it away.

I must admit to having mixed emotions as I awaited Jason Stevens' arrival for what I knew would be the beginning of our last monthly journey together in this yearlong odyssey of discovery. I was elated about the progress Jason had made, and I felt confident and excited about the future he had before him; but I was also struck with the sense of loss that comes at the end of any difficult but meaningful journey.

I felt, in a way, as if I would be losing my longtime friend, Red Stevens, once again because I would not be able to look forward to these monthly visits. On the other hand, if I had learned anything from going through this transformation with Jason, it was a fact that the best of Red Stevens would always be with me.

Miss Hastings called me on the intercom to let me know that Jason Stevens had arrived. I met them in the conference room, and I believe they both, in a way, were sharing the same mixed emotions I felt.

Miss Hastings performed her now familiar ritual of taking the videotape from the box Red Stevens had left in our vault along with his will. She put the tape in the video player at the end of our conference room.

Red Stevens' image appeared on the large screen, and knowing him as well as I did, I believed he was feeling some of the same emotions we all shared.

Red began. "Jason, I want to congratulate you for making it to the last step of the ultimate gift I planned for you. I am very proud that you obviously made it through the learning process involved in the gift of a day from last month. I do not know what you planned for your last day, but I know it was judged acceptable by Mr. Hamilton. I would imagine that the activities you planned for the day were much like mine—very simple and somewhat ordinary.

"If we are living our lives the way we should, everything should be in such an order that we wouldn't change the last day of our life from any other day. Please always remember that none of us is guaranteed a long life. We're not guaranteed anything but today.

"Also, I think if you will consider it, you will realize that there is probably nothing that you would plan for your last day of life that you couldn't do today or tomorrow. Somehow, I think life's tragedies are made up not as much of the great failures as much as of the simple pleasures and kind gestures missed."

Red Stevens paused, and I could feel his emotions and all of ours as we sat in the darkened conference room.

Finally, he continued. "Jason, in this last month, I'm going to introduce you to the one part of my ultimate gift to you that encompasses all of the other gifts as well as everything good you will ever do, have, or know in your life. That is the gift of love.

"Anything good, honorable, and desirable in life is based on love. Anything bad or evil is simply life without the love involved. Love is a misused and overused term in our society. It is applied to any number of frivolous things and pursuits; but the love I am talking about in the gift of love is the goodness that comes only from God. Not everyone believes or acknowledges that. And that's okay. I still know that real love comes from Him—whether or not we know it.

"Since love is a part of each of the other gifts you have experienced throughout this year, during the next thirty days, I want you to explore how love is involved in all the other gifts, and prepare to share what you find with Mr. Hamilton.

"Please remember that your attitude and your performance are still being judged, and if you fail—even in the twelfth month—you will not be receiving the entire ultimate gift I have planned for you. My warning to you is not meant to be threatening, but holding you to the highest standard in my own way is the greatest act of love I can show you."

Red Stevens' image faded, and the screen was, once again, dark.

Jason sat motionless for several minutes. I knew that he was deep in thought. Finally, we all stood and quietly left the conference room. It was almost as if we had been to a memorial service for Red Stevens. I felt it was a fitting tribute to my oldest and dearest friend.

On the last day of the month, Miss Hastings ushered Jason into my office. They both sat in their familiar places, and we exchanged brief greetings. I could tell that Jason had much on his mind.

"Mr. Hamilton and Miss Hastings," Jason began, "I do not have the words to express what this process over the last year has meant to me. I am simply not the same person I was a year ago. I feel that, in many ways, today is my birthday. I want to thank you both for being a part of it."

I noticed that Jason's eyes seemed moist, and Miss Hastings' seasonal allergies seemed to act up at that very moment. I will admit to feeling a lump in my own throat. Jason took a deep breath and launched into his report.

"During the first month of this year, I was angered and very resentful of not receiving an inheritance like everyone else in the family. I was further frustrated when I learned about what I thought then was a crazy plan for the entire year. Then I found myself learning about the gift of work with Gus Caldwell down in Texas.

"At that time, love was the furthest thing from my mind when Gus Caldwell ordered me to dig post holes and build a fence. But as I look back on it, I realize that Mr. Caldwell had a great love for my Uncle Red and passed that on to me. He loved me enough to make sure that I learned the entire lesson that my Uncle Red planned for the gift of work. I also learned that there is a certain love which comes from doing a job well. When you can step back at the end of a long, hard day and watch the sun set over a straight and strong fence that you built yourself, you get the feeling that everything is right with the world.

"During the month when I learned about the gift of money, I learned that loving money leads to a hollow, empty existence. But when you learn how to love people and use money, everything is in its proper perspective.

"From the gift of friends, I learned that you can love others in a way I had never known. When you just worry about yourself, you are always disappointed. But when you think about others and their well-being first, everything works out best for you and for them.

"From the gift of learning, I discovered that people who have no material things—but a passion to learn and a true love of learning—are really quite wealthy. This love for knowledge has come into my life, and I cannot believe that I was so self-centered that I ignored the wisdom of the ages as I pursued my own self-destruction.

"The gift of problems taught me that obstacles are nothing more than a challenge that we face. Before this year, I looked at problems as something that was totally bad, something that had to be dealt with—or, better yet, ignored. But when you look at your problems through a spirit of love, you realize that there is a grand design to this world, and the problem is given to you for the lesson it will teach you and the better person it will make you.

"From the gift of family, I learned that families are present when love is present. People can become a family when they add love to their relationships. Without love, families are just a group of people who share the same family tree.

"The gift of laughter taught me that in order to love life, you have to enjoy it. And when you can laugh at the good things and the bad, you will begin to feel the love life really has to offer.

"During my exploration of the gift of dreams, I came to understand that life has been given to us with a sense of love for everything around us. Our passions and dreams and goals are the outward manifestations of the love we feel inside.

"Before I experienced the gift of giving, I thought that if you gave something away, someone else now possessed it, and you were left with less than you had before. In reality, when you give out of love, both the giver and the receiver have more than they started with.

"The gift of gratitude taught me that we can truly feel and experience love when we remember and enjoy all of the wonderful things we have been given.

"And, finally, from the gift of a day, I learned that if I only had twenty-four hours left to live, I would want to feel and experience as much love as I could and pass it on to as many others as possible."

Jason paused and cleared his throat. I was just about to tell him that I heartily approved of his mastery of the gift of love, when he continued.

"If I were going to really try to define the gift of love in tangible terms, I would have to cite as an example what my Uncle Red did for me and what he gave me during this last year. When we truly love others, our love makes each of us a different person, and it makes each one we love a different person too.

"My Uncle Red's love for me in giving me the ultimate gift forever changed my life and who I am."

Jason rose to his feet and hugged Miss Hastings. He stepped around my desk and hugged me as well. He thanked us both for everything and let us know that he looked forward to staying in touch with us in the future.

As Jason put his hand on the doorknob, I stopped him by saying, "Just a minute, Jason. There is one more step in the ultimate gift that you don't know about."

Fifteen

The Ultimate Gift

In the end,
life lived to its fullest
is its own ultimate gift.

J ason turned with a bewildered look on his face and
said, "I don't know what you're talking about, Mr.
Hamilton. We did all twelve of the gifts that Uncle Red
mentioned, and he said that this month would be the last
one."

"Well, as Red Stevens' attorney and as executor of
his estate," I replied, "I can tell you that he had one last
bequest in his will that would only be made available if all
the conditions were met. As the sole arbiter of each of the
conditions, I can tell you that they have all been met and
exceeded."

Jason continued to appear perplexed and said, "I really
don't know what you are talking about. I thought—"

114

Miss Hastings interrupted and said, "I realize you thought you were done. But there is one more step. If you'll follow me into the conference room, I do believe all things will become clear."

We adjourned to the conference room, and in a few moments, Red Stevens was once again speaking to us from the video screen.

"Jason," he said, "I want to tell you how proud of you I am. You have completed each element and received each part of the ultimate gift I had planned for you. I wish that I had come into possession of all twelve gifts as early in life as you have. Now that you have received the ultimate gift, not only do you have the privilege of enjoying it, but you have the responsibility of living your life to its fullest with each gift in balance. You have the further responsibility of passing along the ultimate gift whenever it is possible.

"I wish I could be with you to simply watch the wonderful things that are going to happen in your life, but somehow—in my own way—I suspect I will be with you.

"Jason, I have done a lot of things in my life, but the best of them may well be passing the ultimate gift on to you. Please don't let me down. Make the gift grow and be fruitful. Make your life an extension of the ultimate gift you have received. If you will do all of these things, you will have—in your own way—given to me your version of the ultimate gift."

The image of Red Stevens faded away for what would be the last time.

As the lights came up, Jason leaped to his feet and, with a confident look on his face, said, "I am going to do it! I am going to use every element of the ultimate gift, and I am going to find a way to pass it on to deprived people who are as I was a year ago. I had no idea that the greatest gift anyone could be given is the awareness of all of the gifts he or she already has. Now I know why God made me and put me on this earth. I understand the purpose for my life and how I can help other people find their purpose."

Jason, once again, headed for the door, and, once again, I stopped him—this time by saying, "Young man, I have never seen anybody in such a hurry to leave."

Jason turned around with that same bewildered expression on his face. "I'm sorry, Mr. Hamilton," he said, "I just thought—"

"I know, you thought we were done," I interrupted. "If you will just sit back down, I will discharge my final duty with regard to Red Stevens' last will and testament."

Miss Hastings handed me the voluminous document, and I turned to the appropriate page. I was just getting my reading glasses out of my pocket when Jason blurted out, "I just thought—"

I interrupted Jason again by scolding him playfully, "Young man, never interrupt a duly appointed attorney when he is trying to discharge his final duty."

Miss Hastings laughed and added, "Especially when the attorney is eighty years old."

We all laughed together, and I read from the document. "And to my great-nephew, Jason Stevens, I leave control of my charitable trust fund. Its current value is somewhere slightly over $1 billion. As my great-nephew has shown himself to be responsible and able in every area of life, he will have the sole control of this charitable trust fund which supports the Red Stevens Home for Boys, the Red Stevens Library Program, several scholarship programs, hospitals, and many other worthy institutions.

"I direct Jason to use the wisdom and experience he has gained as a recipient of the ultimate gift to manage these projects and any others that he deems significant."

Jason sat back in his chair, totally stunned. Finally, after several false starts, he said, "Do you mean that I am in charge of all of those things?"

I gave him a formal look and tone, answering, "As I read the document, it would seem to be the case. You are in charge of all of the aforementioned, and anything else you feel to be important."

Jason lit up. A smile spread across his face. He looked toward Miss Hastings and back to me, saying, "I could use part of the charitable trust to spread the ultimate gift all around the world."

Miss Hastings replied, "If I'm not mistaken, I believe that's what Red Stevens had in mind all along."

Jason hugged both of us again, thanked us profusely, and parted.

Miss Hastings and I sat back down at the conference room table and simply drank in the feeling of elation and success.

"Did you notice," she observed, "that he never asked about his income or wages or anything else like that?"

I nodded with a smile, as we both reflected on the amazing transformation that Jason had made in one year.

Finally, ever vigilant Miss Hastings left the conference room to complete her many duties for the day. I was left alone in the conference room, and I couldn't resist rewinding the videotape and watching Red Stevens' last message one more time.

When it was over, I spoke to the darkened screen. "Well, old friend, I believe this is where we finally do part company. I wish I could tell you how thankful I am to be included in the ultimate gift, and I wish I could tell you all of the wonderful things Jason has done and is going to do."

As I walked out of the conference room, I realized Red did know and—in his own way—would be watching with me as Jason lived out and passed on The Ultimate Gift.

The
Ultimate
Life

Jim Stovall

David C Cook®

transforming lives together

There seems to be a hunger that drives the soul of man, and our choices lead us as surely as if we had followed a map. Some call it luck—whether good or bad.

Others, destination.

~~~~~~

From the personal diary of Joye Kanelakos

Introduction

I want to thank you for the investment you have made in this book and the message contained in its pages. Time is a precious commodity. I am grateful when people are willing to spend some of it with me in one of my books.

Some of you are beginning this journey with these characters and me for the first time today. Others began the journey through *The Ultimate Gift* book or major motion picture. In any event, I'm glad to have you onboard.

When you turn the last page of this book, I believe you will be a different person than you are right now. This story is about the characters you will read about, but the message is about you and me. This is not a journey or a message for a few hours between the covers of this book. It is a message and a journey for the rest of your life. When you have completed the book, the journey will just be beginning.

As you start your *Ultimate Life* journey, please remember to always share this message and the journey with as many others as possible. Please write to me with your stories of how one of the messages in this book has impacted your life or the life of someone you know. Your words are encouraging to me, and they may just help many others around the world through another *Ultimate Life* book in the future.

Thank you,
Jim Stovall

*This book is dedicated to, as always, Crystal,
who is still the best writer who lives at my house.*

*It is also dedicated to Dorothy Thompson without whom
this book would not exist, to my professional team that
makes me look better than I should and makes it fun,
and to my friends and partners at The Ultimate Gift
Experience and* The Ultimate Gift *movie for believing
in me and the message of* The Ultimate Life.

Table of Contents

One

LIFE BEGINS TODAY

*In this life, the most average day can take an extraordinary turn;
therefore, each day should be anticipated and savored as a gift.*

Observing the parade of life from my unique vantage point for more than four decades has allowed me to consider the very best and the very worst that humanity has to offer. That particular morning began much like any other. Little did I anticipate or even imagine that it was the dawning of the day that would change my life and the lives of countless others forever.

Sunrise found me, as it generally does, seated at my ornate monument of a desk. These many years I have allowed the outdated and excessive beast to remain, as people who are supposed to know such things assure me that it is befitting my status and a symbol of my chosen lot in life. If the desk is a compromise to my colleagues and position, my chair is an oasis of self-indulgence. It is a custom-made leather creation that, over the years, has expanded and transformed itself to accommodate only me.

I have heard myself described as imposing and overpowering, among other adjectives. If this is true, it is no doubt a distinct advantage in my chosen profession. Nevertheless, if anything, my legendary leather chair dwarfs even me.

I was attempting to coordinate finishing off the remainder of my second cup of coffee. The anticipated chiming of the historic grandfather clock would announce to everyone up and down the corridor that the beginning of this day would wait no longer. As the majestic clock began to chime ten times, I left the comfortable environs of my chair, traversed around the colossal desk, and made my way toward the ten-foot mahogany door.

"All rise."

I heard the familiar words solemnly intoned that signaled the beginning of my workday.

"Court is now in session. The Honorable Judge Stanford A. Davis presiding."

I stepped through the mahogany doorway, mounted the three steps that rose behind the judicial bench, and settled into my adequate but decidedly less comfortable chair. I gazed out over the assemblage a few beats longer than absolutely necessary, then announced, "You may be seated."

Over the years, I have come to anticipate the gravity or importance of a particular case based on how many participants, observers, and representatives of the media crowd into my courtroom. While not perfect, this barometer has proven itself to be quite accurate over thousands of cases. If it were accurate on this day, I knew that I had never before presided over a case quite like this one.

Each case is unique as the people, situations, and law governing them vary greatly. The law, when adjudicated properly, lies somewhere between a science and an art. A judge must be scientific enough to know the pertinent, repetitive volumes of case law and how they impact every situation while, on the other hand, be artful enough to get into the minds and spirits of those who formed and framed our laws to discern their intent and their lofty ideals as they relate to the modern and current circumstance.

I knew—just as everyone gathered knew, and everyone in the civilized world knew—that the time had arrived for the battle over the estate of Red Stevens. Even though we all recognized this, I stared at the paperwork arranged before me until the courtroom grew deathly silent. Then I pounded my gavel, nodded to my bailiff, and addressed the court reporter.

"The case before the court today is the estate directed by the last will and testament of Howard 'Red' Stevens."

The court reporter's fingers flew unerringly over the mysterious keys just as they had done for many years in my courtroom. I paused reverently, gazing at the counsel and litigants on both sides of the aisle that bisected my marble majestic courtroom.

I knew, in theory, the day I first sat at this bench— and I now know from practical experience—that among the primary roles of a sitting judge is that of appearing, conducting one's self, and acting judicial. When I was first appointed to the bench, I was among the youngest to have ever sat in this position.

I remember commenting to my beloved wife, Marie,

that my walk down the corridor each day was intimidating as I had to pass beneath the portraits of all the solemn and wise judges who had gone before me. As a fresh-faced youth, at least in judicial terms, I felt inadequate to fill their shoes, much less their robes. In the ensuing forty-plus years when I have expressed my concerns about my inevitable aging and my own mortality, Marie has repeatedly admonished me, "You're not getting old, but you are getting very judicial."

I am ever mindful of the fact that the pomp and circumstance surrounding the courtroom is not to elevate me but is, instead, to show the respect and reverence for everything that this courtroom, as a symbol of our law, represents. I concern myself little with what people think of me as I live and move and have my being on the sidewalks and in the streets of our city. But seated here at the bench, attired in my judicial robes, I become a symbol of all that we hold dear.

As such, I demand respect—not for Stan Davis, husband, friend, and neighbor—but, instead, for Judge Stanford A. Davis, symbol and arbiter of the law.

What can I or anyone say about Red Stevens that hasn't already been said, written, or broadcast to every part of the civilized world? Red Stevens was one of those people who became a legend in his own time and a cultural icon after his death.

Generally speaking, a judge would be called upon to recuse himself or vacate the bench, turning the case over to another judge if he had heard as much about the case and the people involved as I had. Fortunately or unfortunately, there was no judge anywhere, or person anywhere, who had not heard about and formed an opinion about Red Stevens, the terms and conditions of his will, and the case to be presented before me.

Red Stevens was a giant human being in person, reputation, and deed. His life had been lived so much in the spotlight that it was hard to separate myth and legend from reality. He had been so famous for so long that his life seemed to have bridged many generations or eras of history.

Red Stevens, as both legend and history tell us, was born into obscurity and unbelievable poverty in the swamplands of Louisiana. As a very young man, he left home headed for Texas with nothing more than the clothes on his back, a head full of dogged determination, and an indomitable spirit full of dreams. Over the next half century, Red Stevens forged an empire in cattle, oil, finance, and industry that rivaled anything the world had ever seen.

Red Stevens did everything in a big way. He was a hard-driving, sometimes ruthless businessman. He was a generous and compassionate philanthropist. He was a valued friend to many and a feared enemy to some. He knew virtually every person of fame and fortune who lived during his time. In many ways, Red Stevens and a handful of people like him defined the twentieth century and established much of what we know as the twenty-first century.

His accomplishments were legendary, but in many ways he was endowed with the human frailties that plague us all. Red Stevens worked unbelievably hard to give his family everything he thought they wanted. Far too late in life, he discovered that mostly what they wanted and needed was him. Near the end of his life, Red Stevens came to realize that, regretfully, he had spent far too much time, effort, and energy at coronations, negotiations, and state dinners and not nearly enough time at Little League games, birthday parties, and family reunions.

He came to this realization at a point in time when he knew he had only a few days or at most a few weeks to live. As he considered the generational dilemma that too much of his money and not enough of his time had created among his relatives, Red Stevens knew that it was too late to help any of his children and most, if not all, of his grandchildren. However, Red in his final days identified what he thought and hoped could be a spark of promise in his young grandson Jason Stevens.

He devised a plan that he executed privately in his last will and testament that became front-page news and popular conversation in every part of our culture. Red left his oil wells, cattle ranches, and financial empire to his children. But, to his grandson Jason, he left through his will a bequest that has become known as The Ultimate Gift.

The Ultimate Gift was a revolutionary idea and was groundbreaking within the field of estate law. It was as unique and special as was Red Stevens. The bequest that Red left to his grandson involved a twelve-month odyssey during which Jason was both encouraged and forced to learn about The Gift of Money, The Gift of Work, The Gift of Friends, and a number of other life lessons. There were a total of twelve gifts that, together, comprised Red Stevens' Ultimate Gift, which he planned for his grandson Jason.

The terms of Red's will called for Jason to learn a real life lesson both through Red's words on video and through tasks Jason was to complete. If Jason successfully completed each task, the will called for Jason to inherit a mysterious Ultimate Gift alluded to by Red Stevens in his will and in the videos he left behind for Jason. Each video message expressed Red's thoughts and experiences pertaining to that individual gift; but the bequest representing Red's Ultimate Gift was never disclosed.

During the year after Red Stevens' death, Jason—under the direction of Red's lifelong friend and lawyer Theodore J. Hamilton—completed to Mr. Hamilton's satisfaction each of the twelve gifts, therefore qualifying to receive Red Stevens' bequest of The Ultimate Gift.

Jason Stevens grew and developed as a person throughout the year, much as a wildflower would flourish that suddenly received the attention of a master gardener. By the time Jason completed the twelfth lesson, which was The Gift of Love, he thought that the lessons themselves were The Ultimate Gift. While this was certainly a major part of Red Stevens' plan for completing The Ultimate Gift, Jason—as a result of accomplishing all twelve tasks—was then directed by Red Stevens' will to receive virtually unlimited control of several billion dollars with which Jason was to help other people experience their own version of Red Stevens' Ultimate Gift.

The seed of an idea that began in Red Stevens' mind was played out as a drama in headlines around the world, and now it had ended up in my courtroom.

On one side of the aisle sat Red Stevens' children and grandchildren who collectively had retained a veritable dream team of high-profile, high-priced lawyers to contest and attempt to overturn Red Stevens' will so they could divide among themselves several billion dollars more than they already had received.

On the other side of the aisle sat Jason Stevens, flanked by one decidedly underwhelming lawyer who, if I had not checked the records, I would have assumed was not old enough or experienced enough to have finished law school. Basically, this looked like a courtroom version of David and Goliath.

Red Stevens' lifelong attorney and friend, Theodore J. Hamilton of Hamilton, Hamilton, and Hamilton, had left the country for an extended sabbatical shortly after Red Stevens' will had been executed and The Ultimate Gift had been presented to Jason Stevens. When last heard from, Hamilton was traveling, lecturing, and studying throughout India and the Far East, and his last communication had come from a remote village in the Himalayas.

The dream team had successfully completed legal maneuvers, freezing all of Jason Stevens' assets, so the totality of Jason's legal firepower in the courtroom before me was embodied in the person of one young Jeffrey Watkins, Esquire. Jeffrey Watkins, my research revealed, had indeed graduated from law school in a somewhat undistinguished manner from a relatively unknown institution of higher learning. As this was virtually his first case, he had no track record to indicate what level of skill or expertise might be hidden behind his unkempt hair, thick glasses, and acne-riddled countenance.

I cleared my throat, waited through a pregnant pause, and then directed my gaze toward the plaintiff's side of the aisle. I inquired, "Are all the parties present and accounted for today?"

An immaculately coiffed and tailored middle-aged member of the dream team rose from the table in front of the Stevens clan. He theatrically gestured, bowed slightly, and spoke.

"Your Honor, if it please the court, I am L. Myron Dudly of the firm Dudly, Cheetham, and Leech appearing before you today representing the rightful and legal claims of the Stevens family, heirs in fact and in law to the estate of Howard 'Red' Stevens."

L. Myron Dudly smiled smugly as muffled applause could actually be heard from the Stevens family scattered throughout several rows behind him. I pounded my gavel forcefully and sat up straight. I peered over my glasses and down my nose at the lawyer who appeared to have just stepped out of the pages of a gentlemen's fashion magazine.

I growled, "Counselor, you will advise your clients to respect the order and dignity of my court and these proceedings. The court will enter into the record that you are Mr. Dudly of Dudly, Cheetham, and Leech and, further, that you represent the Stevens family in this matter. As to who may or may not be the rightful beneficiary in fact or in law to Howard 'Red' Stevens' estate will be a matter to be decided by this court."

I took three deep and audible breaths and pointed the business end of my gavel toward L. Myron Dudly as I asked, "Do we understand one another?"

Dudly appeared to deflate significantly as he muttered, "Yes, sir."

I set down my gavel and continued.

"Counselor, you can save your theatrics and suppositions for an amateur theater night or game of charades somewhere, but in this courtroom, we deal with facts and law."

Dudly nodded once and dropped into the chair behind him. I think he would have welcomed the opportunity to disappear under the table if the chair had not stopped his progress.

I then shifted my gaze to the other side of the aisle and

raised my eyebrows inquiringly. As this elicited no action, I finally had to ask, "Counselor, would you do us the honor of introducing yourself to this court for the record?"

Jeffrey Watkins shakily rose to his feet. His suit had seen better days—I assumed being worn by someone else as it certainly did not fit him. He leaned on the table in front of him as sweat poured down his face. After a few false starts, he finally squeaked out, "Your Honor, I am Jeffrey Watkins representing the defendant, Jason Stevens."

He plopped back into his chair, appearing to have run a marathon as a result of making the one statement before the court.

I was considering the overwhelming mismatch among the legal talent arrayed before me. This was particularly distressing to me as I knew this was going to be an extremely high-profile and complex case with unbelievable assets at stake. Then, without preamble or warning, in one brief instant, the tide turned.

Both of the double doors in the back of my courtroom swung open at the same time. I was reaching for my gavel to admonish my two loyal and long-time bailiffs, Jim and Paul, who knew better than to open the doors while court was in session, when it happened.

Out of nowhere appeared an immaculately dressed gentleman who majestically—almost regally—strode down the center aisle of my courtroom. His ebony skin virtually glowed with energy, and the fire in his eyes was evident to all in attendance. As he slid behind the table on the defendant's side of the aisle, he announced what I and every student of the law already knew.

"Your Honor, I am Theodore J. Hamilton of Hamilton, Hamilton, and Hamilton, for the defense."

TWO

LIFE IS A JOURNEY AND A DESTINATION

*In this life, there is nothing more powerful than
a person who has seen the path to destiny within
their soul and is willing to pursue it.*

The shock of Hamilton's grand entrance reverberated throughout the courtroom. As I pounded my gavel and called for order, I could hear Jason Stevens excitedly exclaim, "Mr. Hamilton, I couldn't reach you. I thought you were lost."

Hamilton smiled wisely and replied, "Young man, there is a vast difference between being lost and simply not wishing to be found."

Before the court could fully come to order, L. Myron Dudly jumped to his feet and declared, "Your Honor, I most vigorously object to this theatrical and disrespectful display exhibited by opposing counsel."

Theodore J. Hamilton slowly rose as the courtroom grew silent. He addressed me but glared across the aisle at Dudly in much the same way that someone would look at an unknown foreign object stuck to the sole of their shoe.

"Your Honor, it was not my intention to upset, intimidate, nor agitate opposing counsel by simply walking into the courtroom."

Mr. Dudly visibly reddened and raised his voice in anger. "Your Honor, I must most vigorously object."

I pounded my gavel for order. I stared sternly at both lawyers then motioned to them as I spoke. "Counsel will approach the bench."

L. Myron Dudly shuffled slightly and then approached the ominous raised judicial bench as if he were a third-grade student preparing to explain how his dog ate his homework. Mr. Hamilton nodded and strode confidently to an area on the polished marble floor directly in front of me. He looked up expectantly.

I certainly knew Theodore J. Hamilton, and he knew that I knew him. Hamilton was nothing less than a legend. When I was in law school and then clerked for old Judge Eldridge, tales of the historic legal exploits of one Theodore J. Hamilton abounded. He had appeared in my court before—always as a consummate professional. He was imposing and intimidating but had the confident aura of someone who knew they had nothing to prove.

Hamilton was like an all-star major-league pitcher. Even though the umpire is trying to be fair, it's hard to call a ball if it's even remotely close to the plate. I glared down at both attorneys.

"Gentlemen, we have a lot of work to do here, and I believe if we will keep the legal matters at hand foremost in our minds and set aside any personal differences, we will be best served."

L. Myron Dudly made the mistake I hoped he would avoid. He spoke.

"Your Honor, Mr. Hamilton seems to think that the rules of law and of this courtroom somehow do not apply to him. We all received ample notice of this hearing to be conducted today and to begin promptly at 10:00 a.m. Maybe Your Honor should instruct counsel in the fine art of telling time."

Theodore J. Hamilton actually chuckled. He paused for an uncomfortable length of time and then he spoke to me while glancing dismissively in the direction of L. Myron Dudly.

"Your Honor, if Mr. Dud—" Hamilton coughed several times, then continued, "—ly ..."

Dudly's eyes actually bugged out as he stammered, "Your Honor, I haven't been referred to as Dud since grade school. I implore you to invoke disciplinary action on opposing counsel for a cheap, demeaning, juvenile gesture."

Hamilton appeared innocent—almost angelic—as he looked up wide-eyed and spoke. "Your Honor, I seem to have developed a tickle in the back of my throat that from time to time manifests itself in the form of a dry cough. It seemed to take hold of me just as I was pronouncing counsel's name, right between the 'Dud' and the 'ly.' I am not familiar with any juvenile antics to which counsel may refer. In fact, as a well-seasoned octogenarian myself, I ask the court's indulgence when my physical ailments from time to time may affect my performance in ways I wish they wouldn't. When Your Honor reaches eighty-plus, I'm sure you will fully understand this."

I heard my always-solemn court reporter, Scott, snicker, and I stifled my own laughter as I responded, "Mr. Hamilton, I have not yet reached eighty, but I am not far behind you, so I do understand your situation; however, the cough did seem to come at a peculiar time.

Hamilton nodded solemnly and said, "Yes, it is quite a curious thing, Your Honor. Unexplainable, actually. And, with regard to my arrival today, I came with all due haste the moment I received word of this hearing."

Dudly interrupted. "Your Honor, our firm received notice of this hearing and copies of the notice received by opposing counsel weeks ago."

Hamilton continued. "Your Honor, I have been traveling extensively throughout India and the Far East on a bit of a sabbatical. Word was forwarded to me as expeditiously as possible by telephone, overnight mail service, facsimile, courier, and finally in the remote regions of the Himalayas via a traveling missionary riding a yak."

Hamilton smiled innocently at Dudly and continued. "Opposing counsel may or may not have any direct experience in executing timely legal documents via yak, but I can assure counsel and Your Honor that a best effort was made by all concerned, and this would, indeed, include support staff, clerks, postal authorities, couriers, the missionary in question, and most certainly the yak himself."

Dudly blurted out, "Your Honor, I am dumbfounded ..."

But all that could be heard was "Your Honor, I am dumb ..." as another coughing fit from Hamilton drowned out the rest.

Dudly pointed violently and continued, "Your Honor, he's doing it again."

Hamilton shook his head disbelieving and solemnly

intoned, "Your Honor, when my young, learned, opposing counsel reaches the august age of eighty and beyond, I hope that he will be able to ply his chosen trade without opposition, fifty years his junior, counting and highlighting each time he coughs."

I couldn't help but chuckle as I tapped my gavel for order.

"Gentlemen, let us proceed with the dignity and professionalism that this court and each of your clients deserves. Please return to your places."

I addressed both attorneys. "Gentlemen, the court will entertain any motions you may have at this time."

L. Myron Dudly stood to his feet and spoke with a recovered sense of dignity.

"Your Honor, this case is a very simple and straightforward one. And when all the evidence has been presented, I am certain that the court will award all of Howard 'Red' Stevens' worldly assets to my clients, in spite of any legal shams or Boy Scout projects that may have been conducted by opposing counsel and his client."

I glanced toward Hamilton, anticipating an objection. Dudly paused as well, assuming he had it coming. Hamilton leaned over toward young Jeffrey Watkins and spoke discreetly. "Son, could you see about getting us some coffee here?"

Watkins replied more shrilly and loudly than necessary, "I didn't go to law school to learn how to get coffee."

Hamilton smoothly responded, "No, I'm sure you didn't learn how to get coffee in law school, but you appear to be a bright youngster, and I have confidence in you."

Hamilton turned toward Dudly as Dudly's motion continued.

"Your Honor, we have filed and this court has granted a restraining order freezing all assets of Jason Stevens that came from Red Stevens either before his death or through that comic book estate proceeding that took place after his death."

I shuffled through my paperwork to locate the pertinent document and responded, "Mr. Dudly, I have that order here before me, and it has been duly executed and recorded. Do you have a point?"

Dudly gestured across the aisle and spoke haltingly. "Your Honor, it's Mr. Hamilton."

I interrupted Mr. Dudly, inquiring, "*What* is Mr. Hamilton?"

At that moment, Jeffrey Watkins scooted back into his seat at the counsel table. He passed a cup of coffee to Jason who slid it over to Theodore J. Hamilton.

Dudly continued, "Your Honor, it is well known in legal circles that Mr. Hamilton charges in excess of 1 million dollars per case, and Mr. Stevens—confirmed by legal audits conducted by our firm—has no financial means of support other than that provided by Red Stevens."

Hamilton looked up as he sipped his coffee and spoke. "Your Honor, if it would be of any help at this point in opposing counsel's motion, I would like to assure the court that I have been adequately retained and promptly paid for my services in this matter; however, I do appreciate Mr. Dud ..."

Hamilton paused to sip his coffee and continued, "... ly being concerned about my fee and my financial well-being."

The courtroom burst into laughter, and I pounded my gavel for order.

Dudly inquired indignantly, "Do you expect this court to believe that you have received your customary compensation from Jason Stevens without benefit of his previous trust or the proceeds from the estate?"

Hamilton smiled, shrugged his shoulders, and stated, "Well, I customarily like to receive a better cup of coffee, but I am willing to accept this one as payment in full for any services rendered or to be rendered in this matter."

I failed to mask my impatience as I said, "If that resolves the issue, I will ask Mr. Hamilton if he has any motions to present to the court."

It was as if an aged boxer came out of his corner for the final round of a championship fight as Hamilton rose to speak.

"Your Honor, I am quite confident that the last will and testament of Howard 'Red' Stevens reflected his intentions and his wishes for his estate. I know this because for more than sixty years Red Stevens was my best friend."

Hamilton paused and continued emotionally, "And, I dare to say that I was his best friend."

Theodore J. Hamilton stopped to collect himself then got down to business. "Furthermore, I can assure this court and all those concerned with this matter that Red Stevens' last will and testament—although informal and somewhat unconventional—was and is valid and binding. I am certain of this as I wrote, filed, and carried out every tenet of the document myself."

Dudly smugly rose to his feet and offhandedly inquired, "Your Honor, does counsel have a point he wishes to make?"

Hamilton fixed Dudly with a stare that would certainly melt a glacier. He paused until Dudly was forced to look away, then spoke.

"I do, most certainly, have a point for opposing counsel and his ..."

Hamilton paused as if searching his mind for the right word to describe something distasteful, then continued.

"... his clients."

Hamilton glanced dismissively at the several rows of greedy relatives arrayed behind Dudly and continued.

"As I do have an intimate personal understanding and professional working knowledge of Red Stevens' intentions and his will, I want the court to recognize the provision that calls for any relative to lose his or her bequest immediately upon arguing, protesting, or contesting this will or the provisions of Red Stevens' estate."

Hamilton paced back and forth in front of the counsel table. He allowed the bomb he had just dropped to take effect. Scattered murmuring and muttering could be heard from the rows of relatives behind Dudly.

"Lose everything?"

"What does he mean, 'Lose everything'?"

Dudly frantically shuffled through paperwork in front of him.

I tapped my gavel and paused for silence to descend.

"Mr. Hamilton, I have, indeed, anticipated your motion and studied the matter thoroughly. It does appear, without a doubt, that the collected beneficiaries gathered here who have all jointly contested the will have, indeed, forfeited their entire inheritance if this will is upheld."

I heard gasps, curses, and sobs emanating from Dudly's side of the courtroom. I pounded for order and continued.

"Mr. Hamilton, your motion is accepted. It would seem that what we have before us is what my friend and mentor, old Judge Eldridge, called a winner-take-all horse race."

I looked down at Scott typing away at the court reporter's station and said, "For the record, let me state that the court recognizes that if Mr. Dudly and his clients are successful in overturning Howard 'Red' Stevens' will, they will divide all proceeds previously awarded to Jason Stevens. However, if on the other hand Mr. Hamilton is successful in defending the bequest received by Jason Stevens, all other inheritances will be forfeited and be added to the trust currently controlled by Jason Stevens."

The gauntlet had been thrown down. Everything was hanging in the balance.

I rose to my feet, tapped my gavel perfunctorily, and stated, "This court will stand in recess for one hour."

I bounded down the steps, through the mahogany door, and found myself trying to catch my breath in the comfortable, familiar confines of my chambers. Rarely had I considered a case that was this simple yet this complicated. This was magnified as there were billions of dollars riding on my decision.

I paced back and forth for the entire hour, considering Red Stevens' life, his intentions for Jason, and the monumental gifts he had provided for his grandson.

I knew, regardless of any personal feelings I might have, that I had to give every consideration to Red Stevens' children who wanted to inherit even more of his estate. It went beyond more. They, in fact, wanted it all. On the other hand, I had to consider Jason Stevens, as to whether or not he had mastered each of the gifts intended for him and, therefore, might be entitled to several billion dollars. And, finally—after hearing all of the opposing arguments——I had to be the voice of the one person whose wishes were paramount but who was not there to speak for himself. I had to put myself in the mind and heart of Howard "Red" Stevens.

———— ∾∾∾∾ ————

As I took my place in the courtroom and nodded for everyone else to be seated, I noticed two additional figures gathered at Mr. Hamilton's counsel table. Next to Jason I recognized his attractive fiancée Alexia. She had been prominent in all of the media coverage surrounding Jason's Ultimate Gift quest over the last year. And seated next to Theodore J. Hamilton—as she had been in a multitude of courtrooms for almost a half century—was his assistant Margaret Hastings. Miss Hastings is one of those regal beauties who was stunning as a young woman, and the ensuing years have settled upon her like age on a fine wine. If anything, she is more beautiful than ever.

I tapped my gavel, gazed out across the assemblage, and began.

"Ruling on the validity of a last will and testament is among the most critical areas of the law, as it calls upon the court to uphold the rights of an individual and speak on behalf of those individuals who are no longer here to speak for themselves. I have reviewed at length the last will and testament of Howard 'Red' Stevens, including the written documents that contained his thoughts, desires, and intentions as he outlined The Ultimate Gift as a bequest to Jason Stevens.

"This court rules that—having heard no evidence to the contrary or dispute—that Howard 'Red' Stevens was of sound mind and body at the time this last will and testament was created. This court also finds that, although unconventional and quite revolutionary, Red Stevens' will is valid and enforceable if all of the terms and conditions are adhered to and met. Therefore, the only remaining question before this court is to determine whether Jason Stevens has, indeed, accomplished each of the provisions set forth in the last will and testament of Howard 'Red' Stevens."

I paused long enough to let either legal team make any objections they wanted to make. Thankfully, hearing none, I continued.

"The will and subsequent trust documents call for several billion dollars to be given over to Jason Stevens to carry out the mission and the message of the twelve elements of The Ultimate Gift as outlined and presented by Red Stevens. It will be the task of this court to determine whether or not Jason Stevens has, indeed, learned sufficiently each of the twelve lessons to an extent that he would be capable of carrying out the mission underlying those lessons, given the resources represented by several billion dollars.

"Therefore, it is my ruling that beginning at 10:00 a.m. tomorrow morning in this courtroom, we will give Jason Stevens every opportunity to explain and demonstrate that he has learned each of the lessons presented to him by Red Stevens in the twelve gifts; and furthermore that he is up to the task of utilizing several billion dollars to pass on The Ultimate Gift to a world that sorely needs it."

I paused and heard the unbelievable tension created by several billion dollars and countless lives hanging in the balance. I pounded my gavel and announced, "Court is adjourned."

My judicial robes billowed and swirled as I rushed from the courtroom into my chambers. I heard the shock, excitement, and anxiety ripple through the crowd.

The overabundance of media present rushed from the courtroom to tell readers, listeners, and viewers around the globe how I had ruled.

I felt somehow unqualified and inadequate to accomplish the daunting task before me. I could only hope and pray that my years of experience on the bench would somehow lead me down the right path and to the proper and just decision.

Only the events of tomorrow and beyond would tell.

Three

THE LIFE OF WORK

*In this life, work is the culmination of all
we are and all we learn that we bring to
others through the marketplace.*

I tossed and turned all night. I could not get my mind away from the case. Every judge in every courthouse throughout the land deals with a voluminous caseload, but in my court and in the minds of people all around the world, the dispute over Red Stevens' estate came to be known simply as *The Case*.

Finally, deep in the middle of the night, I got out of bed, went into my study, and turned on the television. I thought that some mindless TV program might provide escape. As I flipped through the channels, it seemed like everyone everywhere was broadcasting news, commentaries, profiles, conjectures, or tabloid fantasies surrounding Red Stevens, Jason Stevens, and the case.

L. Myron Dudly was prominently featured throughout the media. I had decided early on that this case would unavoidably be a media circus so, instead of trying to control it, I simply let it run its course. But Mr. Dudly was, indeed, making the most of the situation.

As the sun reluctantly clawed its way over the horizon and the stars relinquished their domain, another day came to life. I was in my chambers, reclining in the safety and security of my leather chair, nursing my third cup of coffee as I contemplated what had been and what would be. I gazed out of my window at the cityscape.

Most courthouses were built to last. Many are constructed of limestone or marble. They were designed and prominently placed within the center of communities all across the United States. In the ensuing decades, many of these communities have grown toward the suburbs, leaving their courthouses, including mine, in the middle of a blighted inner city.

Outside my window, I could see several vacant, abandoned buildings and several others that should have been vacated and abandoned. There was a barren city block in the middle of it all where sometime in the distant past, bulldozers had knocked down everything that had been there but nothing had ever come along to take root in that place. There had been talk and rumor for as long as I could remember of putting an inner-city park there, but funding and priorities always seemed to be focused elsewhere.

Even though it was several hours before court would be in session, I knew my part of the day's proceedings needed to begin immediately. I removed from the voluminous case file my printed copy of Red Stevens' last will and testament and my DVD copies of the video messages that Red Stevens had made for Jason as a part of The Ultimate Gift.

I selected the DVD marked *The Gift of Work* and put it into the player built into the wall console. This day's court proceedings would be to determine whether or not Jason had accomplished the tasks set forth for him by Red Stevens with respect to The Gift of Work. Furthermore, I would have to determine whether or not Jason Stevens had the ability to apply the lessons learned through The Gift of Work to benefit the world as a result of the enormous trust fund Red Stevens had left behind.

As the DVD player came to life and Red Stevens' imposing face appeared on the screen, I pressed the pause button and stared at the glowing image before me. Howard "Red" Stevens was, indeed, an historical figure. It was hard to separate the truth from the myth and legend. I thought about the emotions and the turmoil that would exist inside of someone who knew they were coming to the end of life, but hoped to leave behind a message after death that they were somehow unable to convey throughout their lifetime.

I pressed "play" and Red Stevens began speaking from beyond the grave to his grandson.

"Jason, when I was much younger than you are now, I learned the satisfaction that comes from a simple four-letter word: work. One of the things my wealth has robbed from you and the entire family is the privilege and satisfaction that comes from doing an honest day's work.

"Now, before you go off the deep end and reject everything I'm going to tell you, I want you to realize that work has brought me everything I have and everything that you have. I regret that I have taken from you the joy of knowing that what you have is what you've earned.

"My earliest memories in the swamps of Louisiana are of work—hard, backbreaking labor that as a young man I resented greatly. My parents had too many mouths to feed and not enough food, so if we wanted to eat, we worked. Later, when I was on my own and came to Texas, I realized that hard work had become a habit for me, and it served as a true joy all the rest of my life.

"Jason, you have enjoyed the best things that this world has to offer. You have been everywhere, seen everything, and done everything. What you don't understand is how much pleasure these things can bring you when you have earned them yourself, when leisure becomes a reward for hard work instead of a way to avoid work."

I turned off the DVD player and contemplated the words and the spirit of Red Stevens. I couldn't help but think of my own work life and consider how well I had applied The Gift of Work to my life; but the issue at hand was how much had Jason learned and was he capable of passing on The Gift of Work to countless others around the world.

The courtroom was packed. If anything, the electricity and tension had elevated from the day before. I rapped my gavel and got immediately down to business.

"The matter before this court today is the conditions of the last will and testament of Howard 'Red' Stevens relating to The Gift of Work. The court will decide whether Jason Stevens has proven himself proficient in learning The Gift of Work and, more importantly, if he is qualified to manage several billion dollars in trust to pass on this lesson and gift to others."

I glanced quickly at Theodore J. Hamilton who was

calmly taking notes as he listened to my opening remarks. I continued. "Mr. Hamilton, as you are the one who wrote, carried out, and evaluated Red Stevens' last will and testament, the court presumes you find everything to be in order."

Hamilton nodded perfunctorily, and I shifted my gaze to the other side of the aisle. L. Myron Dudly, the rest of the Dudly, Cheetham, and Leech legal team, and the assembled heirs of Red Stevens were in their places. There seemed to be considerably more anxiety present than was in evidence the day before. This was logical as the family previously thought they had nothing to lose and everything to gain, but now they realized that they could quite literally lose it all.

I addressed Mr. Dudly. "Counsel, as your clients are contesting the validity of Red Stevens' last will and testament relating to Jason's completion of the tasks called for, I will let you begin."

Dudly confidently rose to his feet, paused significantly, and then declared, "We call Jason Stevens to the stand."

Jason stood haltingly and tentatively made his way to the witness box. He was seated, and he swore to tell the truth, the whole truth, and nothing but the truth.

Dudly approached the witness box and actually sneered at Jason as he stated questioningly, "You are Jason Stevens?"

Jason nodded and replied sheepishly, "Yes."

Dudly turned to the gallery expansively and said, "Please speak up so everyone can hear you."

Dudly paced back and forth and inquired, "What was the relationship between you and Howard 'Red' Stevens?"

Jason replied cautiously, "He was my grandfather."

Dudly appeared shocked and perplexed. "Are you quite sure he was your grandfather?"

Jason seemed bewildered and repeated, "Yes."

Dudly smiled victoriously and continued. "Can you then please tell this court and everyone assembled why every reference you ever made about Howard 'Red' Stevens, as infrequent as they were, referred to Red Stevens as an obscure uncle or your great uncle?"

Jason reddened and gazed down at his feet. After a long pause, he began. "Howard 'Red' Stevens was my grandfather. He was my father's father. This is something I never appreciated. In fact, I was ashamed of it my whole life until he was already gone. I blamed him for everything that was wrong in my life, and I held him responsible for my father's death. Only after my grandfather was gone did I come to understand that my grandfather was trying to help my father, and my father died as a result of an accident that had nothing to do with my grandfather. Only after receiving The Ultimate Gift am I able to say I am proud to be Red Stevens' grandson and thankful for everything that he taught me."

Jason stared defiantly at Dudly as Dudly continued. "So we are to understand that you feel entitled and deserving of inheriting several billion dollars from someone of whom you were ashamed—and whom you denied being a grandson of—all the years he was alive."

"Yes," Jason croaked.

Dudly smugly looked at the gallery and at me then settled his gaze on Jason and commented, "Shocking. Truly shocking."

Hamilton forcefully interrupted, "Your Honor, I object. Can we please have counsel reserve his opinions and reactions for a time and place more appropriate? Red Stevens' bequests and his reasons for making his bequests are not subject to the approval or the opinions of Mr. Dudly."

I rapped my gavel perfunctorily and sustained the objection in favor of Mr. Hamilton.

Dudly was undaunted and began firing questions toward Jason.

"Have you ever in your life, even once, applied for a job?"

"No," Jason responded.

"Have you ever, even once in your life, held a paying job?"

Jason paused, seeming to think, then shook his head and replied, "No."

"Would you describe for this court and those of us assembled here the brief experience you had at the ranch in Texas last year?"

Jason straightened in his chair and began. "My grandfather taught me The Gift of Work by sending me to work with Gus Caldwell on his ranch."

Dudly smiled and nodded, then inquired, "So, what variety of work experience did you have during that thirty-day period?"

Jason responded, "I dug post holes and built a fence."

"And what else?" Dudly asked.

Jason appeared confused and shook his head, replying, "Nothing else."

Dudly pressed the issue. "So, would it be safe to say that your entire work experience and the totality of your background relating to work is limited to a thirty-day period when you did nothing other than build a fence? Do you feel this, in any way, qualifies you to manage billions of dollars and help other people understand The Gift of Work?"

Jason shrugged his shoulders and stammered inaudibly.

Dudly retreated to his table, exclaiming, "This witness is dismissed. We call to the stand one ..." Dudly paused as he shuffled through his paperwork and announced, "... Gus Caldwell."

It was as if a piece of history or Americana walked down the aisle of my courtroom. Gus Caldwell solemnly put his hand on the Bible and was sworn in. He nodded with respect toward me and Mr. Hamilton.

Dudly barely suppressed a chuckle as he inquired, "So, you are Gus Caldwell."

Gus Caldwell let the silence drag out to an uncomfortable point as only a supremely confident person can do, then replied, "Yes, son, I'm Gus Caldwell. Who might you be?"

Laughter could be heard sprinkled throughout the room. I tapped my gavel for order.

Dudly appeared indignant and replied, "I, sir, am L. Myron Dudly, Attorney at Law, and I am not your son."

Gus Caldwell leaned back in his chair, smiled broadly, and responded, "No, I guess you're not my son. That's just another in the long list of things that I'm thankful to the Almighty for."

The laughter rained down throughout the courtroom, and I couldn't stifle my own chuckle as I pounded for silence and order.

Dudly paused, regained his dignity, and took a different tact.

"Mr. Caldwell, can you describe for this court the nature and extent of your business?"

Gus Caldwell recited the list. "I raise cows, horses. Grow wheat along with a number of other crops. I have oil wells, gas wells, and own parts of banks, shopping malls, and some other stuff I don't know much about."

Dudly nodded as if he understood and continued. "Out of all the tasks, jobs, and positions in all your varied enterprises, can you help us understand the scope and nature of work experience you provided for Jason Stevens?"

Gus nodded and replied brusquely, "He built a fence."

Dudly repeated, "He built a fence. Yes, I see."

Dudly seemed to ponder a moment. "Can you help us understand of what possible benefit thirty days of fence building would be for someone entrusted with billions of dollars for the purpose of helping people, among other things, understand The Gift of Work?"

Gus Caldwell shook his head sadly as if preparing to address a child. "Son, a person who can build a good fence can do anything. The nature of the work is not as important as the nature of the person. Anyone can learn the steps in doing a job, but only a few people understand the pride, the dignity, and the honor that goes with doing a job well. My outfit has grown to be worth a lot of money, and I'm able to handle it all, and I never got that out of a book. I guess I learned a lot about work and a lot about life from hard labor like building miles of fence."

Dudly shook his head, as if he and everyone else in hearing range would be disappointed in the answer, and retreated to his counsel table stating with a dismissive wave, "Your Honor, I believe we have learned all we can and will from this witness."

Gus Caldwell looked up at me questioningly, and I

smiled and nodded, saying, "Mr. Caldwell, the court thanks you for being here today."

Gus rose and replied, "Sir, you don't need to thank me. I'd do anything you can imagine and some things you can't for Red Stevens."

Gus Caldwell walked down the aisle and out of my courtroom with every eye riveted on him.

Eventually, I turned my gaze back to Dudly and inquired, "Mr. Dudly, have you other witnesses?"

"No, Your Honor," he replied. "I believe we've heard more than enough from Mr. Caldwell and Mr. Jason Stevens himself to understand that this young man ..." Dudly jabbed a finger in Jason's direction as he spoke "... does not and could not know anything about the world of work even as it relates to himself, much less the ability and understanding to manage billions of dollars to help others."

I sat back in my chair and stared at Mr. Dudly as I pondered the situation.

Then Hamilton rose to speak. "Your Honor, the matter before the court is not Mr. Dudly's opinion of Red Stevens' will or even Mr. Dudly's opinion of Jason Stevens' work habits. The matter before the court is quite simply, does Jason Stevens understand The Gift of Work and can he pass this lesson on to others through the resources left by his grandfather. I believe—and his grandfather's wishes demand—that he be given a chance to prove his worthiness in this matter once and for all."

Hamilton sat down as if the matter was decided and, indeed, the matter was decided. My eyes settled for a moment on each lawyer in turn, and then I ruled.

"It is the decision of this court that Jason Stevens be given thirty days to prove, by his own means and in his

own way, that he understands The Gift of Work and that
he, indeed, possesses the wherewithal to pass along Red
Stevens' Gift of Work to others. If at the end of thirty
days the court is satisfied in this matter, we will proceed
to the next gift. If not, the last will and testament will be
overturned, and the assets of the Red Stevens' Trust shall
be divided pro rata among the heirs who are a party to this
suit.

"Court is dismissed."

The media coverage in the ensuing days was relentless
and unprecedented. Dudly, Cheetham, and Leech got a
lifetime worth of face time while Hamilton must have found
a place to hide from the media. Jason Stevens' sightings
were recorded here and there with questionable reliability.
Frankly, we were all in the dark.

I wondered if I had done the right thing, considering
Jason Stevens and, more importantly, Red Stevens. Was this
task reasonable, and was it even possible?

I handled the rest of my caseload for the next few weeks
and tried to focus on other matters.

Then an unforgettable day came. As usual, I was sitting
in my leather chair with my cup of coffee as the morning
first became a hint then a reality, when I observed a sight
my mind simply wouldn't register. My normal view out
the picture window of my chambers showed the sun rising
in the east just as it should, and showed the abandoned
buildings and the rundown tenements. It showed the
vacant block where the bulldozers had left their mark, but
something—in fact, everything—was different both in
spirit and in practice.

As the day had barely begun, I observed a Texas-style rail fence materializing around the previously vacant block. Neighborhood youth, actually gang members, were swarming all about the area performing a variety of tasks— some of which were clear to me, while others remained a mystery.

As the day matured, the climbing sun revealed delivery trucks unloading building supplies and playground equipment. Merchants, business leaders, and residents of the area clustered in groups around the perimeter, and several television trucks appeared to cover the unfolding events.

Deep down, I suspected what was happening. I smiled and then laughed out loud in the privacy of my chambers. I simply couldn't wait for the approaching day in my court when the reality of the situation would be exposed.

⁘⸺⸺⸺⸺⸻

I greeted everyone gathered in the courtroom as I tapped my gavel for order.

"Good morning. The purpose of this hearing is to make a final determination regarding Jason Stevens' completion of tasks and suitability for responsibilities with respect to the last will and testament of Howard 'Red' Stevens. The court will ask Jason Stevens to take the stand."

Jason moved confidently to the witness box, was eagerly sworn in, and sat on the edge of the chair. I nodded toward Mr. Hamilton to proceed.

Hamilton casually sat at the counsel table, glanced up at Jason, and said, "Jason, why don't you tell them what happened."

Jason paused, took a deep breath, and began. "Well, in all of my trips into and out of the court building last month,

I had to walk past that vacant block down the street. I heard a number of people throughout the area comment on how, for years, they had wanted to have a park there. Apparently there had been petitions, fund drives, demonstrations, and lawsuits, but nothing had ever happened.

"My grandfather taught me, through his words and through his life, the power of someone with a vision who is willing to simply go to work.

"After court was dismissed last month, I went over to that vacant land and, among the rubble, found a number of old wooden utility poles. I just got some tools, cut up those poles, and did the only thing I knew how to do. I started building a fence around the vacant land. Then kids, teenagers, retired people, and all sorts of others began showing up and asking what I was doing. I let them know that this was going to be a park if we were all willing to believe it and simply work for it. I told them we didn't need the government, or a bond issue, or a lawsuit or a demonstration. We just needed a big dream and a little work.

"While I kept building the fence, some kids started cleaning up the area. Local business leaders made arrangements to have grass planted and trees put in. Several contractors used concrete left over from other projects to build sidewalks and a parking lot. And, well ..."

Jason paused meekly and looked up at me and said, "Your Honor, I think if you'll walk over there, you'll notice that we got a park."

Applause rippled throughout the courtroom. I reached for my gavel to call for silence but decided it could wait a few moments while the applause continued.

I smiled at Mr. Hamilton then down at Jason as I spoke.

"Let the record show that it is the finding of this court that Jason Stevens has demonstrated not only his understanding of The Gift of Work but his uncanny ability to pass it on to others. We will take up the matter of the next gift, being The Gift of Money, at 10:00 a.m. tomorrow. This court is adjourned."

FOUR

THE LIFE OF MONEY

*Money is the fruit of our efforts and
the fuel for our dreams.*

I enjoy a brisk walk, watching a sunrise, and being in a pleasant park. The next morning, I was doing all three at the same time. There is something about watching the sun perched on the horizon that brings an emotional punctuation to the day.

My beloved wife, Marie, shares my sentiments regarding observing the sun on the horizon. However, she feels that the sunset is more in tune with her schedule than the sunrise.

The air felt crisp and clean that morning in the park. It wasn't just any park. I was walking in the new Howard "Red" Stevens Urban Park as the sign at the entrance had proclaimed. The sign also informed me, and anyone else entering, that "This park is dedicated to and provided by the hard work of people in this community."

The sunrise was magnificent from my park perspective. I was just a mere stone's throw from the courthouse. In fact, I could see the sunrise reflecting off the picture window in my chambers; however, I was struck with how a different view can entirely change one's perspective on the world. This seemed to me to be a good thing for a judge to keep in mind, both figuratively and literally. Often, judges are forced to use the law and their intellect to come to a decision that is opposed to the ruling their heart wants them to make.

I settled onto a park bench and observed, among other things, a rather fit young lady wearing some type of space-age form-fitting jogging suit, making her way around the perimeter of the park followed closely by her dog. The dog was some kind of Labrador-terrier mix. When the pair reached the open space in the park across from me, they stopped, apparently having completed their route.

The young woman reached into a backpack and took out a tennis ball. She threw it a short distance, and her dog leapt into action, retrieved the ball, and brought it back to her. She repeated this process several times as I casually looked on. Then she reached into her backpack and withdrew several more tennis balls. This time when the dog returned, she threw out two tennis balls. The dog was quite skilled and was actually able to get both of them situated in his mouth and bring them back to the young woman.

But then she threw out four tennis balls. The dog ran eagerly toward the cluster of tennis balls. He frolicked about excitedly like a child in a candy store, having four tennis balls to retrieve; however, his best efforts repeatedly failed as he tried to get all of the tennis balls in his mouth at once.

As I enjoyed this process from afar, I couldn't help

but allow thoughts of the Stevens' case to enter my mind. Overnight, I had watched several news reports that featured Mr. Dudly with Red Stevens' son Jack in tow. I was struck by the fact that Jack Stevens had inherited several hundred million dollars, but somehow it wasn't enough. He was risking losing it all because he wanted more.

The dog grew more frustrated and agitated as each time he would pick up one or two of the tennis balls, they would slip from his mouth as he tried to retrieve a third one.

As I rose from the park bench and began making my way toward the courthouse in the distance, the dog became so frustrated he ran in circles, howled, and rolled over onto his back with all four paws in the air.

As I passed him, I told him, "You remind me of some humans I know."

He cocked his head and moaned. Somehow I don't think he appreciated the comparison.

I waved at the young lady and smiled as I passed. She pointed at her dog and said, "Sometimes he's not too bright."

I chuckled and replied, "Well, it happens to the best of us."

I was looking forward to having dinner that night with Marie at one of our favorite restaurants. I somehow knew she would be really fascinated with the lesson I had learned from the attractive young woman in spandex and her dog. But I had a day in court with many miles to go before my dinner with Marie.

~~~~~~~

"All rise," Paul, my bailiff, somberly intoned as I climbed the familiar three steps and settled into my place. I gaveled the proceedings to order and organized my thoughts.

I had hoped that counsel for the Stevens' family might let my previous day's ruling stand without protest or objection, but I didn't have much confidence in that happening.

"Your Honor," Dudly beckoned.

I glared at him and inquired, "Yes, what is it?" as I began to realize my fears.

He replied, "We have a number of objections and motions that justice and the gravity of this case require us to make."

I nodded, accepting my fate.

He continued. "Your Honor, first and foremost, we object to Mr. Stevens' escapades in the park being ruled as actual work, pertaining to The Gift of Work as outlined in Red Stevens' will documents. Jason Stevens received no money or other remuneration for his efforts; therefore, we believe that he did not do any work, nor does he have the ability to guide others utilizing Red Stevens' Trust to understand and accomplish their work. For the purposes of this matter, having not earned any money, Mr. Stevens' efforts are worthless."

Mr. Hamilton cleared his throat and made an offhanded comment from his seat. "Your Honor, if not earning money through work makes someone worthless, Mr. Dudly's clients would, indeed, have to be ruled worthless. We believe Red Stevens' desires were very clear and that Jason Stevens far exceeded the requirements of the will."

I nodded toward Mr. Hamilton and replied, "I would have to agree with you, Mr. Hamilton."

I shifted my gaze toward Mr. Dudly. "Objection overruled."

Dudly turned the next page in what appeared to be an ominously lengthy document.

He continued. "Your Honor, we further object to Mr. Stevens' unauthorized, unethical, and indeed illegal activities that he somehow has come to call an urban park."

Mr. Dudly intoned the words *urban park* as if they were somehow distasteful and beneath him.

My patience was growing thin. I pointed my gavel at him and said, "Counselor, if you have a point in all this, I would like you to make it now."

L. Myron Dudly reddened slightly and cleared his throat. He knew he was on very thin ice, but he collected himself and waded in.

"Your Honor, Mr. Jason Stevens would have to obtain building permits, city and county right-of-way zoning variances, and deal with employment issues as well as child labor laws in order to have appropriately conducted his activities over the past month. Furthermore, his trust fund and the proceeds of the estate have all been frozen, and as Mr. Hamilton is working apparently for a fee involving a cup of coffee, there are obviously a number of financial irregularities, if not downright illegal misappropriations, involved here."

Theodore J. Hamilton forcefully cleared his throat and ponderously rose to his full height.

"Your Honor, if you will allow me, I may be able to clear up all of the fog created by Mr. Dud—"

Hamilton experienced one of his brief coughing fits and did not even bother to complete the second syllable of Mr. Dudly's name.

Dudly rocketed to his feet and pounded his clenched fist on the counsel table.

"Your Honor, how long must I suffer these indignities?"

Hamilton looked at Dudly innocently and said, "I'm the one suffering the cough here. Are you experiencing any ailments, counselor?"

Dudly's face achieved the color and hue of one of my beloved sunrises.

Hamilton stated with dignity, "May it please the court, I beg Mr. Dudly's indulgence with regards to any annoyance created by my advanced years."

Dudly shot back, "When I get to be eighty, I can assure you I won't be annoying people in the courtroom."

Hamilton smiled beneficently and announced, "Mr. Dudly, I believe we can all agree you won't have to wait till you're eighty as you have adequately and repeatedly demonstrated your vast ability to annoy people now."

Mr. Dudly's face achieved an even brighter sunrise coloring as he dropped into his chair in frustration.

I pounded my gavel for order, and the courtroom finally grew silent once again.

Hamilton spoke. "Your Honor, I am hoping we can avoid wasting the court's time with each minute detail. I am prepared to stake my reputation as a member of the Bar for well over half a century that the zoning permits, easements, variances, work permits, and all other state, county, and municipal documents are in order and have been duly filed. I can assure the court of this as it was handled most expeditiously by the law firm of Hamilton, Hamilton, and Hamilton."

Dudly whined, "What about the money? Where did all of the funds come from for that so-called park?"

Hamilton smiled magnificently and, with a gleam in his eye, proudly stated, "Yes. Thank you for bringing that to the court's attention and my recollection. There was, indeed, a generous donation made to the newly formed Community Urban Park Fund."

Mr. Hamilton paused opportunely, shuffled through a stack of papers, found the one he apparently had been seeking, and continued as he slipped on his antique reading glasses.

"Yes, here it is. A registered letter, duly signed and notarized, accompanied by a cashier's check made out to the Community Fund."

Dudly interrupted. "Your Honor, I object. Would you please direct counsel to reveal the source of the so-called funds?"

Hamilton indignantly continued after glaring at Dudly.

"Thank you, counselor. I was just getting to that prior to your last eruption. Although the benefactor wished to remain low profile, if not indeed anonymous, I have been authorized to reveal to the court that all outstanding expenses required to complete the Howard 'Red' Stevens Urban Park were donated by a newly formed organization."

Hamilton adjusted his glasses and peered at the document he held.

"This newly formed organization is known as the Alpine Texas Fence Builders Corporation. Your Honor, the ownership of this newly formed corporation seems to be covered by a number of trusts and shell corporations, but I can assure the court that the corporation itself, and the funds received for the Community Park, are legal and well accounted for."

Dudly lowered his head onto the counsel table in front of him. The other members of the Dudly, Cheetham, and Leech team seemed perplexed and agitated. Grumblings and mutterings could be heard from the assembled Stevens clan arrayed in the rows of seats behind Mr. Dudly.

I let the silence draw out for several moments and spoke.

"Hearing no other motions or objections, I believe we can press on with today's business before the court. Today with respect to Red Stevens' last will and testament, we will be hearing arguments surrounding Jason Stevens' response to The Gift of Money portion of The Ultimate Gift as well as the court's findings with respect to Jason Stevens' ability to manage several billion dollars in Red Stevens' Trust to benefit society relating to The Gift of Money."

I gestured toward Mr. Hamilton.

He responded as a matter of fact, "Your Honor, we are satisfied that Jason Stevens did, indeed, perform sufficiently regarding The Gift of Money, and he is, therefore, qualified to manage the trust as outlined in the last will and testament of Red Stevens."

My gaze had barely settled on Mr. Dudly when he spoke. "Your Honor, we call Jason Stevens."

Jason was seated in the witness box, and I informed him and everyone present that he was already sworn and would still be under oath with regard to his testimony in the matter.

Dudly began. "Mr. Stevens, have you ever earned any money in your entire life?"

Jason shook his head slowly.

Dudly bore in, saying, "Please answer the court."

Jason said, "No."

"Have you ever managed or invested any money?" Dudly inquired.

"Not really," Jason responded.

"Then can you please tell this court how any reasonable person could trust you to earn and manage your own money, much less several billion dollars that should rightly be inherited by my clients?"

Dudly gestured to the assembled relatives on his side of the courtroom.

When Jason did not answer, Dudly shrugged and commented, "Well, I guess we have our answer. We have no further questions."

Hamilton approached Jason. "Jason, isn't it true that after you spent a month in Texas building a fence for Gus Caldwell, that you were given a certain amount of money as directed by your grandfather's will?"

Jason replied, "Yes, I guess they figured that I would have earned about fifteen hundred dollars for that fence I built, so I was given that much and told to go out and find people whose lives could be helped by the money."

Hamilton nodded and said, "So, what did you do then?"

Jason gazed off into the distance as if remembering a different time and place, and then he spoke as if recalling a fond memory.

"Well, first I found a group of Scouts who were two-hundred dollars short in their fund-raising to go to their Jamboree. Then a woman with a baby was having her car repossessed, and I gave her four hundred dollars to keep her car. Next, I found a family shopping in a toy store. The parents told the children that Santa would not come this year. When the children were in another area of the store, I gave the parents three hundred dollars to make sure Santa would make it to their house. Next, I found an old lady sitting on a bench crying because she didn't have the money to buy her husband's heart medication."

Jason paused and looked up at me. There were tears in his eyes as he continued.

"They'd been married fifty-seven years, and she told me they had never missed a payment in all those years. I gave her two hundred dollars, which would cover three months of the heart medication with twenty dollars left over for her to take her husband, Harold, out to lunch at his favorite place. And last, I discovered a car broken down at the side of the road where I met a young man named Brian. He needed his car to get back and forth to work or he was going to lose his job. The mechanic said it was going to be seven hundred dollars, so I gave him the money."

Hamilton smiled as if looking at a son of whom he was most proud. Hamilton glanced up at me and then out at the gallery and said, "I believe that meets the terms and conditions of Red Stevens' will."

Dudly sprung to his feet and said, "Your Honor, we object."

He was holding an adding machine tape dangling from his left hand. One of the Dudly, Cheetham, and Leech clerks at the end of the counsel table actually had an adding machine in front of him.

Dudly smirked defiantly at Hamilton and stated, "Your client was directed to spend fifteen hundred dollars but claims to have spent eighteen hundred. This points out the fact that Jason Stevens cannot take care of his own money, much less billions of dollars which my clients are lawfully entitled to."

I glanced over at Mr. Hamilton.

He responded, "Jason, can you explain the three-hundred-dollar discrepancy in this matter?"

Jason seemed at a loss and spoke. "Well, he really needed the car, and it cost seven hundred."

Hamilton continued. "So where did the other three hundred dollars come from?"

Jason seemed nervous but spoke forcefully. "I got the three hundred out of my pocket."

Dudly blurted out, "I object. Obviously, this does not meet the criteria set forth by Red Stevens. He was to distribute fifteen hundred dollars and, in doing so, demonstrate he could manage money. I don't find that he accomplished this."

I pounded my gavel and ruled, "Well, I do find that he met both the spirit and the letter set forth in the document, and if during the next thirty days Jason Stevens can demonstrate he can pass along The Gift of Money to others, this portion of the case will be duly resolved. Court is adjourned."

Back in my chambers, Red Stevens spoke to me from the DVD just as he had spoken to Jason about The Gift of Money.

"Today, we are going to talk about what may, indeed, be the most misunderstood commodity in the world. That is, money. There is absolutely nothing that can replace money in the things that money does, but regarding the rest of the things in the world, money is absolutely useless.

"For example, all the money in the world won't buy you one more day of life. That's why you're watching this videotape right now. And it's important to realize that money will not make you happy. I hasten to add that poverty will not make you happy either. I have been rich, and I have been poor—and all other things being equal— rich is better.

"Jason, you have no idea or concept of the value of money. That is not your fault. That is my fault. But I am hoping in the next thirty days you can begin to understand what money means in the lives of real people in the real world. More of the violence, anxiety, divorce, and mistrust in the world is caused by misunderstanding money than any other factor. These are concepts that are foreign to you because money to you has always seemed like the air you breathe. There's always more. All you have to do is take the next breath.

"I know that you have always flashed around a lot of money and spent it frivolously. I take the responsibility for this situation because I deprived you of the privilege of understanding the fair exchange between work and money."

They were lined up along the wall, shoulder to shoulder, across the back of my courtroom. They were lined up along either side of the gallery from the back of the room to the front. There were three sides of a perimeter made up of all shapes, sizes, and descriptions of young women.

A month had come and gone quickly since I had sent Jason Stevens out to prove himself regarding The Gift of Money. I had called the court to order and, like everyone else present, was curious about the gathering of young women, but before I could make any inquiries, predictably, Dudly spoke.

"Your Honor, I object. What kind of outrageous display or grandstanding tactic of opposing counsel is this?" Dudly gestured to either side then behind as he continued. "My clients and I would like to know the meaning of this."

I shrugged and commented, "I would like to know the meaning of this as well."

Hamilton chuckled and spoke. "Your Honor, I know the meaning of this but feel it would be best explained by my client."

Jason took the stand. Hamilton approached as he asked, "Jason, would you like to inform everyone about the gathering of young ladies lined up around the courtroom today?"

Jason smiled shyly and replied, "I didn't tell them to come here."

Dudly blurted out his objection. "Your Honor, are we to believe that Jason Stevens had nothing to do with this gathering?"

Jason continued as he glanced up at me. "Well, I know who they are, and I know why they're here, but I didn't tell them to come."

Hamilton encouraged Jason, asking, "Can you tell us, then, who they are?"

Jason looked at the ring of young ladies around the room and began. "I heard in a news story that single mothers are among the most financially disadvantaged people in our society. So I went around in some low-income areas—through day-care centers, schools, community centers, and low-income housing—and found a number of single moms. I asked them about their specific needs, and ..." Jason seemed to struggle for the right words.

"Well, I guess we came up with sort of a program."

Hamilton smiled and asked, "Can you tell us about this program?"

Jason continued. "Well, the first and biggest problem seemed to be that they are spending a lot of money on day care, and they don't have enough time with their kids. So we came up with a day-care co-op where the mothers take care of one another's children while they're trading off working day shifts, night shifts, and weekends. This gives them more time with their kids and saves a lot of money on day care."

Hamilton nodded for Jason to continue.

"Next, we got them all wills, guardianship power of attorney documents, and all of the things that single moms running a household would need. We helped them shift high-interest credit card debts to lower interest cards, and a lot of them just got rid of credit cards all together. We've started financial classes where we bring in volunteer experts from the community to help them learn about managing money and moving ahead in their careers and lives."

Hamilton was beaming. He gave a thumbs-up gesture to Jason, turned, and actually bowed to Mr. Dudly, announcing, "Your witness, Counselor."

Dudly stalked Jason, who leaned back in his chair defensively. Dudly attacked. "Mr. Stevens, what if anything qualifies you to help these young women or anyone with legal documents, credit problems, or financial planning?"

Jason shrugged and said, "Really, nothing at all. Mr. Watkins and Miss Hastings helped out."

Jason nodded toward the counsel table.

Dudly glared up at me and declared, "Your Honor, Jason Stevens didn't help anyone with money. He got other people to do it for him. He's simply not qualified to ..."

The pounding of my gavel interrupted Mr. Dudly.

"Mr. Dudly, it is a long-recognized fact in our society that people who need to accomplish complex or specialized tasks seek the expertise of others. This is why firms such as Dudly, Cheetham, and Leech exist."

I gazed at the long line of young ladies ringing my courtroom. They were clean and presentable, but the cost of their combined wardrobes would not have paid for one of the outfits worn by the Stevens clan seated behind Dudly. But the women somehow seemed to have a pride and dignity I couldn't quite define. Maybe it was simply hope.

I looked down at my court reporter, Scott, and stated, "Let the record show that Mr. Stevens has duly and admirably completed all tasks to this court's satisfaction with regard to The Gift of Money."

A hearty cheer rose from all sides of my courtroom. I couldn't bring myself to pound my gavel for order.

I looked at Hamilton and Dudly, in turn, and declared, "Gentlemen, tomorrow is another day. Court is dismissed."

Five

THE LIFE OF FRIENDS

*No one can be considered a failure who has a friend, and
no one can be considered a success without one.*

The media coverage that I hoped would die down was, instead, accelerating. Images of the young single mothers lined up around my courtroom were inescapable on television and in the print media.

I sought legal precedent for high-profile cases of this nature that would be carried out over an entire year or more. Unfortunately, there was no precedent, so I had the dubious honor of breaking new legal ground.

One of my favorite nightly news interview programs featured Mr. Dudly and Red Stevens' younger son Bill. The program captured my attention before I could change the channel.

Bill first stated innocently that this case wasn't about the money. Along with phrases like "The check's in the mail" and "I'm from the government, and I'm here to help you," the phrase "It's not about the money" must be prominent in the Liar's Hall of Fame somewhere. More than four decades on the bench have taught me "It's always about the money."

The host of my favorite nightly news interview program failed to press Bill on the money issue and let him ramble on about what a worthless, irresponsible playboy Jason Stevens had been his whole life and how the rest of the family was regrettably forced to come together to fight Jason in court so that they could each receive their legitimate inheritance.

Bill explained, "Depriving rightful heirs of the fruit of our beloved father's efforts—to give it over to someone like Jason—simply cannot be allowed, no matter how much time and money it takes to stop this injustice."

The host asked, "Bill, are you concerned that you've lost the first two phases of this twelve-step case?"

Bill waved his hand dismissively and quipped, "No, it's no big deal, because it's like we have twelve hurdles. Jason and his old lawyer have to get over all twelve of the hurdles in order to win. We, the rightful heirs, only have to win one hurdle in order to get our inheritance."

As the program was drawing to a close, the host inquired, "Mr. Stevens, are you concerned that if you lose this case you not only don't get Jason Stevens' portion of the estate, but you lose everything you had previously inherited? Wouldn't this leave you and your family penniless?"

Bill chuckled nervously. The hot TV lights seemed to be causing him to perspire at that very moment. He cleared his throat and croaked, "We are very confident, with the able help of Mr. Dudly, that justice will be served."

The theme music for the show began playing, signaling

the end of the program. The interview had reminded me that it was, indeed, a long road ahead with many potential hazards along the way. And Jason's position reminded me that the hunter can make many mistakes but the hunted can make only one.

───────

My bailiffs, Jim and Paul, stopped me in the corridor. We didn't get to speak very often considering that we worked in the same room all day, every day.

Jim blurted out, "We're sorry."

I must have appeared not to understand as Paul explained, "We should have done something about those women or told you before court began."

I patted them both on the shoulder and said, "Gentlemen, it's a public building and an open court. No explanations necessary."

I laughed as I voiced my thoughts. "Somehow, I fear the atmosphere will be lacking in the courtroom today."

Indeed, as I entered the courtroom and took my place, although the courtroom was packed, the long line of young women was no longer in evidence. It had been a sight I would not soon forget.

I rapped my gavel, took a deep breath, and began. "Today, we will be exploring The Gift of Friends."

I looked at Theodore J. Hamilton and inquired, "Counselor, are you prepared?"

I smiled to myself as I thought, *Asking Theodore J. Hamilton "Are you prepared?" is like asking a hungry lion if he would like to eat.*

Hamilton simply nodded, and Jason took the stand.

Then, Hamilton inquired, "Jason, would you tell the court what you learned from your grandfather about friendship?"

Jason licked his lips, took a deep breath, and began. "I had never understood the real definition of a friend or the depth of friendship before my grandfather gave me The Gift of Friends."

Jason seemed to be struggling with his thoughts as Hamilton nodded for him to continue.

"I guess a friend is someone you can count on, no matter what happens. They applaud the best things you do and accept the worst things you do."

Hamilton proceeded, "During the month that Red Stevens taught you about The Gift of Money, you went out and met someone that you had never been introduced to before, and you subsequently became friends."

Jason nodded and said, "Yes."

Hamilton continued, "Are you still friends to this day?"

Jason nodded and said, "Yes. We don't talk as often as we'd like, but we are friends."

Hamilton looked up at me and said, "Your Honor, I believe this does accomplish everything Red Stevens set forth in The Gift of Friends. There is simply nothing more or less required of a friend."

Mr. Hamilton returned to his seat as Mr. Dudly inevitably rose. "Your Honor, if I may."

I nodded at the unavoidable situation.

Dudly continued, "We have a few questions. Jason, you reportedly met a young man named Brian when you were asked to demonstrate The Gift of Money."

Jason nodded and replied, "Correct."

Dudly smiled conspiratorially and asked, "Would you please tell the court the circumstances under which you met Brian and how you became friends?"

Jason shrugged and began. "I was driving away from Mr. Hamilton's office after I had watched the video made by my grandfather telling me about The Gift of Money. His words and examples had really affected me. Then I noticed a car stalled at the edge of the road. I pulled over, and that was how I met Brian. I helped him get a new engine, and we began to talk and do things together, and now we're friends."

Mr. Dudly laughed out loud and said, "Let me get this straight. You found someone broken down at the side of the road, you bought him a new engine, and you think you have a friend."

Jason nodded and stared directly at Dudly, replying, "Yes, sir. I do."

Dudly inquired, "Jason, have you ever had a friend in your life that you didn't give your grandfather's money to or whom you didn't buy things for?"

Jason answered, "Well, there was Emily."

Dudly appeared reverent as he asked, "Are you referring to the late daughter of your fiancée?"

Jason answered, "Yes."

Dudly glanced at me and at Alexia seated at the counsel table. "With all due respect, I believe that would be classified as more of a family relationship."

Dudly shifted like a chameleon. "So, Jason, back to my question. Have you ever had a friend in your life that you didn't give your grandfather's money to or whom you didn't buy things for?"

Jason seemed to think back into his past, then he shook his head and said, "No, thanks to my grandfather I always had a lot of money, so I always bought things and helped my friends out."

"And that's the same way you met Brian?" Dudly asked.

Jason replied, "Well, I guess so."

Dudly shot back, "How many of these friends have you seen and how many have contacted you since all of your grandfather's assets were frozen?"

Jason looked down at the floor and said, "Well, not really any."

Dudly appeared triumphant and declared, "Witness dismissed. Your Honor, anyone would act like a friend as long as someone was giving them money, paying their expenses, and buying them things. This is not the definition of a friend nor does it meet the criteria set forth in the last will and testament of Red Stevens."

Hamilton blurted out, "Your Honor, we object to counsel's assertion that having money or sharing money necessarily eliminates the elements of a true and lasting friendship. You can't buy a friend with money, nor can you lose their friendship simply because you've shared what you have."

I was torn. Both Hamilton and Dudly had scored significant points. The evidence was not overwhelming as it had been in The Gift of Work and The Gift of Money.

I took a deep breath stalling for time, and then I remembered old Judge Eldridge's words: *Never make any decision before you have to.*

I smiled and mentally thanked my mentor for the thousandth time and spoke: "At this time, the court does not find evidence to conclusively support the fact that Jason Stevens has mastered The Gift of Friends."

A cacophony of shouts, whistles, and cheers rose from the assorted Stevens clan arrayed behind Dudly. I pounded my gavel mercilessly and glared at them until the silence of a tomb descended.

I growled, "Counselor, inform your clients that we will have order in this court. This is not a football game or even a polo match."

I let the silence draw out before I continued. "On the other hand, the court finds no conclusive evidence to demonstrate that the friendships formed by Jason Stevens are not legitimate; therefore, the court will reserve judgment and hope the evidence will be more clear in thirty days when Mr. Stevens can demonstrate that he has the ability to not only make friends but pass along The Gift of Friends to others.

"This court is adjourned."

In my chambers, I gazed at the many photos on the wall. There were pictures from law school and a number of photos with associates and colleagues. I wondered how many, if any, of these people would meet the courtroom criteria of a friend. I was hoping for clarity and inspiration as I slid the DVD labeled *The Gift of Friends* into the player.

Red Stevens appeared as if he had always been there and always would be. He spoke. "Friend is a word that is thrown around far too easily by people who don't know the meaning of it. Today, people call everyone they know their friend. Young man, you're lucky if you live as long as I have and can count your real friends on the fingers of both hands.

"I am now going to share a story with you, Jason, that I promised I would never tell as long as I lived. Since you are watching this after my death, and in the presence of the one whom I promised, I feel comfortable sharing it.

As you know, I lived past my seventy-fifth birthday and enjoyed what to most people was a long and healthy life. But this was not always a sure thing.

"I remember when I had just turned thirty-eight years old and was hospitalized with an extreme fever. The doctors weren't sure what was wrong with me, so they brought in every specialist from across the country. Finally, I was diagnosed as having a rare kidney disease, which was incurable. The only hope they gave me was a new procedure called a kidney transplant.

"You've got to realize that this was unheard of at that time, and donors were not readily available as they are today. I called Mr. Hamilton, who has always acted as my attorney, and told him we would need to start a nationwide search to find a kidney. I was very frightened because the specialist had told that without the transplant I might not have more than a few weeks. You can imagine my relief when Mr. Hamilton called me two days later and told me he had located a kidney on the East Coast.

"Well, as I'm sure you can guess, the operation was a success and gave me back almost half of my adult life. What I'm sure you couldn't guess, and what no one has known until now, is that the kidney that Mr. Hamilton found was his own.

"There's only one way in the world to explain something like that, and it's called friendship."

I sat back in my familiar leather chair and tried to catch my breath. I thought about the emotions involved with giving someone one of my kidneys, and I further thought about having a friend at a level so deep that they would give up their kidney for me.

The image haunted me. I was questioning whether

I had anyone like that in my life when the phone on my desk rang. I had told the switchboard to hold all my calls, so I knew who it was. As I picked up the phone and said, "Hello, Marie," I knew beyond a shadow of a doubt that I had someone like that in my life and she, in turn, had me. I would continue thinking about The Gift of Friends and how it related to my life, but I knew that I first and foremost would always be grateful for the fact that I had found my best friend and asked her to marry me.

The month dragged by, but eventually I found myself back in court dealing with *The Case*.

As I called the court to order, I just stared at Theodore J. Hamilton. I couldn't get the story Red Stevens had told out of my mind. I had always considered Theodore J. Hamilton an incomparable practitioner of the law. Now I knew him to have been an incomparable friend. He stared back at me, and somehow I was sure that he knew that I was aware of his Gift of Friendship with Red Stevens. I nodded at him in greeting, and he smiled and actually winked at me.

I gestured for him to proceed. Jason took his now-familiar place on the witness stand, and Theodore J. Hamilton asked, "Jason, during the last month, have you had an opportunity to explore and demonstrate your ability not only to understand friendship but to impart that gift to others?"

Jason nodded, and Hamilton said, "Please share your experience with us."

Jason cleared his throat and started, "When I left here last month, I wasn't sure what to do since Mr. Dudly doesn't seem to count people who know you have money as friends. With all of the TV reports and everything because of this trial, everybody knows me.

"Then I remembered a young man I met last year named David Reese. David is a blind guy I met while learning about The Gift of Laughter. I heard that David was teaching over at the school for the blind across town. I called him, and he told me he was teaching sort of an introduction class for newly blinded people or those just entering the school. I told David I was looking for a group of people to discuss The Gift of Friends with, and David thought this would be a really good part of his class."

Jason looked toward Hamilton for approval, but Hamilton was reviewing notes. Miss Hastings, seated next to Hamilton, smiled at Jason angelically, and Jason continued confidently.

"Well, I thought that since all the people would be blind, they wouldn't have seen me on TV and wouldn't know who I was or that I might be rich. So I went to the class and, after David introduced me, I told about twenty-five blind people that I couldn't imagine having to make the adjustment they were all making and I really respected their efforts. I also told them that I thought if I were going through something like they were, that I would want and need my friends around me.

"They all agreed, but some of them shared that after becoming blind they had lost a lot of their friends. They felt it was probably because people were uncomfortable and just didn't know how to react to them. We went around the room and talked about what we needed from friends and what we each thought we had to offer. I connected with several people that day who I hope will be my friends in the future.

"One of the things we all discovered was that in order to have a friend, you have to be a friend. I was struggling to think of how these people could reach out and be a friend to others. Then I remembered the senior citizens' center I had driven past on my way to the school for the blind. I told them that there must be hundreds of people there who would really appreciate and welcome a telephone call. Some of these calls would just be a pleasant encouragement, while others might blossom into friendship."

Jason reached into his inside jacket pocket and withdrew a folded sheaf of papers. He looked up at me questioningly as he continued.

"Your Honor, I'm not sure who to give this to, but this is a list of all the people who are making regular phone calls to the elderly and a number of letters from the elderly people describing how making new friends has made their lives better."

I followed the direction of Jason's gaze and observed Miss Hastings with tears in her eyes smiling back at Jason.

Hamilton quipped, "I believe the young man has spoken for himself."

Jason was glancing between me and the court reporter, holding out the bundle of papers questioningly.

Dudly interceded, "I'll take that, and I do have a few questions."

Dudly rifled through the pages quickly and said, "So, Jason, let me get this straight. In order to find friends, you went to a school for blind people and a nursing home. Wouldn't you agree these are not traditional places to find friends?"

Jason shrugged and answered, "I don't know. I just went to the school for the blind so that I could meet people who hadn't seen my picture on TV or in the papers. I thought I could stay anonymous."

Dudly smirked and inquired, "Well, did you stay anonymous, or did you or your friend David let all these people know that you stand to gain control of several billion dollars if you somehow deprive my clients of their inheritance?"

I glanced over, anticipating Hamilton's objection, but he just smiled and waved his hand dismissively.

Jason responded, "Well, I didn't tell them who I was, but they kind of found out."

Dudly pressed the issue. "And how, pray tell, did this breach of security involving your identity occur?"

Jason chuckled and replied, "Well, it was after the class and the times we spent together coordinating the calls with the senior citizens when David and several students at the school for the blind actually laughed at me quite a bit and told me how ridiculous I was to think they wouldn't recognize my voice from the TV and radio. They all knew me instantly, and they asked about the case."

Dudly continued down this path, asking, "Just exactly what did they ask about the case?"

Jason shook his head and mumbled, "Oh, nothing really specific."

Dudly drew himself to his full height and demanded, "Young man, you are under oath. What specifically did they ask you about these proceedings?"

Jason responded innocently, "They wanted to know if you really worked for a firm named Dudly, Cheetham, and Leech."

Laughter could be heard throughout the courtroom as I tapped my gavel for quiet.

Dudly recovered some of his dignity and changed course. "Mr. Stevens, exactly what formula or recipe do you feel you followed at the school for the blind or the nursing home that could indicate to this court that you have the ability to find or create friendships?"

Jason glanced up at me then back at Mr. Dudly, answering, "I couldn't guarantee anybody anything. Friendship and friends are gifts we receive. The only thing we can do is plant the seeds and help other people plant them; and occasionally when we're really fortunate, a friendship will grow and blossom and provide seeds for more friendships in the future."

Dudly just stared at Jason dumbfounded.

Finally I broke the silence, inquiring of Dudly, "Counselor, any further questions?"

Dudly shook his head and returned to his counsel table. I smiled at Jason and told him that would be all.

I stared at Mr. Hamilton as I ruled. "I believe we've all learned something about friendship in this place today. The court wishes to thank Jason Stevens for his lesson and commend him on not only being a friend but helping others become friends as well. I would encourage everyone here to think on these things.

"This court is adjourned until 10:00 a.m. Monday."

Six

THE LIFE OF LEARNING

Learning lights a candle in the darkness
that illuminates our dreams.

It was a blessed weekend. Some weekends are merely accustomed parentheses at the end of a work week. Other weekends are a needed prescription for an overburdened soul.

Marie informed me Friday night as we were dining at one of our favorite restaurants that she had scheduled some *family activities* for us over the weekend. The term family activities could otherwise be loosely translated into chores. My family activities, among other things, were to involve raking leaves, cleaning out guttering, and trying to rearrange the garage so it might hold two cars this winter instead of one. I was about to lodge a complaint as I considered all of that work with the only prize being to get one additional car in the garage when I remembered that the additional car in the garage this winter would be mine.

Marie and I had a delightful dinner remembering good times past and planning trips and holiday celebrations in the future. I am always amazed and thankful that after knowing this person over fifty years, we have yet to run out of things to talk about. In fact, the years—instead of exhausting the possibilities between us—have opened vistas we can still explore together.

I think we both tried to avoid it as long as possible, but like an elephant in the living room, it was simply unavoidable, and eventually we settled on the topic of *The Case*. Marie knows that I am opposed to discussing ongoing cases other than the aspects of the trial that may have been introduced into the media. The media coverage of the Red Stevens' contested will case had been so thorough I felt comfortable in discussing any and all matters surrounding *The Case*.

Marie asked, "Why do you think the family can't just be satisfied with hundreds of millions? Why do they have to go after the billions of dollars Jason was to manage through the charitable trust?"

I thought for a minute and then offered a possible explanation. "After seeing thousands of people come and go through my courtroom, fighting over money, property, and all manner of personal possessions, it has come to my attention that there is a disease rampant among humans. The disease is called *more*. It is a veritable epidemic.

"People who have nothing want something. People who have something want a lot. People who have a lot want everything. And people who have everything want more. It just never ends. Otherwise contented and well-adjusted people can learn that someone else is receiving something, and all of a sudden what they had is no longer enough. They want still more."

Marie frowned and shook her head. She commented, "It's too bad those kinds of people can't travel abroad as you and I have and see the abject poverty in which most of the world is living."

I nodded, thinking about some of the heart-wrenching sights of poverty I had seen as I spoke. "That would seem to be logical; however, some of the wealthiest people I have ever known will step over a wounded homeless person in the gutter as they rush to a meeting to try to make their next million.

"There is a balance that must be achieved. The drive to be successful is what has made our country great. Scientific breakthroughs and medical advances are a part of this ongoing effort and striving. On the other hand, people must come to understand how, in a global sense, we are all wealthy beyond imagination."

Marie sipped her coffee and said, "It's sad, because you are in a roomful of Stevens' family members, all of whom have enough wealth for a hundred lifetimes. But their greed has put them in a position where someone is going to walk away with absolutely nothing."

I chuckled as I thought about that eventuality.

"These are people who have never learned how to make it without money. Being poor is a skill that must be learned and cultivated."

Marie laughed and said, "Your Honor, I remember those days very well. Law school wasn't cheap, and we both learned how to sleep on the floor and eat whatever was on sale during double coupon day. I wouldn't want to go back to that."

I responded, "I agree, but some of our best times were then, and we both know if we had to we could survive on next to nothing. The Stevens family simply doesn't know what they don't know. There's a whole world out there that they've never been exposed to."

Dessert arrived, which called for lighter, more pleasant table conversation. We settled into talk of grandchildren and gardening.

As we were walking out of the restaurant arm-in-arm, I commented, "I needed that."

"The food was good," Marie said.

I stopped and looked deeply into those familiar and still-fascinating eyes and said, "I don't mean the food."

As I climbed up to the bench and settled into my chair, I noticed that I was quite sore in my lower back. A remnant, no doubt, of the several hours of raking leaves, otherwise known as *family activities*.

I tapped my gavel for order, nodded a greeting to the overflowing courtroom, and announced, "Today we will take up the matter of The Gift of Learning. I want to remind everyone of the gravity of this case and the fact that this is an ongoing matter that, unlike most estate cases, will not be resolved in a day or two. This case will be heard periodically over an entire year and holds serious consequences for the parties involved.

"If the Stevens family, represented by Mr. Dudly ..." I paused, glanced toward Dudly, and motioned to that side of the courtroom, "... is successful in overturning the Red Stevens' will and attached Ultimate Gift provisions, they will divide among themselves several billion dollars currently frozen in the Red Stevens' Charitable Trust.

"On the other hand ..." I looked toward Mr. Hamilton, Jason, his fiancée Alexia, Hamilton's able assistant Miss Hastings, and the ever-present but silent Jeffrey Watkins and announced, "... on the other hand, if Mr. Jason Stevens, represented by Theodore J. Hamilton, is successful in defending the last will of Red Stevens, including The Ultimate Gift provisions, the charitable trust will remain in place and be under the sole direction of Jason Stevens; and the resources inherited by the Stevens family members will be forfeited as they have contested the will, and those resources will be added to the Red Stevens' Charitable Trust.

"Although this case is very unorthodox and I have granted extreme latitude in the display and demonstration of evidence, I caution counsel and all those present that this is, indeed, a most serious court proceeding, and I will expect everyone to act accordingly."

I gazed judicially about my courtroom and then glanced toward Hamilton.

"Mr. Hamilton, I call on you and your client to make your case before this court that Jason Stevens has, in fact, lived up to the provisions of The Ultimate Gift as outlined by Red Stevens with respect to The Gift of Learning."

Theodore J. Hamilton, following my admonition to treat this matter as a formal court proceeding, rose in a dignified manner and intoned, "Your Honor, we call Jason Stevens to the stand."

Jason rose from his chair, moved around the counsel table, and took his place in the witness box.

I reminded everyone that Jason Stevens had already been sworn in this matter, and he was still under oath with regard to his testimony in these proceedings.

Hamilton began. "Jason, as a part of your grandfather's Gift of Learning, you made a trip to South America."

Jason nodded affirmatively, and Hamilton encouraged him. "Would you tell us about your experiences there?"

Jason replied, "I traveled to a rather remote village where my grandfather had established a library for the people of the region. I worked on reorganizing and categorizing books in the library."

Hamilton inquired, "What did you discover about The Gift of Learning while performing your duties in the library?"

Jason paused to reflect before continuing. "First, I learned that the people of the region have a hunger for learning. They don't have access to schools, books, libraries, and computers like we do. I was surprised when I first got to the library to learn that most of the books were gone. The librarian told me that the majority of the books were always checked out and were distributed among even more remote villages encompassing an area of many miles."

Hamilton directed the testimony by asking, "Isn't it true that you were actually kidnapped during your time in South America and imprisoned by a group of drug lords?"

Jason recounted, "Yes. It was the most frightening experience of my life. I fully expected to be killed at any time."

Hamilton inquired, "Did you acquire any knowledge about The Gift of Learning during your imprisonment?"

Jason nodded and spoke, "While I was in my prison cell, occasionally pages of a book would be passed to me by other prisoners. They were in Spanish, which took me a long time to decipher. I came to treasure the moments when these pages would appear, as they seemed to be my lifeline to the outside world and any hope of being free again. I will never forget the value of even one page of a book."

Hamilton nodded as if thoroughly satisfied and announced, "That will be all."

Theodore J. Hamilton returned to his accustomed spot at the end of the counsel table. I looked across the aisle and gestured at Mr. Dudly.

He spoke. "Yes, Your Honor, we have several lines of inquiry regarding this so-called learning experience or field trip into the jungle that Jason Stevens took last year."

I looked at Hamilton anticipating an objection, but he just smiled at me and shook his head as if it didn't really matter.

Dudly continued, "Mr. Stevens, isn't it true that you flunked out of or were otherwise expelled for disciplinary reasons from ..." Dudly referred to a file folder and continued. "... at least nine different prep schools before you allegedly graduated from high school?"

Jason shrugged and replied, "I don't know the exact number, but that's probably about right."

"Mr. Stevens," Dudly continued, "it appears to me that you had the benefit of attending some of the finest private schools in the United States. How is it that with all of these advantages you either failed to perform even minimally or, in many cases, were removed for disciplinary reasons?"

Jason cleared his throat and spoke. "Well, I guess you could say I wasn't very motivated when I was a school-aged kid."

Dudly glared at Jason, replying, "I think that would be a gross understatement, but let us go on. The story seems to be even more fascinating."

Dudly paced back and forth. His momentum was building.

"You apparently somehow, thanks to the generous contributions of your grandfather, got into several elite universities and somehow walked away with a sketchy and dubious degree that seems to correspond with a sizable gift from your family to the endowment of that institution. But, once again, you apparently did not attend class and, when you did show up, you failed to perform at a level that achieved anything other than failing grades."

He stared at Jason and inquired, "Is that about right?"

Jason nodded reluctantly and admitted, "Yes."

Dudly continued pacing back and forth and spoke. "Now let us focus our attention on this little trip to South America. Mr. Stevens, did you have any knowledge of the culture, customs, or even the language of the people served by the Red Stevens' Library in South America?"

Jason shook his head and stated, "No. I had never heard of the place. I didn't know anything about it, and I couldn't speak the language."

"So," Dudly continued, "we are to understand that you worked in a library and somehow organized books that were written in a language you could not even read."

Jason nodded his head and said, "Yes."

Dudly built to a crescendo. "We will not even address your so-called kidnapping and confinement relating to any scraps of paper you may have received. It would be absurd to put any of that activity in the context of The Gift of Learning."

Hamilton announced automatically, "Your Honor, we object. If counsel is not going to address the matter, please ask him to save his commentary for someone who might care."

I glanced at Mr. Dudly and said, "Objection sustained.

Mr. Dudly, please confine your cross-examination to questions for this witness."

Dudly waved dismissively and stated, "Your Honor, we have no further questions for this witness as nothing he has ever done or said here today could lend itself even slightly toward demonstrating that he understands The Gift of Learning, much less is he equipped and prepared to pass this learning on to others."

Dudly took his seat at the counsel table across the aisle from Mr. Hamilton. Both lawyers and everyone in the courtroom looked toward me with great anticipation. I felt the tension building.

Old Judge Eldridge's words came back to me once again. *Never make any decision before you have to.*

My gaze rose to the giant ornate clock on the back wall of the courtroom.

I spoke. "As it is approaching midday, court will stand in recess until 2:00 p.m."

I struck my gavel once and retreated to the sanity of my chambers.

As Red Stevens' countenance appeared on the video screen, I hoped he would have some answers for me about The Gift of Learning.

"As you know, I never had the benefit of a formal education, and I realize that you have some kind of degree from that high-toned college we sent you to that is little more than a playground for the idle rich.

"Now, before you get your feelings all hurt, I want you to realize that I respect universities as well as any type of formal education. It just wasn't a part of my life. What was a part of my life was a constant curiosity and desire to learn everything I could about the people and world around me. I wasn't able to go to school very long after I learned to read, but the ability to read, think, and observe made me a relatively well-educated man.

"But learning is a process. You can't simply sit in a classroom and someday walk offstage with a sheepskin and call yourself educated. I believe the reason a graduation ceremony is called a *commencement* is because the process of learning begins—commences—at that point. The schooling that went before simply provided the tools and the framework for the real lessons to come.

"In the final analysis, Jason, life—when lived on your own terms—is the ultimate teacher. My wealth and success have robbed you of that, and this is my best effort to repair the damage."

At 2:00 p.m. sharp, I reentered the courtroom and couldn't help but notice the Stevens clan eagerly assembled in their customary seats. There appeared to be great anticipation on that side of the aisle. Dudly was beaming.

I pounded my gavel and declared, "Court is back in session. With respect to the ruling on The Gift of Learning, I find that Mr. Dudly is correct in that Jason Stevens has never demonstrated even an average aptitude for school or the formal pursuit of learning."

A cheer and smattering of applause could be heard from the Stevens family. I glared at them until silence resumed.

"However ..." A corresponding moan could be heard from Dudly's side of the courtroom. "... Howard 'Red' Stevens had some nontraditional and informal ideas regarding The Gift of Learning. Red Stevens felt that education was a lifelong process, not a brief activity or accomplishment; therefore, it is the finding of this court that Jason Stevens has demonstrated that he understands The Gift of Learning. During the next thirty days, he will be given an opportunity to demonstrate that he can impact others with this Gift of Learning received from his grandfather.

"This court stands adjourned. This matter will be taken up again in thirty days."

I rapped my gavel.

~~~~~

It was thirty days later. Jason Stevens was, once again, in the witness box as Theodore J. Hamilton approached.

"Jason, over the past month, have you had the opportunity to pass along The Gift of Learning shared with you by your grandfather?"

Jason nodded and said, "Yes," as Hamilton motioned him to continue. "I was struggling to decide how my grandfather would pass on The Gift of Learning. I decided to take a walk in the Howard 'Red' Stevens Urban Park. Sometimes I feel closer to him there."

Jason looked timidly toward Mr. Watkins seated next to Miss Hastings at the counsel table. They both nodded encouragingly as Jason continued.

"While I was walking through the park, I noticed a group of ten- or twelve-year-old boys gathered there. This struck me as strange as it was a school day. I went over and talked to them and asked why they weren't in school. They shared with me that they didn't care about school, and you couldn't learn anything important in that school anyway.

"I asked what school they went to and found out the name of their teacher. I went to the school and waited for class to be out and then went in to meet their teacher."

Jason loosened his tie slightly and sat back in the witness chair. He glanced up at me briefly and went on.

"It's a really rundown inner-city school. It looks like they spend more money on armed guards than they do on teaching the kids. The teacher I met was a young guy my age named Tom. Tom has spent his whole life preparing to be a teacher, and he is totally dedicated to these kids; but Tom told me most of their parents aren't involved, and the kids just don't see anything in his lessons relevant to the world they know.

"I asked what subjects these kids were studying. Tom told me they were learning fractions, geometry, beginning economics, and they all had to prepare a science fair project. I worked it out with Tom for me to create a supplemental Saturday School in the inner-city park every week."

Mr. Hamilton nodded as if in approval of the progress that Jason had made and inquired, "How has your Saturday School been going?"

Jason smiled with pride and said, "Well, we've had class for four weeks. In order to get into my Saturday School, you have to have a library card and a note from the teacher that you have been in class every day the previous week. We invited kids from surrounding schools and older kids in the day care run by the single moms' co-op."

Jason paused to organize his thoughts and then discreetly counted off the four weeks' activities on his fingers as he spoke. "The first week, I got all the kids to come because I announced that the shortstop for the area Major League baseball team would be at the Saturday School that first week. He talked about batting averages, and he and Tom worked together so kids began to understand and be excited about learning percentages and fractions. He gave all the kids signed baseball cards.

"The second week, we met at the basketball court in the park, and the starting forward for the NBA franchise showed up to help us demonstrate geometry. He made shots from all angles of the court using the backboard to demonstrate the various angles and how they changed, depending on where he was shooting from.

"The third week, we had a lesson in economics. A self-made millionaire businessman, who had attended their school thirty years ago, showed up in a limo and explained why it was important to understand business and finance. The kids all got to ride in the limo, and Tom said they are really interested in beginning economics now.

"Last week, I had a NASCAR driver come to the park and bring his race car. He told the kids and demonstrated how a high-performance engine works. He explained that you can't be a race-car driver or much of anything else unless you understand basic science. The kids got energized and excited about their science fair projects, and things are getting a lot better at the school."

I looked at Mr. Hamilton and inquired, "Any further questions, counselor?"

Hamilton grinned and replied, "Your Honor, I believe that's more than enough."

Dudly rose and barked, "Your Honor, a number of questions regarding this whole situation are begging to be asked."

I sighed and responded, "Please ask your questions."

Dudly was undaunted as he approached Jason.

"Mr. Stevens, do you have a teaching certificate from this state or any jurisdiction?"

Jason shook his head, appearing bewildered and replied, "No."

"Does your baseball player, basketball player, businessman, or race-car driver have teaching certificates or credentials that this court might recognize?"

Jason shrugged and said, "I don't know, but I doubt it."

Dudly continued. "Does this teacher named Tom you refer to have permission from the school board to conduct official sanctioned classes in this so-called urban park?"

Jason shrugged again and responded, "I'm not sure. It is just a bunch of kids who need a new way to learn in order to get excited about school, combined with a few high-profile individuals who are willing to volunteer their time to help."

Dudly swirled about grandly as if addressing everyone seated in the courtroom. "Well, I certainly don't find anything educational or approaching The Gift of Learning in that."

"Well, I do," I ruled. "Counselor, do you have any further questions in this matter?"

Dudly appeared deflated and shook his head in defeat.

I concluded, "Then this matter is resolved. This court will be in session at 10:00 a.m. to take up The Gift of Problems."

Seven

THE LIFE OF PROBLEMS

*Problems viewed in the future appear to be obstacles while
problems viewed in the past are revealed as blessings.*

I f my chambers in the court building, with the
exception of my own leather chair, were designed by
people to impress other people, my study at home
was designed by me to impress no one other than me. The
photos displayed are for the sole purpose of helping me
to recall times, places, and people who matter only to me.
While the array of pictures might not impress anyone else,
they are, without a doubt, the photographic milestones of
my life.

My desk is huge, but unlike the one in the court
building, it is functional. Every inch of the surface is
covered with what appears to be chaotic debris; but, in
reality, I know where everything is and can put my fingers
on it whenever I choose. The fact that the disorganization

would baffle anyone else is somehow comforting to me.

There are a number of well-worn law books that share shelf space with books on everything from golf to fishing and novels ranging from westerns to science fiction. My Labrador retriever, Rex, has found his own familiar and comfortable spot on the ancient rug in front of the fireplace. Like me, he doesn't ask for anything during his time in the study other than to be left alone and to have everything left permanently as it is.

I was breaking one of my study's unwritten rules as I was thinking about the day in court; however, since it's one of my rules and since it's my study where I have sole and absolute jurisdiction, I can suspend or amend rules whenever I wish.

Rex and I were preparing to watch a football game on the large television nearby. It wasn't just any football game, but the hometown team was playing the evil instate rival. I realize there are many sections of the United States that do not even have a professional football team, but I still feel one of the great developments in the game was when they put two pro teams in the same state. I had the hometown jersey on and my refreshments arrayed before me.

The aforementioned jersey has been the subject of several debates with my beloved Marie, as the jersey is now older than the oldest player currently in the League. Approximately a decade ago, Marie informed me that my football jersey should be donated to a charity resale shop. In recent debates, she has downgraded its proposed disposal to inclusion in our family rag bag for washing the cars.

Since the jersey is worn only in my study where I have supreme jurisdiction, she has relented but has laid down a ruling pertaining to her jurisdiction, which includes everywhere outside of my study. Marie's ruling states that the football jersey in question can never be worn outside of the study, particularly if we're going anywhere or having people come over.

Since I didn't want to go anywhere or see anyone, the football jersey was an ideal wardrobe selection. I had asked Rex the Wonder Dog if he disagreed. Hearing no comments to the contrary, I knew we were in one accord.

I was tuned in to the appropriate channel waiting for the ball game. Then just before the pre-game broadcast, the network went for a news update.

There she was, standing next to L. Myron Dudly. It was Sarah Stevens—Jason Stevens' mother and one of the litigants opposing him in the Red Stevens matter.

Sarah was asked, "Why would you oppose your own son in the court case?"

She smiled for the camera and spoke as if discussing a delightful dinner party or fashion accessory.

"Jason is a good boy. He's just confused. This is not really an argument. We're just clearing up some of those nasty, nagging legal things."

The reporter continued, "Don't you feel Jason should be allowed to give away your father-in-law's money as Red Stevens intended through the charitable trust?"

Sarah giggled and offered her comments. "Well, charity's fine, but this is money that my father-in-law worked for, and it should go to his children. Besides, we do a lot for charity."

"How much do you do for charity?" the reporter fired at her.

Sarah seemed perplexed. Dudly stammered as if to stop Sarah, but Sarah answered, "Well, I know I help a lot of charities. Just last week, I donated a whole bag of clothing, and we always buy a table for the opera, ball, and the ballet, and ... well, you know. All the right things."

The reporter asked, "Sarah, are you in communication with your son, Jason?"

Sarah smiled and said, "Well, we don't talk any less now than we always have."

As the reporter was beginning to thank Sarah Stevens and throw it back to the anchor, Dudly interrupted authoritatively, "I believe my client has answered all the questions she needs to. We will have no further comment on this matter."

The reporter appeared bewildered as the screen faded to black and the football game came on.

I was totally distracted and reaching for the remote control to turn off the game when I noticed that Rex was focused on the TV in anticipation. Since I had promised him all week we would watch the game together, I tossed him a pretzel and kept my commitment.

<hr>

The next morning, as usual, I greeted the sunrise as it appeared through the window of my chambers. I located the DVD copy of the video Red Stevens had made for Jason labeled *The Gift of Problems.* I was thinking that the phrase "The Gift of Problems" seems to be ironic when Red Stevens began to speak.

"Jason, life is full of many contradictions. In fact, the longer you live, the more the reality of life will seem like one great paradox. But if you live long enough and search hard enough you will find a miraculous order to the confusion.

"All of the lessons I am trying to teach you as a part of The Ultimate Gift left through my will are generally learned as people go through their lives facing struggles and problems. Any challenge that does not defeat us ultimately strengthens us.

"One of the great errors in my life was sheltering so many people—including you—from life's problems. Out of a misguided sense of concern for your well-being, I actually took away your ability to handle life's problems by removing them from your environment.

"Unfortunately, human beings cannot live in a vacuum forever. A bird must struggle in order to emerge from the eggshell. A well-meaning person might crack open the egg, releasing the baby bird. This person might walk away feeling as though he has done the bird a wonderful service when, in fact, he has left the bird in a weakened condition and unable to deal with its environment. Instead of helping the bird, the person has, in fact, destroyed it. It is only a matter of time until something in the bird's environment attacks it, and the bird has no ability to deal with what otherwise would be a manageable problem.

"If we are not allowed to deal with small problems, we will be destroyed by slightly larger ones. When we come to understand this fact, we live our lives not avoiding problems but welcoming them as challenges that will strengthen us so that we can be victorious in the future."

I thought about the perspective of actually welcoming problems. I remembered many of the good things that had happened in my personal and professional life and had to admit they were each accompanied by a number of problems.

The appointed hour arrived. I donned my black judicial robes, made my way through the mahogany door, and mounted the three steps to my familiar perch above the courtroom. I settled in and asked everyone to be seated. I reviewed my case notes, removed my reading glasses, and gazed at the overflowing crowd.

The ensuing months of this case had not diminished the media frenzy nor the curiosity surrounding Red Stevens and his last will and testament.

I cleared my throat and began. "Today, we are beginning the fifth of twelve provisions outlined in the estate of Howard 'Red' Stevens. This hearing will focus on The Gift of Problems. I will call on counsel for Jason Stevens, Mr. Theodore J. Hamilton, to bring us up to date on how the provisions were handled in this matter."

Hamilton rose with amazing grace and agility for a gentleman well past eighty. He sensed my more formal demeanor with respect to this hearing and acted accordingly.

"Thank you, Your Honor. Once again, the matter before this court is to determine and verify that each tenet of the last will and testament of Howard 'Red' Stevens was carried out appropriately and the bequest awarded to Jason Stevens was, and is, in order."

Hamilton paused for effect, but Dudly jumped in. "Your Honor, counsel should understand after five monthly hearings that the purpose of this case is to scrutinize the absurd bequest in the form of a charitable trust given to Jason Stevens depriving the three children and other heirs who are direct descendants of Red Stevens of their rightful inheritance."

Hamilton laughed aloud and responded, "That may be your purpose in being here, Mr. Dud ..." The now-familiar coughing fit erupted. Hamilton regained control and continued. "... but my purpose here is quite different. I would ask opposing counsel to make his own case and allow me to make mine."

I was forced to intervene as if dealing with two squabbling children. "Counselors, I fully understand why you each are here and the positions of the parties you represent; therefore, if we can suspend the superfluous soliloquies I will ask Mr. Hamilton to make his case."

Hamilton motioned for Jason to take his place, and he began his questioning.

"Jason, do you recall the month you spent, under the direction of your grandfather's will, exploring The Gift of Problems?"

Jason responded solemnly, "Yes, sir. I do. I think I can safely say it was both the best and the worst time in my life."

"Can you explain that?" Hamilton inquired.

Jason glanced cautiously toward his fiancée, Alexia, seated next to Miss Hastings at the counsel table. Miss Hastings placed her hand atop Alexia's hand as Jason spoke.

"My grandfather said that I should go out and find people who were experiencing real problems in their lives, and I should learn the lessons that came with their problems."

Hamilton nodded in understanding and asked, "So what did you do?"

Jason was fighting emotion as he spoke. "I went for a walk to think about The Gift of Problems. I passed a park and noticed a young girl swinging, while her mother watched her with a somber look on her face. I went to meet them and found out that Emily, the daughter, had terminal cancer."

I couldn't help but notice a few tears on Alexia's face as Jason continued.

"I got to know Emily and her mother, Alexia ..." Jason pointed toward his fiancée. "... during the time Emily had left."

"Can you help us understand what you learned from little Emily during the last months of her life?"

Jason's voice broke and tears began to form as he remembered that time. "Emily got sicker and sicker, no matter what anyone did. I know it had to be painful and terrifying for a little kid like that. She never complained, and she taught me so many things through her problems and suffering.

"First, she taught me about joy—that no matter what the circumstance, people can be happy simply because they have decided to be happy people. Then she taught me about courage—that there's really nothing to be afraid of that is any worse than living a life full of fear. And, finally, she taught me how to love. I learned to love her as an unforgettable and special part of my life. And she taught me how to love her mother, and she left us both with that special love. I hope to spend the rest of my life with Alexia, learning how to love and live out all of the lessons I learned from Emily and her problems."

Hamilton was emotional and touched Jason's hand, which lay atop the rail in front of him.

He said, "Thank you, son. That wasn't easy, but it was important."

Hamilton cleared his throat, looked at me, and said, "Your Honor, we will let that be enough for now."

Dudly rose to speak. He actually restored some of my faith in lawyers as he said, "Your Honor, we accept these provisions regarding this matter as stated."

I nodded with some new respect for Mr. Dudly and said, "Thank you, Mr. Dudly."

I wiped my eyes and stated, "Mr. Stevens has demonstrated to this court beyond a shadow of a doubt that he has fully experienced and learned The Gift of Problems. During the next thirty days, he will be given the opportunity to demonstrate that he has the ability to utilize the Red Stevens Charitable Trust to impart an understanding of The Gift of Problems to other people. This court is adjourned."

I rushed into my chambers and engaged in an emotional display that would not be becoming the dignity of a sitting judge, but it was the thing to do. I thought about a special little girl who, through her dying, taught me and everyone in the courtroom a lot about how we should be living.

A month later, we were all back in our places. Jason, under the direction of Theodore J. Hamilton, was recounting his recent activities with respect to The Gift of Problems.

"Alexia and I decided that we had to help other people who were going through what we went through." Jason smiled at Alexia, and she returned the gesture. He pressed on. "We decided that one of the biggest problems that anyone could ever face would be a parent losing a child. Alexia and I felt compelled to help these people as I believe they can only be helped by someone who has faced that same tragedy.

"A book or a lecture or some well-meaning person who hasn't been there isn't going to cut it. You never really get past it or through it, but we believe that with the help of someone that has gone ahead of you, you can learn to live with it and actually grow as a result of it."

Hamilton nodded in agreement and understanding.

Jason continued. "Alexia and I went around to hospitals, clergy, and nursing homes and let them know that if and when they encountered parents experiencing the tragedy of losing a child, we would welcome the opportunity to just talk with them and share our experiences. In the last month, we have met with seven families who have lost or are losing a child. Some of them we've met with more than once. It's probably the hardest thing I've ever done, but I think it may be the best thing I'll ever do."

Hamilton nodded with approval at Jason. He turned to me and said, "Your Honor, that will be all."

I motioned toward Mr. Dudly inquiring, "Counselor, have you anything to add to the proceedings?"

Dudly spoke from his seat behind the counsel table. "We have no questions or arguments to put before the court."

L. Myron Dudly, his legal team, and even the Stevens family situated in the first few rows behind them all seemed to be moved. No one in the courtroom that day, including me, could escape the emotional impact and the life-altering message left by a little girl named Emily.

I tapped my gavel and ruled. "This matter is resolved by consent of counsel and ruling of the court. Tomorrow morning at 10:00 a.m., we will take up the matter of The Gift of Family."

EiGht

THE LIFE OF FAMILY

*Some families are formed by birth, others by legal
documents, and still others are formed through love.*

That next morning in my chambers, I prepared
myself for what I knew would be a hotly contested
issue surrounding The Gift of Family. Mr. Dudly
and his team had wisely avoided any futile conflicts
regarding The Gift of Problems, but I knew they would put
on the pressure this day in the courtroom.

I kept my mind open and free from prejudice as any
judge should do, but—at the same time—I allowed my
thoughts to wander through the possibilities and the
potential arguments I might hear.

The Stevens family was unique in many ways and
dysfunctional in many other ways. Their money, power,
influence, and occasional celebrity status had given them
many advantages along with many disadvantages.

I couldn't help but think about my own family and the relatively simple life we have led. We had been forced to do without a lot of things that are available to rich and famous people, but we had experienced a depth of commitment and love that we would not trade for all the riches and fame the world has ever known.

I was so deep in thought that the time just escaped me. I said, "Come in," in response to a tap on my door, and Jim, my bailiff, stuck his head in and said, "Your Honor, everyone's ready whenever you are."

I glanced up at the clock as I was reaching for my robes. The official day in court was already two minutes old as I settled into my seat and gaveled the proceedings to order.

"Today, we are going to consider The Gift of Family. As this entire case is between family members, and related to family wealth, I anticipate that emotions may run high throughout these proceedings. As always, I want to caution counsel, clients, and everyone in the gallery that this is an official court proceeding that will be carried out with the order and respect it deserves. The court calls on Theodore J. Hamilton to address this matter."

Hamilton made his way around the counsel table and approached Jason who was already settling into the chair in the witness box.

Hamilton began. "Jason, can you share with us what you learned as a result of the lesson your grandfather, Red Stevens, gave to you through The Gift of Family?"

Jason nodded and began. "I went to the Red Stevens Boys' Home in Maine and spent an entire month working with a group of boys. Some of them had families that were not a part of their lives. Others had no family at all.

"It took me a while to learn that these kids at the Boys'

Home had formed their own family. They worked together, played together, and encouraged one another in amazing ways. They taught me that a family is not always the traditional storybook family that we all wished we had, but sometimes a family is wherever you can find it."

Hamilton nodded as if satisfied, waved toward Dudly, and said, "Your witness."

L. Myron Dudly turned into a ferocious shark sensing blood in the water. He, along with his legal team and the Stevens family, knew this was one of the so-called hurdles where they had a good chance to prevail. This emotion was fueled by the fact that, if they could overturn just one of Jason's gifts that were a part of The Ultimate Gift in Red Stevens' will, they would divide several billion dollars among them. On the other hand, the fear of knowing that if they were defeated they would lose everything clung to them like a living thing.

Dudly attacked. "Mr. Stevens, you are before the court today apparently expecting us to believe that you understand The Gift of Family and are in a position to help others with this gift."

Jason nodded and simply replied, "Yes, sir."

Dudly continued. "It would be hard to think of anyone less qualified to speak to The Gift of Family than you."

"Your Honor," Hamilton thundered, "if counsel has a question, please encourage him to ask it or sit down."

I glared at Dudly, ruling, "Sustained. Mr. Dudly, do you have questions for this witness?"

Dudly bore in. "Mr. Stevens, you have testified before this court that you were so disconnected and so ashamed of Red Stevens that you would not even recognize the fact and admit that he was your grandfather."

Jason nodded feebly and almost whispered, "That's true."

Dudly had the grin of a shark sensing victory. "Mr. Stevens, your own family ..." Dudly motioned toward his side of the courtroom, "... has come together in this matter in opposition to you. They have had to mount a legal case for the sole purpose of protecting family assets that should rightfully be inherited by the direct descendants of Howard 'Red' Stevens. Don't you feel like you're tearing apart your family instead of displaying any understanding of The Gift of Family?"

Jason sighed and glanced toward Hamilton. He croaked, "I don't know how to answer that."

Dudly slapped his hands together and said, "I'm sure you don't know how to answer that. I wouldn't either."

Dudly paced back and forth, framing his next question. "Now, can you tell us how—even though you have no real relationship with your family—you became proficient in understanding the importance of families by simply spending a few weeks at some sort of boys' camp?"

Jason blurted out, "It's a Boys' Home."

Dudly mocked him as he bowed slightly and intoned, "Please excuse me. We will call it a Boys' Home."

Jason appeared to gain some momentum, stating, "I learned a lot of things there that would be hard to learn from people who have a good family life. I think it's difficult to know how important something is until it's not there. Without some of the lessons I learned from my grandfather and through the Boys' Home in The Gift of Family, I could not have made the beginning of a family with Alexia and Emily. I think when you get right down to it, the value of a family can only be judged by the people in the family."

Dudly rubbed his hands together and concluded, "Well, young man, in this case someone is going to have to judge you with respect to family, and I am imploring this court to rule on behalf of the Stevens family as the rightful heirs and natural family of their beloved patriarch, Howard 'Red' Stevens."

This matter was far from clear-cut, and I wanted to get some time and distance from the arguments before I made a decision. My head and the law I cherish so much were leaning one way. My heart and emotions were leaning the other way. I rapped my gavel and announced, "This court is in recess for lunch. We will resume these proceedings at 2:00 p.m."

I made my way into my chambers, threw off my judicial robes, and grabbed the DVD marked *The Gift of Family*. As I slid it into the player, I hoped and prayed that Red Stevens' message would somehow give me clarity and direction.

Red spoke to Jason. "Now, Jason, I realize that our family is about as messed up as a family can be, and I accept my full share of responsibility for that. However, the best or worst family situation can teach us a lesson. We either learn what we want or, sadly, we learn what we don't want in life from our families. Out of all the young men in the world, I have selected you. I have asked Mr. Hamilton to undertake this monumental task on my behalf for you. It's hard to understand why that means something, but I want you to know that it does.

"Families give us our roots, our heritage, and our past. They also give us the springboard to our future. Nothing in this world is stronger than the bond that can be formed by a family. That is a bond of pure love that will withstand any pressure as long as the love is kept in the forefront.

"It's important for you to realize that families come in all shapes and sizes. Some very blessed people are able to live their whole lives as part of the families they were born into. Other people, like you, Jason—through a set of circumstances—are left without family other than in name. Those people have to go out and create family."

As I was leaning back in contemplation of Red Stevens' powerful words, the intercom on my desk buzzed. I pressed the button and said, "Yes," and heard the always able and efficient voice of my court reporter, Scott, say, "Your Honor, we're all gathered in the conference room for lunch."

"I'm on my way," I responded, hoping that he didn't realize I had forgotten.

For many years, I had hosted a monthly luncheon for my courtroom colleagues, and the luncheon date was today. I rushed into the conference room generally reserved for judges and lawyers but also the site of my monthly luncheons. I took my seat at the head of the table beneath the portrait of my treasured late mentor and friend Judge Eldridge. For years, sitting in this spot, I had felt his presence and somehow believed it to be fitting that Judge Eldridge was a part of our monthly luncheons.

Seated to my right was Paul, my bailiff. Most people consider Paul to be a virtual giant. I have never asked the exact measurement but would guess that his height is probably closer to seven feet than it is to six feet. The fact that he is an imposing figure has helped us many times in the courtroom when we are confronted with particularly agitated or even potentially violent people. Although we all know Paul wouldn't hurt a fly, somehow his presence has kept us out of a number of uncomfortable situations.

Seated to Paul's right was my other bailiff, Jim. If

Paul is imposing and intimidating, Jim is accommodating and a calming presence everywhere he goes. He seems to understand people at a deep level and be able to communicate with them. I have seen him over the years subdue many angry litigants with nothing more than a calming smile and a kind word.

Across the table from the bailiffs and seated directly to my left was my longtime court reporter, Scott. As we were preparing to eat our lunch, Scott was organizing all of his pills and various medications that he constantly took for his ongoing fight with cancer. When we all heard that Scott had been diagnosed with cancer, everyone was devastated and distraught. Everyone except for Scott, that is. He has shown a grace, a dignity, and a perseverance that has kept me in constant awe.

As we began to eat, the discussion flowed from our families to sports and even politics. We shared many common emotions and experiences as a result of being in the constant firing line together inside the courtroom. In a way that would be hard to explain, it is almost like we have been to war together. We trust each other and understand each other at a deep and significant level.

As my three colleagues were bantering back and forth in a good-natured way, I sat back—along with Judge Eldridge above me—and simply enjoyed being in their company.

As our luncheon time drew to an end and the afternoon's session in court loomed, my thoughts returned to Red Stevens and his words about the unique and wonderful nature of family. As I pushed away from the table, I realized that—right here in this special room around this special table—we had somehow formed our own family.

Back in the courtroom, I called the proceedings to order and directed my comments toward L. Myron Dudly and the Stevens family.

"The court does, indeed, appreciate the arguments of counsel for the Stevens family and agrees that Jason Stevens has little or no experience in what anyone would define as a traditional family."

Murmurs of excitement rocketed through that side of the courtroom as the family anticipated victory.

"On the other hand, after reviewing Red Stevens' thoughts and beliefs surrounding The Gift of Family, a wonderful, natural family experience—while priceless—is not necessary."

I glanced toward Jason and Hamilton across the aisle and ruled. "This court finds that, while unique and unconventional, Jason Stevens has demonstrated an understanding of The Gift of Family as defined by Red Stevens. He will be given the customary thirty days to demonstrate his ability to pass this gift on to other people in need of all the things family can bring."

During the next month, I thought about the concept of family in new ways. I was more thankful for my biological family and more aware of and grateful for my work family and the other people who make my life so special.

Jason was back on the stand, and Hamilton had directed him to explain his actions during the last month surrounding helping others understand The Gift of Family.

Jason explained, "I thought a long time about different people I have come in contact with who need the things family can bring. The kids at the Saturday School in the park don't all have good home lives, but Tom and everyone at the Saturday School seem to be beginning to fill in that role. The single moms have been struggling for a stable family life, but the day-care co-op and the things they are doing together are really making a difference. So, I decided to focus on the seven families Alexia and I helped who had lost or were losing children.

"Since last month, we've been contacted about even more families facing that horrible situation. We organized a brief and informal support-group session so that the pain, the joy, and the lessons learned could be spread among all the hurting families.

"It went over really well, so we are going to make it a monthly event. A lot of the families who lost children a number of months ago are able to begin helping those who are just beginning to face the reality of the struggles before them. These families who are being torn apart are able to come together and begin to find a way to try and fill the tremendous void left behind in a family when a child is gone."

Hamilton had no further questions and turned it over to Mr. Dudly.

Dudly inquired, "Are any of these people related in any way?"

"No," Jason responded. "Not other than the fact that they are sharing the same pain and suffering."

"So, really," Dudly questioned, "you have possibly started a successful support group and, as worthwhile as this may be, how can you call this a family?"

Jason paused for several seconds then spoke with conviction. "My grandfather believed, and I believe, that a family is nothing more or less than people in our lives that provide the love, support, and encouragement that we all want and need from a family."

Dudly dismissed Jason and spoke directly to me before I made my ruling.

Dudly pleaded, "Your Honor, this court must rule on behalf of my clients on this point of law as it pertains to The Gift of Family outlined in Red Stevens' last will and testament. While Mr. Jason Stevens may be accomplishing some laudable work, it could not in any way be called or defined as helping people with The Gift of Family.

"These people ..." Dudly pointed toward his side of the courtroom. "... are family in every sense of the word, and they deserve to be recognized as such by having this court restore their family assets to them."

I thanked Mr. Dudly for presenting his motion, nodded in thanks to Mr. Hamilton, and spoke for the record.

"The court agrees that Jason Stevens has not been working in an area that would generally be defined as family. It does not meet the legal definition of family as well; however, it does meet Red Stevens' definition of family as he intended it for his grandson in The Gift of Family. This court rules in favor of Jason Stevens and will be recessed until 10:00 a.m. tomorrow when we consider The Gift of Laughter."

Nine

THE LIFE OF LAUGHTER

*It is impossible to experience fear, hate,
or defeat when we are laughing.*

After the final decision on The Gift of Family, I returned to my chambers to clean up a bit of paperwork. I was going to stay downtown at the court building and wait for my hot dinner date for the evening to arrive. Marie and I feel that our relationship has stayed as fun and exciting as it was in the beginning because we talk and go out on dates just like we did from the start.

I had almost completed the voluminous pile of paperwork the clerks had placed before me when Marie came through the mahogany door.

She smiled and said, "Your Honor, you'd better be on your best behavior this evening, because I have another offer."

I smiled and inquired, "What kind of offer are we talking about?"

"Well," she explained, "when I came into the court building, there was a new guard on duty downstairs, and he didn't know me. I told him I was here for a dinner date, and he said he would be off in forty-five minutes if I wouldn't mind waiting."

I pounded on my ridiculous judicial desk as if using my gavel and exploded in mock anger, "I'll have that man's job!"

Marie laughed raucously and said, "Your Honor, I don't think you'd make a good guard, and I don't think anyone would trust you with a loaded weapon. You'd better stick with this judge gig you've got going here."

Marie asked me how my day in court had gone, so I told her all about the Stevens' case and The Gift of Family.

Marie asked, "So what's next on that case?"

I explained that in the morning we would be looking into The Gift of Laughter that Red Stevens had outlined for Jason in his last will and testament.

Marie was curious and asked how I knew exactly what Red Stevens wanted for his grandson. I told her about the videos that Red had made to deliver the various gifts to Jason after Red's death.

Marie asked, "How does that work exactly?"

I considered for a minute, picked up the DVD marked *The Gift of Laughter*, and replied, "Well, I'll show you. Or better yet, Red Stevens will show you."

I slid the disk into the player, and Red Stevens appeared. I pressed *pause* so I could get back to my chair, and Marie could settle into one of my guest chairs.

She stared at Red Stevens on the screen and asked, "How long before his death was this video made?"

"As I understand it, it was completed just a few weeks before his passing," I responded.

Marie thought aloud, "It's really rather sad that someone has to talk to a video camera instead of their grandson when they're so near the end of life."

I considered her perspective then said, "It's sad, but I believe Red knew that this was the only way he had a chance of reaching Jason."

As silence fell over my chambers, I finally pushed *play*, and Red shared his thoughts and feelings with Jason.

"This month, you are going to learn about The Gift of Laughter. The Gift of Laughter I want you to learn about is not a comedian in a nightclub or a funny movie. It is the ability to look at yourself, your problems, and life in general and just laugh. Many people live unhappy lives because they take things too seriously. I hope you have learned in the last six months that there are things in life to be serious about and to treasure, but life without laughter is not worth living.

"This month, I want you to go out and find one example of a person who is experiencing difficulties or challenges in his or her life but who maintains the ability to laugh. If a person can laugh in the face of adversity, that individual will be happy throughout life."

Marie and I walked arm-in-arm out of the court building, through the urban park, and toward our favorite Greek restaurant. We remembered times past, both good and bad, and laughed at them all. Some of the worst times we had experienced financially, and the hardships we endured, now just seem petty and humorous. We enjoyed a wonderful dinner and listened to the life-affirming Greek music provided by a strolling violinist.

Near the end of the evening, I excused myself and went to the restroom. I returned shortly and slipped back into my place at the table. I will never in my life figure out how she did it, but when I looked across at Marie, she lowered her dessert menu and there before me sat my beloved bride wearing a giant rubber nose, a goofy fake mustache, and ridiculous comedy glasses.

She said with total dignity and solemnity, "Your Honor, may it please the court, this is your Gift of Laughter."

<hr>

I heard Paul intone the always-familiar "All rise."

I made my way up the three stairs as I had done countless thousands of times. I often thought I could do this in my sleep if ever called upon to do so. I settled into my chair and pounded the gavel, calling the court to order. I realized that there needed to be a certain amount of pomp and circumstance surrounding my duties as a judge, but Marie's Gift of Laughter was still in my memory, so it was hard to take myself too seriously.

I greeted Mr. Hamilton and asked him to open the proceedings. He steered Jason through his testimony of how Red Stevens had required Jason to go out and find someone who was experiencing struggles or difficulty in their life but dealt with it through laughter. Jason explained how he had met his friend David Reese, a blind young man, who dealt with his blindness and everything else in life through his humor.

Mr. Hamilton dismissed Jason, who stepped down from the stand, then Hamilton called on David Reese to testify.

A handsome young man wearing dark glasses and using a white cane moved confidently and quickly toward the witness stand. He tapped his cane on the one step up into the witness box and then negotiated it deftly. He slid into the witness chair, and my bailiff, Jim, asked him to place his hand on the Bible. David Reese did so and swore to tell the truth, the whole truth, and nothing but the truth, then Theodore J. Hamilton approached and said, "Hello, Mr. Reese. Thank you for being here today."

David Reese smiled and said, "It's good to see you again, Mr. Hamilton. In fact, as I always say, it's good to see anybody."

Tentative laughter could be heard filtering through the courtroom.

David continued. "I don't know who designed that step up into the witness box, but I'll bet it wasn't a blind guy."

David faced directly toward Hamilton and said, "Another great tie, Mr. Hamilton. How many of those do you have?"

The laughter built and rose pleasantly in my courtroom until Dudly shouted, "Your Honor, we most vigorously object to this slapstick comedy routine that opposing counsel has obviously orchestrated."

."I didn't know we had an orchestra," David shot back. He asked, "And who is this guy? Is he with the string section?"

Dudly became indignant and announced, "Young man, I am L. Myron Dudly of Dudly, Cheetham, and Leech."

David laughed and quipped, "Wow, people like you are hard on a poor blind guy like me trying to spread a little cheer. I have to work at making people laugh at me, and it just comes naturally to you."

The laughter roared about us, and David Reese asked, "Is that your real name, or did you hire comedy writers?"

I chuckled, myself, but finally had to pound my gavel and call for order.

I addressed David Reese. "Mr. Reese, while your humor may be a breath of fresh air here in my courtroom, and even though we are exploring The Gift of Laughter, I will have to ask you to confine yourself to the questions addressed to you by counsel."

David Reese smiled innocently, shrugged his shoulders, and nodded, saying, "Good enough. Let's do this thing."

Hamilton resumed questioning. "Mr. Reese, is it true that as a result of Jason Stevens' search for The Gift of Laughter as directed by Red Stevens, he met you on a subway train?"

"Yes, sir, that is correct-a-mundo."

Dudly began to rise, and I glared at him, motioning for him to be seated.

Hamilton continued. "From that time to this, have you formed a relationship with Jason Stevens?"

David nodded and said, "Absolutely."

"What is the nature of your relationship?" Hamilton inquired.

"Well, we're friends. We get together from time to time and talk on the phone a lot. Jason met with me and some of my students at the school for the blind just recently. We know different people and move in different circles, so we kind of exchange jokes with one another. When I see something funny—no pun intended—or Jason finds something good, we share it."

"And why is humor important in your life?" Hamilton asked.

David Reese sighed deeply and was serious for the first time that day. "Sometimes laughter and my humor is all I have. Being blind can be depressing and unbelievably difficult. People don't know how to deal with you, and they're afraid of saying or doing something wrong, so they just avoid you. But laughter is the universal language. It's just like here in the courtroom today. I'm sure a lot of people were nervous and didn't know what to think when I walked up here wearing my shades and using my white cane. But a couple of jokes later, and we're all comfortable and, well, we're just friends."

Mr. Hamilton thanked David for his appearance and stated, "Your Honor, I have no further questions for this witness.

Mr. Dudly got to his feet and began. "Mr. Reese, do you have any psychological training in your background?"

David laughed and responded, "No, but I have been to a psychologist; however, I was more of the therapee and not the therapist."

A few chuckles could be heard from the gallery, but Dudly ignored them and continued. "Would you say Jason Stevens has helped you better understand or deal with your situation through laughter?"

David responded, "Jason is my friend, and we laugh together. We all deal with our own situations, but sometimes it's nice to have someone who cares enough to share a good laugh."

David paused and then asked, "Does anyone ever call you Dud?"

I joined in the laughter that overflowed the courtroom. Mr. Dudly was beet red and shaking. He stammered and pointed his finger at me, then Mr. Hamilton, and finally David Reese before he simply sat down. When order was restored, I inquired of Mr. Dudly if he had any further questions. He shook his head vigorously with disgust and busied himself with some paperwork in front of him.

I addressed myself to my court reporter, Scott, saying, "Let the record show that the court finds that Jason Stevens has demonstrated he understands The Gift of Laughter as set forth in the last will and testament of Howard 'Red' Stevens. Thirty days from today, we will rule upon Jason Stevens' ability to share his Gift of Laughter with others. This court stands adjourned."

In the intervening month, either there were a lot more humorous episodes in my life than normal, or exploring The Gift of Laughter through Red Stevens and Jason had made me more aware of all the opportunities to enjoy laughter.

"Let the record show that today the court will be ruling on the matter pertaining to Red Stevens' last will and testament relating to Jason Stevens' ability to pass on The Gift of Laughter."

I waved toward Theodore J. Hamilton and asked, "Mr. Hamilton, can you get the ball rolling for us here this morning?"

"I would be pleased to, Your Honor."

Hamilton waved Jason toward the witness stand. Jason settled in, and Hamilton inquired, "Jason, in the last month, have you had an opportunity to pass along The Gift of Laughter that your grandfather shared with you?"

Jason nodded emphatically and began. "Yes. I thought a lot about The Gift of Laughter and who might need it the most. When I visited the senior citizens' center to see how the periodic calls from the students at the school for the blind were going, I felt I had my answer.

"The senior citizens at the center are often suffering

from chronic physical pain, and many of them have lost a spouse and a great number of their lifelong friends. They don't get to see their children or grandchildren as often as they wish, so I felt they needed The Gift of Laughter."

Hamilton prompted, "So how did you facilitate this?"

Jason continued. "Well, after breakfast each day at the center, a lot of the senior citizens gather together in regular groups around the television or on the sun porch or just in the hall near one another's rooms. I went around to each of these groups and let them know that we had a new activity called the Monday Morning Circle of Laughter."

Jason paused and then explained, "These senior citizens had gotten into the habit of getting together each morning and sharing complaints, fears, or just their aches and pains; but I told them from now on, Mondays were dedicated to the Circle of Laughter.

"All of the informal groups would allow each senior citizen, in turn, to share something humorous that had happened to them recently or a funny memory they have from the past. Nothing other than humor is allowed on Mondays."

Hamilton nodded and asked, "So what have the results been from this Circle of Laughter?"

"It's really been amazing," Jason explained as he reached inside his jacket and drew out an envelope. "Here is a letter from the senior citizens' center's administrator. She explains that they are compiling data from the doctors and nurses, but the preliminary results have shown that the residents rest better, require less medication, and report an overall improved sense of well-being on Mondays than other days of the week. One of the physicians is actually planning to produce a report for a geriatric medical journal outlining the success of the Circle of Laughter."

Hamilton thanked Jason and spoke to Mr. Dudly. "He's all yours."

Dudly nodded perfunctorily and began. "Mr. Stevens, did you actually teach these senior citizens anything about humor or laughter?"

Jason shook his head and admitted, "No, not really."

"Did you facilitate or lead the discussions in these groups?" Dudly asked.

"No, not really," Jason stated.

Dudly began to pace and shook his head as if disappointed in Jason's answer then asked, "So other than suggesting that these people get together and discuss laughter, what did you really accomplish?"

"Nothing," Jason said. "My grandfather taught me—and I realize—that humor exists in all of us. It surrounds us every day. Potential laughter is everywhere if we just find it and share it, but as my grandfather taught me through The Ultimate Gift, unless we look for and expect all of the good things and gifts of life, we will miss them. I simply helped a group of people focus on laughter instead of pain, suffering, and loneliness."

Mr. Dudly waved at Jason and mumbled, "Dismissed."

Dudly focused on me and said, "Your Honor, it is clear that Jason Stevens did not pass on or bring anyone The Gift of Laughter. These people at the center had it all along. I ask this court to rule on behalf of my clients, the rightful heirs to Red Stevens' fortune."

I nodded as Dudly returned to his seat and stated for all present to hear, "Mr. Dudly, I agree with you ..."

Excited whispers could be heard from the Stevens family.

I tapped my gavel and began again. "I agree with you in that Jason didn't bring these senior citizens anything they didn't already have, but as I have come to understand Red Stevens' intentions with respect to The Gift of Laughter, the fact that Jason allowed them to understand and express the laughter inside of them may, indeed, be the greatest gift of all."

I rapped my gavel and ruled, "This court finds in favor of Jason Stevens. We will resume tomorrow and consider The Gift of Dreams."

Ten

THE LIFE OF DREAMS

Dreams are the essence of all we can become.

T he next morning found me—with cup of coffee in hand—leaning back in my comfortable leather chair and staring out the window toward the east in time for the sunrise. While I was in my usual place, the sun wasn't. Or at least I could not have sworn to it under oath in a court of law. There was a filmy layer of clouds and fog lying atop the city. The most solid and permanent structures looked temporal as viewed from the window in my chambers that morning.

Reality is not always easy to define, and everything is not as it appears. These are good things for a presiding judge to remember both personally and professionally.

I held the DVD labeled *The Gift of Dreams* in my hand as I contemplated the ironies of life and what Red Stevens might reveal about dreams. The familiar image of Howard "Red" Stevens materialized on the video screen.

"Jason, this month you're going to learn about a gift that belongs to all great men and women—The Gift of Dreams. Dreams are the essence of life—not as it is, but as it can be. Dreams are born in the hearts and minds of very special people, but the fruit of those dreams becomes reality and can be enjoyed by the whole world.

"You may not know it, but Theodore Hamilton is known far and wide as the best lawyer in the country. I know that performing at that level was a dream of his when I met him, and he has been living that dream for over fifty years. The dream came true in his heart and mind before it came true in reality.

"I can remember wandering through the swamps of Louisiana, dreaming about becoming the greatest oil and cattle baron in Texas. That dream became such a part of me that when I achieved my goals, it was like going home to a place I had never been before.

"I have been trying to decide, as I have been formulating this Ultimate Gift for you, which of the gifts is the greatest. If I had to pick one, I think I would pick The Gift of Dreams because dreams allow us to see life as it can be—not as it is. In that way, The Gift of Dreams allows us to go out and get any other gift we want out of this life.

"One of the first truly great dreamers I ever met in my life had a passion to create places and things that would touch the imagination of people. This passion was with him all the days of his life. He had his share of setbacks and failures as well as many detractors. I never saw him or talked to him at a time when he didn't want to share his latest project with me. He was in the habit of creating huge dream boards that he would hang on the wall and draw out the plans for each of his projects on.

"I remember that when he was on his deathbed, he had arranged to tack the plans for his newest project onto the ceiling of his hospital room. That way, he could continue to look at his dream as he constructed it in his mind.

"A reporter came to visit him while he was in the hospital, and my friend was so weak he could barely talk. So he actually moved over and asked the reporter to lie on his bed with him so the two of them could look at the plans on the ceiling while my friend shared his dream.

"The reporter was so moved that a person would have that much passion while dealing with a serious illness in the hospital. The reporter concluded his interview, said good-bye to my friend, and left the hospital.

"My friend died later that day.

"Please do not miss the point. A person who can live his entire life with a burning passion for his dream to the extent that he shares it on his deathbed—that is a fortunate person. My friend had his dream with him all the days of his life. It continued to grow and expand. When he would reach one milestone of his dream, another greater and grander one would appear.

"In a real way, my friend taught a lot of people how to dream and imagine a better world. His name was Walt Disney.

"But let me warn you. Your dreams for your life must be yours. They cannot belong to someone else, and they must continue to grow and expand.

"I had another friend whose name you would not know. He said it was his dream to work hard and retire at age fifty. He did, indeed, work hard and achieve a degree of success in his business. He held on to that dream of retiring, but he had no passion beyond that.

"On his fiftieth birthday, a number of us gathered to celebrate both his birthday and his retirement. This should have been one of the happiest days of his life—if his dream had been properly aligned. Unfortunately, his entire adult life had been spent in his profession. That is where he had gained a lot of his pride and self-esteem. When he found himself as a relatively young man without his profession to guide him, he faced the uncertainty of retirement. It was something he thought he had always wanted, but he discovered quickly it created no life-sustaining passion for him.

"A month later, my second friend committed suicide.

"The difference between one dreamer who was still energized by his lifelong passion while on his deathbed and another dreamer whose goal was so ill-fitting for his personality that he committed suicide should be apparent to you.

"Jason, it is important that your dream belong to you. It is not a one-size-fits-all proposition. Your dream should be a custom-fit for your personality, one that grows and develops as you do. The only person who needs to be passionate about your dream is you."

I thought about the relationship between dreams and reality in my own life. As I was contemplating my own long-held dreams—some that had come true, others that were unrealized—the sun broke through the clouds. What had been totally obscured earlier was now revealed as the most glorious sunrise I had witnessed in many months. It had been there all along.

The tension was high in my courtroom that day as Theodore Hamilton led Jason Stevens over each of the hurdles. The stakes seemed to grow even greater in this winner-take-all race to the finish.

I reminded everyone that Jason Stevens was still under oath with respect to his testimony in this case.

Mr. Hamilton began the questioning. "Jason, when your grandfather shared The Gift of Dreams with you, what was the task he asked you to undertake as a part of the process?"

Jason collected his thoughts and began. "My grandfather asked me to think about my life, my goals, and my dreams to determine what it was I wanted to accomplish in my life."

Jason fidgeted a moment in his seat, put his hand on his forehead in concentration, and then looked above the gallery. He seemed to be focused on that time and place in the past.

"I thought about a million things I could do with my life, but when I boiled them all down, they seemed to each take the same direction."

Hamilton nodded in understanding and encouraged Jason. "Please share that direction with us this morning."

"Well, it's pretty simple in a way," Jason responded. "I want to help deprived young people. I don't simply mean young people who don't have money or who come from difficult circumstances; but I want to help those who don't understand all the things that they have in their lives. I guess, in simplest terms, I want to spend my life sharing The Ultimate Gift with everyone I can."

Hamilton smiled and said, "Thank you for sharing that, Jason. That's what your grandfather wanted for you as well."

"I object," Dudly thundered. "It is for this court to decide what Red Stevens' intentions were, not Mr. Hamilton."

Hamilton mocked Dudly with a brief bow and formally intoned, "Very well, counselor, I shall leave this witness to you, and we will allow this court to decide."

Dudly moved toward the witness box and actually leaned over the rail toward Jason.

"Mr. Stevens, doesn't it seem a little too convenient for the dream you have for your own life to be to help other people with The Ultimate Gift? Could it be that you simply want control of several billion dollars?"

Jason smiled and said, "I have been sharing The Ultimate Gift with everyone I can since my grandfather gave it to me. I will be doing that for the rest of my life, no matter what else happens."

"I see," Dudly said with great skepticism. "Do you have any experience living life in poverty?" Dudly asked.

Jason shook his head and laughed, "No, quite the contrary, actually."

Dudly continued, "Do you have any experience in your life with any sort of disability or infirmity?"

Jason shook his head and replied, "No, I've been very fortunate to be healthy my whole life."

"Then how can you reasonably expect anyone to think you are the person to help others with their dreams? You can't even undertake your own dreams without your grandfather's money that should legally and morally be the property of my clients."

"Object," Hamilton said. "Your Honor, apparently Mr. Dudly wants to not only be the lawyer and the witness but judge, jury, and executioner as well."

I tapped my gavel. "Sustained."

"I have no further need to question this witness," Dudly remarked offhandedly as he confidently strode to the counsel table, smiled at his clients assembled in the first three rows, turned, and took his seat.

"A dream is quite different from reality," I began. "There

need not be any evidence to support a dream for it to be valid. In fact, the aspect that makes dreams so remarkable is the fact that they are rarely, if ever, realistic. I find that Mr. Jason Stevens' dream is both reasonable and admirable in light of his grandfather's wishes and desires as outlined in Red Stevens' last will and testament."

A collective groan could be heard and felt from the gallery behind Dudly. Dudly sat open-mouthed, thinking that he had this one in the bag.

I continued, "Jason Stevens will be given a thirty-day period to demonstrate his ability to pass on The Gift of Dreams to others. This court stands adjourned."

Jason Stevens carried a sizable box with him to the witness stand and set it on the floor near his feet. Hamilton directed him to share his activities pertaining to The Gift of Dreams over the last month, and Jason spoke.

"I began the month thinking about young people who most need The Gift of Dreams. Then I realized I had ready access to a group of kids who come from impoverished, dysfunctional, and disadvantaged backgrounds."

Jason paused, looked down at the box at his feet, and continued, "I went to the Saturday School in the park, and I told all of the kids about The Gift of Dreams. We had several discussion groups and exercises. Finally, I asked each of them to write down the dreams that they have for their life."

Hamilton smiled expansively and said, "Very good. Would you be able to share some of their dreams with us today here in the courtroom?"

Jason nodded confidently and reached into the box. He pulled out a handful of papers and began. "Taylor is age eight. He wants to play shortstop for the New York Yankees.

Nicole is nine, and she wants to be an astronaut. Marcus is also nine and wants to be an actor. David is eleven, and his dream is to be a successful businessman so he can buy his mom a house and car. Laurie is seven, and she wants to be president of the United States."

Hamilton interrupted, stating for the benefit of all present, "Thank you, Jason, I think that is more than enough to demonstrate your point in this matter. I have no further questions."

"Mr. Stevens," Dudly began, "what would you say are the odds of any one child growing up to play shortstop for the New York Yankees, becoming an astronaut, or—much less—being elected president of the United States?"

"I have no idea." Jason shrugged as he spoke.

Dudly fired back, "Well, wouldn't you say it's highly improbable?"

Jason considered and then said, "Yeah, maybe."

Dudly went for the throat, asking, "Then please tell the court what the point is of this entire exercise?"

Jason placed the paperwork respectfully back into his box, sat up straight, and spoke. "The point is not what these kids are dreaming. The point is that coming from their helpless and hopeless backgrounds that they have a dream at all. My grandfather taught me that dreams can grow and change. It's not as important what dream you have as it is that you have a dream."

Dudly rested his case, and I confidently ruled, "Jason Stevens has, to the satisfaction of this court, proven that he has the ability and desire to pass along The Gift of Dreams. Monday, we will consider The Gift of Giving."

Eleven

THE LIFE OF GIVING

*In this life, we often lose everything we try to keep, and
get to keep everything that we try to give away.*

The media vultures descended on the Saturday
School the next morning. The obscure inner-city
kids became instant celebrities across the country
and around the world.

I watched an in-depth interview with nine-year-old
Marcus who had a dream of being an actor. The reporters
took turns shouting questions at him, flashbulbs exploded
all around him, and a score of microphones were thrust in
his face. Marcus was calm, cool, and collected. He handled
every question as if the answer had been scripted for him,
his voice never faltered, and his gaze never wavered.

At the end of his few minutes of fame, I was certain
that if I were ever casting a major motion picture, Marcus
would be on the top of my list.

Then Laurie appeared before the cameras. She was frail and seemed a bit bewildered. The graphic at the bottom of my TV screen reminded me that Laurie was only seven years old; but when the first question was fired at her, Laurie more than rose to the occasion.

A reporter opened with, "Laurie, what makes you want to become president?"

Laurie articulated her platform. "The street lights are out, the school needs to be painted, there are scary people on my street, and everybody is always fighting."

The reporter followed up, asking, "Well, Laurie, what are you going to do about it?"

"I'm going to change it," Laurie proclaimed in a manner that convinced me to mark my ballot for her. I wouldn't be surprised to have the opportunity to vote for Laurie in the future.

The weekend offered some needed rest, but far too soon Monday rolled around, and everyone was back in their familiar places in my courtroom.

I called for order and stated, "Today, we are going to review The Gift of Giving as it was presented to Jason Stevens by his grandfather. This court will hear evidence with respect to whether Jason Stevens has an understanding and working knowledge of his grandfather's wishes regarding The Gift of Giving. As usual, we will first hear from Mr. Hamilton, representing Jason Stevens."

Jason took his place in the witness box and, as directed by Mr. Hamilton, explained that Red Stevens had challenged him—each day of the month—to find people to give gifts to that came from Jason, himself. These could not be gifts bought by the money provided to Jason by his grandfather but instead had to be something from Jason.

Hamilton inquired, "So what did you do?"

Jason said, "Well, I found things that I could get on my own or already had that I could give away."

Hamilton nodded and said, "Can you share them with us?"

Jason pulled a folded sheet of paper from his pocket. He unfolded it and read, "On the first day, I stopped at a shopping center and found a parking space on the first row. As I was getting out of my car, I noticed an elderly couple looking for a space. I backed out and allowed them to park in my space, and I parked in the back of the lot.

"On the second day, I got caught downtown in a thunderstorm. I shared my umbrella with a young lady who didn't have one. One the third day, I went to the hospital and donated a pint of blood. On day four, I called a man in my neighborhood who had told me he needed to buy new tires. I let him know there was a really good sale going on across town. On day five, I helped an elderly woman carry her packages to her car. On day six, I agreed to watch a neighbor's children for her while she went out with some friends. On day seven, I went to the Center for the Blind and read articles to visually impaired students. On day eight, I served lunch at the soup kitchen, and on day nine I wrote a note and sent a poem to a friend.

"On day ten, I agreed to take my neighbor's kids to school. On day eleven, I helped box and move donated items for the Salvation Army. On days twelve and thirteen, I let some visiting foreign exchange students stay in my home. On day fourteen, I helped a local Scout troop with their weekly meeting. On day fifteen, I found a man with a dead battery and jump-started his car. On day sixteen, I wrote letters for several people who were in the hospital.

On day seventeen, I went to the local animal shelter and walked several of their dogs in the park. On day eighteen, I gave the frequent flyer miles I had earned with an airline to a high school band planning a trip to a parade in California. Day nineteen, I worked with a local service organization and delivered meals to disabled people.

"Days twenty, twenty-one, twenty-two, and twenty-three, I took a group of inner-city kids who had never been camping and fishing on a trip with the Scout troop. I had never been camping or fishing either. On day twenty-four, I helped a local church with their rummage sale. Days twenty-five and twenty-six, I worked with a crew on a Habitat for Humanity house. Day twenty-seven, I let a local charity group use my home for a reception. Day twenty-eight, I helped one of my neighbors rake the leaves out of his yard. Day twenty-nine, believe it or not, I helped to bake cookies for the elementary school's bake sale."

Theodore J. Hamilton actually applauded as he stood in front of the witness box. He said, "Very impressive, son, but what did you do on day thirty?"

Jason chuckled and replied, "Well, Mr. Hamilton, if you'll remember I gave some of the leftover cookies I had baked for the bake sale to you and Miss Hastings."

"Yes, you did," Hamilton remarked. "And I can attest to the fact that they were quite delicious. No more questions."

Hamilton retreated to his seat as Dudly prepared to attack.

"Mr. Stevens, what would you say—in your opinion—was the combined monetary value of all the gifts on your little list there?" Dudly pointed to Jason's paper as if it were unclean.

Jason looked bewildered, shrugged, and said, "Well, sir, I don't have any idea."

Dudly pressed. "Wouldn't you agree that most of those items had little, if any, relative worth in the real world?"

"Probably," Jason admitted.

"Then how can you hope to manage several billion dollars, based on that?" Dudly jabbed his finger toward the page in Jason's hand.

Jason pondered for several moments then said, "My grandfather told me to give away things I had gotten on my own. I didn't have any choice but to give away a part of myself." Jason paused, found his stride, and continued. "But I think it's a lot easier to manage money than it is to manage ourselves."

Dudly looked at Jason and appeared shocked. "You have got to be kidding." He looked at the ceiling and held out his hands palm upward as if he were imploring the heavens for relief from this absurdity.

I finally had to interrupt the theatrics, asking, "Mr. Dudly, do you have any other questions for this witness?"

Dudly intoned dramatically, "No, Your Honor. This matter seems more than clear."

Dudly sat down.

I nodded to Jason, thanked him for his testimony, and told him he could step down. I organized my thoughts into a ruling and spoke. "The last will and testament of Howard 'Red' Stevens called for his grandson to give away something of himself each and every day for a month. It is the finding of this court that Mr. Jason Stevens duly accomplished this task.

"During the next thirty days, he will be given the opportunity to demonstrate that he can pass along The Gift of Giving to others."

My gavel sounded with finality, and I made my way through the mahogany door into the private world of my chambers. I leaned against the monstrous desk and wondered if I could think of something of myself to give away every day for a month.

I watched Red Stevens appear on the screen before me and discuss The Gift of Giving.

"This month, I want you to learn about The Gift of Giving. This is another one of those paradoxical principles like we talked about several months ago. Conventional wisdom would say that the less you give, the more you have. The converse is true. The more you give, the more you have. Abundance creates the ability to give; giving creates more abundance. I don't mean this simply in financial terms. This principle is true in every area of your life.

"It is important to be a giver and a receiver. Jason, financially, I have given you everything that you have in this world. But, I violated the principle involved in The Gift of Giving. I gave you money and things out of a sense of obligation not a true spirit of giving. You received those things with an attitude of entitlement and privilege instead of gratitude. Our attitudes have robbed us both of the joy involved in The Gift of Giving.

"It is important when you give something to someone that it be given with the right spirit, not out of a sense of obligation. I've learned to give to people my whole life. I cannot imagine being deprived of the privilege of giving things and part of myself to other people.

"One of the key principles in giving, however, is that the gift must be yours to give—either something you earned or created or maybe, simply, part of yourself."

During that whole month, I looked at giving and receiving in ways I never had.

Even though I had seen it once before, the sight still amazed me. I took my seat in the courtroom, pounded my gavel, and called the court to order. I smiled at everyone assembled and said, "I want to welcome everyone to these proceedings. The law is a sacred part of our lives and culture. I'm always glad to see people participate in the process."

Once again, running from front to back on either side of my courtroom and standing shoulder to shoulder against the back wall were the single moms who had appeared in my courtroom once before during The Gift of Money hearing.

I motioned to Mr. Hamilton and Jason Stevens, and they took their places and opened the proceedings.

Hamilton inquired, "Jason, over the past month, have you had the opportunity to share The Gift of Giving as outlined by your grandfather, Howard 'Red' Stevens, with other people?"

Jason nodded and said, "Yes."

"Please fill us in on your progress," Hamilton said.

Jason gazed down the long line of single women who made an amazing silent statement just by being there, then he began. "I tried to think about The Gift of Giving and felt giving should be both creative and automatic. It needs to be something we constantly think about in new ways; but, on the other hand, it's important to develop the habit of giving regularly."

Jason looked up at me and said, "As you know, when we talked about The Gift of Money I set up a sort of financial class for all the single moms participating in the day-care co-op and support group. Those classes have continued, and we've learned that we should always do three things with every dollar we receive.

"We should first save some so that we will have money for hard and difficult times or special opportunities. Second, we should spend some to wisely and prudently take care of our immediate and future needs. And, finally, we should regularly and consistently give away a part of each dollar.

"When we discussed giving among the single moms, there was a lot of frustration, because they are on such tight budgets there was a feeling that they couldn't really accomplish anything with their individual gifts."

Jason smiled and looked around the perimeter of the room with anticipation.

Hamilton smiled as well and asked, "So what did you do, Jason?"

Jason announced, "All of the single moms in the group got together and pooled their money. Collectively, they have made a monthly pledge toward building a community center with day-care facilities at the Howard 'Red' Stevens Urban Park."

Jason reached into the inner breast pocket of his jacket and drew out an envelope. He continued, "Here is their first check written from the Single Moms Benevolence Fund and made out to the Howard 'Red' Stevens Urban Park Community Center."

A cheer rose from the single moms around the courtroom.

Old Judge Eldridge had always stressed to me the important responsibility of keeping order in the court. Somehow I knew he was looking down on us and would approve of the fact that I let the applause run its full course.

Hamilton waved at the single moms, thanked Jason, and turned the witness over to Mr. Dudly.

Dudly asked, "Mr. Stevens, do you have an estimate of the cost of this community center with day-care facilities to be built at this so-called park?"

Jason displayed an impish grin and clarified. "Mr. Dudly, do you mean the Howard 'Red' Stevens Urban Park where we are going to build the community center with the day-care facilities?"

"Yes, whatever," Dudly responded impatiently.

Jason continued. "Yes, I have a preliminary estimate, and it will cost several hundred thousand dollars. We are factoring in some of the variables and details to get a final number."

"So how long will it take for ..." Dudly waved his hand at the ladies standing around the room and continued, "... you to pay for such a center with these monthly checks?"

"Not nearly as long as it would take without these checks," Jason stated.

Another cheer rose from the single moms. I halfheartedly tapped my gavel but wanted to applaud, myself.

Dudly tried to ignore the display dismissively and said, "No further questions."

I tried to look each of the single moms in the eye as I slowly gazed around the room.

I spoke directly to them, "Many times in this courtroom I am called upon to make a ruling because it is my sworn duty and my legal obligation. While this ruling is, indeed, my duty and obligation, it is also my distinct pleasure to acknowledge the contribution made by each of you ..." I looked at the single moms, smiled, and continued, "... in this matter and to rule on behalf of Jason Stevens in the portion of this case relating to The Gift of Giving."

As I dismissed the court, a third and more rousing cheer erupted.

It had been a good day.

Twelve

THE LIFE OF GRATITUDE

Gratitude provides a balance between the
things we have and those we want.

One of the cable news channels carried a live remote broadcast of the groundbreaking ceremonies for the community center and day-care complex in the Howard "Red" Stevens Urban Park. Jason spoke briefly but allowed the spotlight to shine on the group of single moms who had committed funds and the residents of the community who had built the park.

I will never forget a statement made by one of the single moms. She timidly approached the lectern, stared into the blinding TV lights, and said, "In a lot of ways, life has not been kind to me. I have three children, aged two, five, and seven, and I work two jobs just to make ends meet. This park has become a safe haven where my kids and I can come to play and just spend time together. The community center with day-care facilities will mean my family—and others to come—will have opportunities that have just not been around for us.

"But more important than the change in the neighborhood is the change that has taken place inside of me. I have spent many bitter years waiting for someone else to do something for me. Now I get up every day and think about what I can do for myself and what I can do for others around me."

From my chamber window, I could view the park in the distance with the crowd surrounding the temporary platform and a number of satellite trucks ringing the perimeter. It made me think about the possibilities for my own life. It would be hard to calculate the difference we can make in the world if we simply select a goal, make a beginning, and keep on going.

In preparation for my day in court, I located the DVD marked *The Gift of Gratitude*. I slid it into the player as I anticipated Red Stevens' message for his grandson.

"When you prepare your will and a video like this, you automatically have to think about your entire life. I have been so many places and experienced so many things, it is hard to remember that I have only lived one lifetime.

"I remember, as a young man, being so poor that I had to do day labor for food to eat and had to sleep along the side of the road. I also remember being in the company of kings and presidents and knowing all of the material things this life has to offer. As I look back, I am thankful for it all.

"During what, at the time, I considered to be some of my worst experiences, I gained my fondest memories.

"Jason, this month, you are going to learn a lesson that

encompasses something that has been totally lacking in your life. That is gratitude.

"I have always found it ironic that the people in this world who have the most to be thankful for are often the least thankful, and somehow the people who have virtually nothing, many times live lives full of gratitude.

"While still in my youth, shortly after going out on my own to conquer the world, I met an elderly gentleman who today would be described as homeless. Back then, there were a lot of people who rode the rails, traveling throughout the country doing just a little bit of work here and there in order to get by. It was during the Depression, and some of these so-called hobos or tramps were well educated and had lives full of rich experiences.

"Josh and I traveled together for almost a year. He seemed very old at that time, but since I was still in my teens, I may have had a faulty perspective. He is one of the only people I ever met of whom I could honestly say, 'He never had a bad day.' Or if he did, there was certainly no outward sign of it. Traveling about as we did, we often found ourselves wet, cold, and hungry. But Josh never had anything but the best to say to everyone we met.

"Finally, when I decided to settle down in Texas and seek my fortune there, Josh and I parted company. Settling down was simply not a priority in his life. When we parted, I asked him why he was always in such good spirits. He told me that one of the great lessons his mother had left him was the legacy of The Golden List.

"He explained to me that every morning before he got up, he would lie in bed—or wherever he had been sleeping—and visualize a golden tablet on which was written ten things in his life he was especially thankful for.

He told me that his mother had done that all the days of her life and that he had never missed a day since she shared about The Golden List with him.

"Well, as I stand here today, I am proud to say I haven't missed a day since Josh shared the process with me almost sixty years ago. Some days I am thankful for the most trivial things, and other days I feel a deep sense of gratitude for my life and everything surrounding me.

"Jason, today, I am passing the legacy of The Golden List on to you. I know that it has survived well over one hundred years simply being passed from Josh's mother through Josh to me, and now to you. I don't know how Josh's mother discovered the process, so its origins may go back much further than I know.

"In any event, I am passing it on to you, and if you will be diligent in the beginning, before long it will simply become a natural part of your life, like breathing."

Once again, I called the court to order in the matter of the last will and testament of Howard "Red" Stevens. After the formalities were out of the way and Jason Stevens had taken the stand, the legendary Theodore J. Hamilton went to work.

"Jason, isn't it true that—as a part of your grandfather's bequest of The Ultimate Gift to you—he taught you about The Gift of Gratitude?"

Jason nodded and replied, "Yes, sir."

Hamilton continued. "Isn't it also true that Red Stevens shared with you a process called The Golden List?"

Once again, Jason nodded in agreement and said, "Yes, sir."

Hamilton smiled as if understanding and asked,

"Could you please share with this court about the process of The Golden List."

Jason nodded, cleared his throat, and began. "My grandfather told me about a process he had learned many years before that had made his life better. Each day, you simply think of ten things that you are thankful for."

Hamilton inquired, "Did you perform this task within the thirty days allotted to you for The Gift of Gratitude?"

"Yes, sir," Jason confirmed.

Hamilton retrieved a page from his counsel table and returned to Jason, asking, "I have here a copy of the list you made of the things you were thankful for during your Gift of Gratitude month."

Hamilton held the list out in front of Jason and said, "Can you please confirm for the court that this is a copy of the list you made in your own handwriting?"

Jason looked over the list carefully, glanced up at me, and stated, "That's my list."

Dudly interrupted, "I'll take a look at that, if you don't mind."

"Be my guest," Hamilton said with mock cordiality.

L. Myron Dudly glared at the page in contempt, retorted, "Whatever," and stomped back to his seat.

Hamilton slipped his out-of-date reading glasses onto his nose and held the page at arm's length. "I see here on that day you were thankful for your friends, your family, and The Ultimate Gift, among other things."

Hamilton looked up at Jason over the reading glasses and asked, "Does that seem right to you?"

"Yes, sir," Jason confirmed.

Hamilton folded his glasses and put them into their

ancient leather case. He glanced up at me and said, "That will be all, Your Honor."

I waved at Dudly.

L. Myron Dudly approached the witness box as if he were a homerun hitter who needed several runs in the late innings.

"Mr. Stevens, would it be true that for the majority of your life you took your wealth, position, prestige, and opportunities provided by your grandfather totally for granted?"

"That's true," Jason admitted.

"Furthermore," Dudly pressed, "isn't it true that during his life you never once thanked your grandfather and actually were ashamed of him to an extent that you wouldn't even claim him as your grandfather but wanted to palm him off as some kind of distant great uncle or something?"

Jason sighed and slowly nodded his head, stating, "Yes, that's right."

Dudly shook his head as if disappointed in an unruly child and inquired, "Then how can you expect this court to believe you understand gratitude because you made up one little list of things anyone should be grateful for on one particular day?"

"It wasn't one day," Jason replied defiantly. "I have a Golden List for every day."

Dudly exhibited false shock, saying in a ridiculous falsetto voice, "Well, excuse me. I guess you feel qualified to manage several billion dollars because you wrote down a list every day that month."

Jason shook his head and reported, "No, I have made a Golden List every day since my grandfather shared the idea with me."

Dudly laughed mockingly and asked incredulously, "You want to sit there and have us believe that every day since your grandfather's death, well over a year ago, you have taken the time to mentally formulate a list of ten things for which you are grateful?"

Jason reached inside his jacket as he spoke. "I not only thought about what I was grateful for, but I wrote it down."

A worn leather diary could be seen in Jason's hand. He held it lovingly.

Dudly quickly masked the shock he felt and said, "Let me see that book."

Jason held it out toward him. Dudly flipped through a few pages and sighed as if feeling great impatience and frustration.

"Mr. Stevens, you want to tell this court, under oath, with penalty of perjury, that you have written in that book ten things you're thankful for every day since the time your grandfather presented you with the idea of The Gift of Gratitude?"

Jason shook his head and said, "No, sir."

Dudly slapped his hands together and exclaimed, "I thought so."

But before Dudly could continue, Jason said, "This is actually my third book. The first two got filled up."

Dudly shook his head in disbelief. He said haughtily, "Well, why don't you just read us your supposed entry for today?"

Jason reverently turned the pages and began to read. "Today, I am grateful for the groundbreaking for the community center in the park. I am grateful for the single moms who made it possible. I am grateful for the people of the community who built the park. I am grateful for Jeffrey

Watkins who was willing to take my case when no one else would. I am grateful for my friend David Reese who helps me keep laughing through this difficult court case.

"I am grateful for Miss Hastings for always being there for me. I am grateful for the class at the school for the blind and the people at the senior citizens' center for teaching me a lot. I am grateful for Mr. Hamilton for being my lawyer and my friend. I am grateful to Alexia for loving me when I'm not always lovable." Jason closed the book, putting it back into his pocket, concluding, "And I'm grateful to Emily for teaching me, through her dying, how I should be living."

Dudly shuffled toward his chair, mumbling, "That's all."

The silence stretched out across my courtroom. Finally, I broke it, ruling, "It is the finding of this court that Jason Stevens has adequately demonstrated The Gift of Gratitude in his life as defined by Red Stevens. We will reconvene this hearing in a month to judge his ability to pass on his Gift of Gratitude."

Before I did anything else that day, I sat at my ridiculous behemoth of a desk in my chambers and jotted down my Golden List. I called Marie to tell her that I loved her and let her know that she was number one on my list. I knew this would be a habit that would stay with me all the days of my life.

Another month had flown by. Back in my courtroom, Jason was on the stand being questioned by Mr. Hamilton.

"Jason, how did you pass along The Gift of Gratitude this month?"

Jason recounted the story. "This month was homecoming at my Ivy League university. I never exactly graduated with any particular class, so from time to time I just show up at homecoming to see a few friends I met during my time there.

"They have a banquet each year after the football game for the alumni who are back on campus. Since this court case has gotten so much media attention, the dean of the university asked me if I would like to say a few words of greeting to everyone after the meal. I got up onstage and told them all about The Gift of Gratitude and The Golden List.

"A lot of these people are like I was. They've been given everything they ever thought they wanted so they haven't gotten a lot of what they really needed. I told them that the next step toward moving into their future and getting what they want is to reach into their past and express gratitude for what they have.

"I showed them my diary." Jason patted his pocket where the diary was kept and continued. "Many of them started jotting down lists on napkins or the backs of programs. The Gift of Gratitude I presented received a standing ovation."

Hamilton smiled and nodded confidently and then inquired, "And then what happened, Jason?"

"Well, it was a few days later that I got a call from the president of the Alumni Association. Every year, they raise money for scholarships. This year, they have endowed the Red Stevens Memorial Scholarship—which will be awarded each year—to a deserving student from the inner-city park Saturday School."

"Thank you for everything, Jason," Hamilton said warmly.

I looked toward L. Myron Dudly and the assembled legal team from Dudly, Cheetham, and Leech. Arrayed behind them were the various assorted members of the Stevens clan. There seemed to be a lot of anxiety among the entire group. It was as if they realized that the time on the ticking clock of their case, representing billions of dollars, was rapidly running out.

Dudly shakily stood and croaked, "No questions."

I stated for the record, "Hearing no opposition, this court accepts Jason Stevens' presentation of The Gift of Gratitude as presented. This court stands adjourned until 10:00 a.m. tomorrow."

Thirteen
THE LIFE OF A DAY

The ultimate life is nothing more than a series
of ultimate days. Today's the day!

I could feel the marathon known as The Red Stevens Last Will and Testament Case approaching the finish line; but as any great marathoner will tell you, just before the final phase of the twenty-six-mile ordeal, you hit an invisible but very real obstacle known as *the wall. The wall* has stolen the hopes and dreams of many a competitor.

Rex the Wonder Dog and I were taking a vigorous walk around the Howard "Red" Stevens Urban Park. Rex was expertly leading me by his leash. Since he could feel me trying to restrain him with the leash, he felt confident enough to explore any direction or change course at any time.

In life, and most certainly in walking Rex the Wonder Dog, control is an illusion. Rex and I have spent many such hours with him leading the way and me contentedly following behind. He is not nearly as young nor as fast as he used to be, but then neither am I. A veritable match made in heaven between pet and master. Rex and I just aren't sure who fills which role in that relationship.

The seasons of my life have been punctuated by first owning and then growing to love a series of loyal dogs. I have kept an informal list of things that I absurdly think I would do differently if I were King of the World. I realize that the odds of this happening are not great.

Among the many things on my list are: If I were king, we would enjoy the energy of youth when we had the wisdom of age to temper it. If I were king, winter would be shortened to a period just long enough so that we would fully appreciate spring, summer, and fall. And not the least of these, if I were king, a beloved dog would live long enough to be with you all the days of your life.

I shared with Rex my concerns and inadequate feelings surrounding the Red Stevens case. Rex listened attentively, as he always does, and looked at me with those big brown eyes that communicate, "I may not understand what you're talking about, but I know that you are more than capable of doing whatever needs to be done."

It's wonderful to have someone who always believes in you. Between Marie and Rex the Wonder Dog, I am doubly blessed.

The time finally came for me to get back to the court building and for Rex to get home and perform his unknown, but no doubt vital, tasks for the day.

~~~~~~~

I had thought the courtroom had been filled to capacity during the ten months of this case, but as we entered the eleventh and next-to-last month, Jim and Paul had to set up additional folding chairs, covering every square inch of the available space.

"Good morning," I said to everyone. "Today, we are here to consider The Gift of a Day as outlined in The Ultimate Gift left as a bequest from Red Stevens to his grandson, Jason. It's all yours, Mr. Hamilton."

Theodore J. Hamilton called Jason Stevens to the stand, and I reminded Jason and everyone that his testimony was still under oath.

Hamilton began. "Mr. Stevens, were you given a lesson and an opportunity to perform tasks by your grandfather regarding The Gift of a Day?"

Jason nodded and confirmed, "Yes, I was."

"Share that experience with us," Hamilton prompted.

"My grandfather told me to think about how I would spend the last day of my life."

Hamilton smiled, encouraging Jason as he continued. "Well, I decided I wanted to get up early in the morning and think about my Golden List of things I was thankful for, but on my last day, it would be a lot longer than ten things. I would want to have a really nice breakfast with a group of friends outside on a patio. I hope we would talk about how all of us could get the most out of our day and our lives. Then I decided I would call a lot of people who have meant a great deal to me in my life and thank them—like Gus Caldwell, the people at the library in South America, and the kids at the Red Stevens Boys Home."

Jason paused, took a deep breath, and sighed heavily. He looked at his extended family members across the courtroom and said, "I decided I would like to call all of my family members, thanking them for the good times and apologizing for the bad ones. Next, I decided I would take a friend to lunch and talk about the dreams he has for his life.

"That night, I decided it would be good to have a special banquet for all my friends. I would tell them how much they meant to me and share with them all the gifts in The Ultimate Life. We would videotape the banquet so that we could share that time and message with other people as they consider their lives."

Hamilton paused and then said, "Jason, I want to thank you for sharing that."

Hamilton returned to his seat at the counsel table, and I offered Mr. Dudly an opportunity to question Jason.

"So, Mr. Stevens, let me get this straight. To prove that you understood The Gift of a Day, you made up a group of activities that you thought were important to do on your last day."

Jason nodded and confirmed, "Yes, sir."

Dudly continued. "If these items are so important that you would want to be sure you did them on your last day, how many of them have you done to date?"

Jason fidgeted for a few moments, cleared his throat nervously, and said, "Well, I haven't done them all. It's not easy to master The Gift of a Day, but I have done a lot of them. I've called and written friends I wouldn't have contacted without learning The Gift of a Day. I am more conscious about thanking everybody for what they have done for me in my life, and I have dedicated myself to passing on my grandfather's Ultimate Gift."

Dudly, sensing weakness, circled for the kill. "So, Mr. Stevens, if it is so important to pack as many things as possible into each day of our lives—and certainly the last

day of our lives—can you tell us why, after your grandfather's
lesson and after having a whole month to think about it,
you didn't plan anything for the entire afternoon of your
mythical last day of life?"

Dudly beamed triumphant, and Jason looked down at
his feet and mumbled, "I did have plans for the afternoon."

"Oh, you did, did you?" Dudly stated confrontationally.
"Well, if it's so important, why don't you share those plans
with us now and tell us why you didn't present them when you
were asked to as a part of your sworn testimony."

Jason glanced uneasily toward the counsel table, let
out a long breath, and said, "More than a year ago when,
through a video, my grandfather taught me about The Gift
of a Day, I prioritized every minute of what I would have
planned then for the last day of my life. I had intended to
include plans of spending the afternoon in the park, at a
museum, and out on a sailboat in the harbor."

Dudly rubbed his hands together in glee and asked,
"Well, Mr. Stevens, if all that's so important, why did you
fail to even mention it in your sworn statement earlier?"

"I had planned to do all those things with Emily," Jason
said as a tear rolled down his cheek.

The sounds of several people softly crying could be
heard as Jason continued. "But I guess what I really learned
from planning my last day is the fact that everything's
important because for some of us, like Emily, it really is our
last day."

Dudly looked like a giant balloon that had just lost all
of its air. He shook his head and plopped into his chair.

I tapped my gavel and spoke. "This court finds in
favor of Jason Stevens. We will reconvene in thirty days to
conclude the matter relating to The Gift of a Day."

I watched Red Stevens teaching his grandson on the screen before me.

"Jason, I want you to know that as I was contemplating the ultimate gift I wanted to present you through my will, I spent a lot of time thinking about you. I think you gained a permanent place in my Golden List each morning. I am thankful that you and I share a family heritage, and I sense a spark in you that I have always felt in myself. We are somehow kindred spirits beyond just our family ties.

"As I have been going through the process of creating my will and thinking about my life and my death, I have considered all of the elements in my life that have made it special. I have reviewed many memories, and I carry them with me like a treasure.

"When you face your own mortality, you contemplate how much of life you have lived versus how much you have left. It is like the sand slipping through an hourglass. I know that at some point I will live the last day of my life. I have been thinking about how I would want to live that day or what I would do if I had just one day left to live. I have come to realize that if I can get that picture in my mind of maximizing one day, I will have mastered the essence of living, because life is nothing more than a series of days. If we can learn how to live one day to its fullest, our lives will be rich and meaningful."

I thought about The Gift of a Day and what I would do with my last day on earth. I told the court clerk to reschedule any hearings I had the next day, and then I called Marie and told her that tomorrow was reserved for The Gift of a Day.

During dinner that night, we talked about all the special things we wanted to do the following day.

We were up early in the morning. We had a special breakfast and walked, talked, and enjoyed a show in the company of some special friends. That night, we watched the sunset together, as it is Marie's favorite time of the day.

As the special day drew to a close, we were both struck by the fact that—although the day had, indeed, been a gift—all of the things we did could have been done on most any other day. I knew the rest of our lives would be different because the rest of our days would be different.

~~~~~

Thirty days came and went, and Jason Stevens was back in my courtroom in the witness box. Hamilton asked him to explain how he had passed on The Gift of a Day.

Jason said, "I thought about the people that might benefit most from The Gift of a Day, and I realized it would be people who didn't have many days left.

"There is a place called The Crossroads Center run by a wonderful family. They help hospice patients experience one special day. I decided to help them with their work so more people could experience The Gift of a Day."

Jason organized his thoughts and went on. "There was a one-hundred-year-old man who wanted to ride a motorcycle. We got him in a sidecar with a helmet and goggles and toured him around the countryside. He had an amazing experience, and his picture riding in the sidecar made it into the newspapers. I think a lot of other people will begin thinking about each day as a gift.

"Then there was a terminal cancer patient who had never seen the ocean. I helped make arrangements for her to travel to the shore. She strolled up and down the beach and just looked out at the vast ocean.

"There was a person with just a few days left to live who wanted to meet a well-known singer and entertainer. I got in contact with the record company, and they made arrangements for the patient to sit on the front row at a concert and go back stage afterward to have dinner with the star.

"And, finally, I asked the Crossroads people to work with me on teaching The Gift of a Day to people who have not been diagnosed with a terminal condition. Once a week, they do a seminar on The Gift of a Day. They will be teaching it next week at the Saturday School. I think this is important for everyone."

"I do, too," Hamilton agreed and passed it on to me to tell Dudly to ask his questions.

"Mr. Stevens, if I understand your story, you didn't really help these people directly. You worked with an existing organization."

"Yes, sir," Jason stated.

"So what did you do on your own to help other people understand The Gift of a Day that your grandfather gave you?"

Jason was flustered. "I didn't do anything on my own. Just like I didn't build the park on my own. I believe my grandfather would say that The Gift of a Day is too big to pass along all by yourself, so I got some help."

Dudly asked doubtfully, "So, do you believe you have passed on The Gift of a Day, and are you convinced you have an understanding of it yourself?"

Jason chuckled and said, "About all I can say is I understand enough for today, but I'm still learning because, if I'm lucky, tomorrow will be another day."

Dudly knew he was beaten on this hurdle, and he retreated—hoping for better results later.

"Let the record show that Jason Stevens is deemed to understand and to have passed on The Gift of a Day. This court stands adjourned until 10:00 a.m. tomorrow when we will conduct a hearing on the final element—The Gift of Love."

Fourteen

THE LIFE OF LOVE

The ultimate life is locked away inside each of us.
Love is the key.

The TV networks were carrying around-the-clock coverage of the final stages of the Red Stevens case. As I was flipping through the channels, I noticed a panel of law school professors debating the issues. It got very heated, and the only thing all of the legal scholars agreed upon was the fact that this case was like a twelve-round heavyweight championship fight. You could lose eleven rounds in a row and score a knockout punch in the twelfth and walk away with the prize.

I couldn't help but feel the gravity of what hung in the balance, dependent upon my decision. Either the entire Stevens family would lose the millions of their inheritance, or Jason would lose the control of billions that Red Stevens had set aside in trust to do good work.

There just didn't seem to be any middle ground.

I spent a lot of time seeking the wisdom to find some sort of compromise, but when it was all boiled down, it seemed there was no way out other than the fact that there would be a winner and a loser. I couldn't believe that this was what Red Stevens would have wanted.

I stared at the clock in my chambers. Time seemed to stand still; but, finally, it was 10:00. I slipped on my judicial robes, paused for a brief moment of silence and reflection, and then went through the mahogany door.

As I climbed up to the bench, I could feel the tension in the room. I had never been in a situation where, financially, there was this much at stake. I wasn't sure if any other judge had either.

I settled into my chair and wondered what the results would be when I once again stood up from my seat. I pounded my gavel and declared, "Ladies and gentlemen, this court is now in session. It has been a long road for all of us to get to this final matter in the Red Stevens' Last Will and Testament Case.

"I want to thank the attorneys involved for working professionally and tenaciously to represent their various clients. I, also, want to thank my courtroom family, Jim and Paul, who ably serve this court as bailiffs, and Scott, who I believe to be the best court reporter in the business. Finally, I want to thank my mentor and friend Judge Eldridge who presided over this courtroom for many years. He gave me a priceless example and some enormous shoes to fill. I do my best each day, as I will today, to live up to the standard he set.

"All of us here today know what is at stake. Indeed, thanks to our media friends both here in the courtroom and elsewhere, everyone around the world knows what is at stake. I would still caution everyone that this is an official and legal court proceeding. I will hold each person involved to the standard of respect and order this matter deserves.

"First I will call on Mr. Theodore J. Hamilton of Hamilton, Hamilton, and Hamilton to make his case."

I locked eyes with Hamilton and said, "Sir, it is, indeed, a privilege to have you in our courtroom and in our profession."

Hamilton nodded and said in acknowledgment, "Your Honor, I want to thank you and everyone involved in this case for giving my client nothing more or less than an opportunity to plead his case and have it judged fairly."

Hamilton paused, shuffled a few papers arrayed on the table before him, and intoned, "Your Honor, once again we call Jason Stevens to the stand to give testimony in this matter."

Hamilton strode toward Jason seated in the witness box and asked, "Mr. Stevens, in the final month of the yearlong quest that your grandfather bequeathed to you in his will, did you have occasion to learn about The Gift of Love?"

Jason nodded solemnly, replying, "Yes, sir, I did."

"And did you then have the opportunity to undertake a task that would help you experience The Gift of Love for yourself?"

Once again, Jason acknowledged, "Yes, sir."

Hamilton walked back to the counsel table and stood next to his chair. He said, "Jason, can you share that experience with this court today?"

Hamilton sat down as Jason began.

"My grandfather taught me that you can't have love in one area of your life without having love in all areas of your life. So, for The Gift of Love, I was asked to consider for the month each of the gifts I had been given and how love played an integral part in each of them."

Hamilton inquired, "And Jason, were you able to complete that task successfully?"

"Yes, sir, I was," Jason responded.

Hamilton prompted, "Jason, would you share briefly how The Gift of Love played out in each gift you received from your grandfather?"

Jason thought for a minute and said, "Well, in The Gift of Work, I learned that Gus Caldwell and my grandfather had a true respect and love for one another, and I learned how important it is to love your work. In The Gift of Money, I learned that to love money is a dead-end path; but if you love people and use money, you can truly make a difference. In The Gift of Friends, I learned that in order to have a friend you've got to be a friend. You must be willing to give love before you demand to receive it. In The Gift of Learning, I found out that the love of learning is a lifelong pursuit. It simply never ends. In The Gift of Problems, I learned that—while the circumstance may be difficult or even seem impossible—when you love yourself and those around you and focus on the things you have been given, a problem viewed through love is an opportunity. In The Gift of Family, I discovered the difference between what we like and what we love. We don't always like our family, but we can always love them through every problem and circumstance.

"In The Gift of Laughter, I learned that hatred disappears when you laugh, and then love can find its way into every situation. In The Gift of Dreams, I discovered that we each have passions and destinies inside of us. Love can unlock the potential that we have on the inside. In The Gift of Giving, I found out that we should always love everyone enough to be a giver, and love is the one thing that the more you give, the more you have. It is an inexhaustible fountain. In The Gift of Gratitude, I learned that we have received many blessings in our lives, and the only way we can show true love is to be grateful for what we've been given. In The Gift of a Day, I learned that it is impossible to love life unless you love today. If we fill each day with love, we will always have enough of everything."

I couldn't believe that, with so many people in my courtroom, there was a total prolonged, absolute silence.

Eventually, Theodore J. Hamilton rose and declared, "Your Honor, I shall not diminish the power of what we have heard by going on any farther. We rest our case with respect to this matter."

I nodded to Mr. Hamilton then swung my gaze to L. Myron Dudly. I stated, "Sir, you now have the floor in this proceeding."

Dudly sat motionless for an uncomfortable length of time. I wondered if he had heard me call on him, but eventually he stood and inevitably made his way toward the witness box like a man walking his last mile. As I look back on it, I will have to admit that Dudly actually did an admirable job against formidable odds.

He cleared his throat, nodded to me, and leapt in. "Mr. Stevens, as this is your grandfather's last will and testament that is being argued and contested before this court, let's examine your relationship with him as it relates to The Gift of Love."

Dudly paced back and forth gaining confidence and momentum. "Mr. Stevens, would you say before this court that you loved your grandfather for the years of your life that he was with you?"

Jason sighed deeply, leaned forward in his chair, and explained, "I didn't know how to love anybody, including myself, until I got The Gift of Love from my grandfather, so I would have to say honestly I did not love my grandfather while he was alive."

Dudly sensed a glimmer of hope. It seemed to be somehow communicated to the Stevens family as they appeared immediately hopeful.

Mr. Dudly pounded the rail in front of Jason and thundered, "Young man, if that be the case as you have testified under oath, how in the name of all we hold to be legal, fair, and just can you say that you loved your grandfather as outlined in his Gift of Love and that you are entitled to this inheritance?"

Dudly glared at Jason, anticipating victory.

Eventually, Jason spoke. "Mr. Dudly, I will admit I did not love my grandfather when he was alive, nor did I in any way deserve the love he had for me; but somehow through his death and The Ultimate Gift he left to me, I learned to love him and everyone around me. None of us can ever deserve love. We can just treasure it and give it away."

Dudly was shaken but was still hoping for a long shot. He addressed me.

"Your Honor, we have no further questions for this individual. As he has already admitted in his sworn testimony that he never loved his grandfather during all the years of his grandfather's life, we can do nothing other than ask this court to make a swift and certain ruling on behalf of my clients and restore to them their rightful inheritance."

Dudly slid into his seat behind the counsel table.

Several of his Dudly, Cheetham, and Leech colleagues patted him on the back and flashed him the victory sign. The Stevens clan collectively leaned forward in their seats with anticipation.

I was torn as I weighed the issues before me. Love is impossible to define, so it defies judgment.

I pounded my gavel and stated, "This court will take our noon recess and reconvene at 2:00 p.m."

I fled through the mahogany door into my chambers. I spoke aloud to the DVD marked *The Gift of Love* I held in my hand, saying, "Red, if you ever had anything profound to say on the subject, there's an old judge here that would really appreciate it."

I slid the final DVD into the player and welcomed Red Stevens to my chambers for the final time.

"Jason, in this last month, I'm going to introduce you to the one part of my Ultimate Gift that encompasses all of the other gifts as well as everything good you will ever do, have, or know in your life. That is The Gift of Love.

"Anything good, honorable, and desirable in life is based on love. Anything bad or evil is simply life without the love involved. Love is a misused and overused term in our society. It is applied to any number of frivolous things and pursuits; but the love I am talking about in The Gift of Love is the goodness that comes only from God. Not everyone believes or acknowledges that. And that's okay. I still know that real love comes from him—whether or not we know it.

"Jason, we've come a long way in this Ultimate Gift. I want you to know, above all, that in spite of all the mistakes I made and the many times I failed you, Jason Stevens, that your grandfather loved you."

I spoke aloud to Red Stevens on the screen. "Thank you for your help."

I hoped that somehow he knew that I would do the very best I could for his whole family.

———————

At 2:00 sharp, I heard a brief rap on my mahogany door. It opened enough for Scott, my court reporter, to stick his head in and say, "Your Honor, they've all been sitting and waiting for almost a half hour. I've never seen anything like it."

Back in the courtroom, I prepared to deliver—if not the most important—what I knew would become the most famous judgment of my life. I tapped my gavel, but it was wholly unnecessary as the court was in order, and every eye was focused on me.

"It is the considered decision of this court that Jason Stevens did not love his grandfather at any point during Red Stevens' life. Only after his death was Red Stevens able to teach The Gift of Love to Jason, therefore making it possible for Jason Stevens to love his grandfather. Although this arrangement is highly unconventional and completely undesirable, it does meet both the letter and the intent of the last will and testament of Howard 'Red' Stevens."

It was at that point I did have to pound my gavel repeatedly for order. Shouts of protest and anger could be heard from the Stevens family. My bailiffs, Jim and Paul, materialized at the front of the courtroom, and I felt glad for their presence.

I produced an ominous stare that I leveled at those assembled in my courtroom and spoke.

"Let me be absolutely clear that we will have order in this court, or these gentlemen before you will clear this courtroom, and a few of you may have the opportunity to experience the hospitality of our official house of detention next door."

I let my words settle over everyone and concluded, "This court will stand adjourned for thirty days, during which time Jason Stevens will be given an opportunity to demonstrate that he has the ability and aptitude to pass along The Gift of Love he received from Howard 'Red' Stevens through The Ultimate Gift."

Although we had finished for that day in the courtroom, the matter was far from settled.

Fifteen

THE ULTIMATE LIFE

A life lived well is The Ultimate Gift.

I would not have believed it possible, but the media intensity increased, the tension and anxiety built, and it was hard for me or anyone else in the court building to get anything done that whole month.

Finally, it was the last day. For better or worse, it would all be finished this day. I was still searching my heart, my mind, and my soul for that elusive middle ground or some way to pull off one of Judge Eldridge's famous win/win decisions.

I pounded my gavel and called the court to order, and then it happened. The legend himself, Theodore J. Hamilton, rose and beckoned, "Your Honor, may it please the court, I have a written motion to present that has direct bearing on these proceedings."

Mr. Hamilton walked toward me holding out one

single sheet of paper. L. Myron Dudly jumped to his feet and cried, "Your Honor, we object to any motions being made or heard by the court without said motion being reviewed by counsel for my clients."

Hamilton paused in mid-stride, lowered the single sheet he held in his hand, and said, "Your Honor, I beg the court's indulgence in this matter, but I will stake my entire reputation as a jurist and practitioner of the law. If Your Honor will merely review this brief document, I believe it will all become clear."

Dudly repeated, "I object."

As Hamilton began to speak, I raised my hand to both of them for silence.

"Mr. Dudly, I am going to allow this motion to be presented in this fashion, giving Mr. Hamilton the widest possible latitude based on his experience and reputation before this court."

Dudly slammed his open hand on the counsel table in frustration and dropped into his chair in resignation.

I then pointed the business end of my gavel at the one and only Theodore J. Hamilton and continued, "But, Counselor, let me warn you, if you are leading this court down an inappropriate path, I will react with every measure and course open to me to the full extent of the law."

Hamilton nodded, agreeing to the conditions, stepped forward, and handed the single sheet to me. I scanned it once then read it again and, finally, reviewed it a third time to be sure my eyes were not deceiving me.

I nodded to Mr. Hamilton and said, "This motion is accepted as presented. You may call Mr. Stevens to the stand."

Dudly sprang from his chair, knocking over a pitcher of

water, and nearly upending the counsel table. He spread his arms wide, pleading, "Your Honor, there has been a motion before this court, both presented and accepted, without my clients having their right to due process in the matter."

I nodded in understanding and remarked, "Mr. Dudly, I do acknowledge your position and ask you and your clients to indulge the court for a few moments."

Jason Stevens had taken the stand, and Hamilton approached, asking, "Jason, would you please share with the court your expression of The Gift of Love as presented to you by your grandfather, Red Stevens."

Jason said, "I did not learn how to love my grandfather or anyone else in my family until, through The Ultimate Gift, I received The Gift of Love. Love both gives and receives forgiveness, so at this time, I would like to ask each member of my family to forgive me for many years of not showing them respect, much less love."

Dudly thundered, "Your Honor, that's all well and good, but ..."

I pounded my gavel and held up my other hand for Dudly to be silent.

"Your objection is overruled, counselor," I stated. I looked back down at Jason, and he continued.

"In addition to asking for forgiveness, I also wanted to ask the judge if I could try to, in some small way, express my Gift of Love to my family."

Jason looked up at me and asked, "Can I tell them?"

I nodded yes, and Jason Stevens testified.

"I asked Mr. Hamilton to prepare a document and present it to Judge Davis so that, if the judge ruled in my favor, my family would not lose all of the assets they have inherited."

A multitude of questions and uncertainty could be heard throughout the courtroom. I pounded my gavel for order and nodded toward Mr. Hamilton.

"Jason, in order to clarify, are we to understand that you are asking your family to forgive you and you're giving them back their entire inheritance, regardless of the outcome of this case?"

Jason's gaze moved to each member of his family in the courtroom as he stated, "Yes. These people are my family, and at the end of this day, no matter the outcome, they will still be my family, and I want them to know I love them, and I want them to have the inheritance my grandfather gave to them."

Everyone sat in stunned silence. Finally, Jason turned to me and spoke.

"Your Honor, can I ask you a question?"

I chuckled and said, "Son, after a year of answering everyone else's questions, I think you're entitled to one."

Jason asked, "Is it true that judges can marry people? I mean can you perform a wedding?"

I laughed aloud and replied, "Son, I haven't married anybody since before you were born, but it doesn't mean I can't do it."

Jason declared, "Well then, sir, if it's agreeable to Alexia, I think we would like you to do the honors as soon as possible."

Alexia rose from her chair at the counsel table, nodding her head vigorously, saying, "Yes. Yes. Yes."

Applause rose from the gallery. I let it die down and then rapped my gavel and declared, "We will address the marriage situation shortly, but first I have a decision to hand down.

"It is the judgment of this court after reviewing each aspect of The Ultimate Gift as set forth in the last will and testament of Howard 'Red' Stevens that Jason Stevens is, indeed, the legal heir of his grandfather's estate and entitled to be awarded with all of his grandfather's assets by this court.

"His earlier motion has been accepted by the court, thus restoring all previously held assets to the Stevens family.

"Jason Stevens, you will have full control of several billion dollars in the Red Stevens Charitable Trust. This court hopes you will act responsibly with it as your grandfather would were he here."

I smiled at Jason and concluded, "And son, after spending more than a year with you here in the courtroom, I don't believe there's a better man anywhere for the job."

That which was the end was also the beginning.

It was only a few days later that I was enjoying a glorious sunrise in the Howard "Red" Stevens Urban Park. I couldn't believe so many people had gathered at that hour. All of the single moms and their kids from the day-care co-op had showed up, along with two busloads of students from the school for the blind. There were numerous wheelchairs and walkers in evidence, demonstrating a great turnout from the senior citizens center. The inner-city kids from the Saturday School were down front, along with many other friends and guests. I recognized the Stevens clan, fully decked out for the occasion. Of course, Theodore J. Hamilton and Margaret Hastings were there, along with Jeffrey Watkins. And, most amazing, was the fact that all of the partners and support staff from the entire legal firm of

Dudly, Cheetham, and Leech were there.

Despite the best efforts to keep the media back from the proceedings, many of them had filtered through into the crowd. And standing before me, with as much joy and promise as the sunrise, were Jason and Alexia.

After welcoming everyone and making a few initial statements, I asked, "Jason, do you take Alexia to be your lawfully wedded wife?"

"I do," Jason declared.

"And Alexia," I asked, "do you take Jason to be your lawfully wedded husband?"

She gazed up at him lovingly and promised, "I do."

I concluded, "I now pronounce you husband and wife. You may kiss the bride, and please accept my most sincere wishes for a healthy, happy, and Ultimate Life."

About the Author

Jim Stovall is among the most sought-after motivational speakers anywhere. Despite failing eyesight and eventual blindness, Jim Stovall has been a national champion Olympic weight lifter, a successful investment broker, and an entrepreneur. He is the cofounder and president of the Narrative Television Network, which makes movies and television accessible for America's 13 million blind and visually impaired people and their families. Although NTN was originally designed for the blind and visually impaired, more than 60 percent of its nationwide audience is made up of fully sighted people who simply enjoy the programming. The network's programming is also available free of charge, 24 hours a day, via the Internet at www.NarrativeTV.com.

Jim Stovall hosts the network's talk show, *NTN Showcase.* His guests have included Katharine Hepburn, Jack Lemmon, Carol Channing, Steve Allen, and Eddie Albert, as well as many others. The Narrative Television Network has received an Emmy Award and an International Film and Video Award among its many industry honors. It has grown to include more than 1,200 cable systems and broadcast stations, reaching more than 35 million homes in the United States, and it is shown in eleven foreign countries.

Jim Stovall joined the ranks of Walt Disney, Orson Welles, and four U.S. presidents when he was selected as one of the Ten Outstanding Young Americans by the U.S. Junior Chamber of Commerce in 1994. He has appeared on *Good Morning America* and CNN and has been featured in *Reader's Digest, TV Guide,* and *Time* magazines. He is the author of previous books titled *You Don't Have to Be Blind to See*, *Success Secrets of Super Achievers*, *The Way I See the World*, and the prequel to this book entitled *The Ultimate Gift*. *The Ultimate Gift* has sold in excess of 2 million copies in more than a dozen languages and has been made into a major motion picture starring James Garner, Lee Meriwether, Brian Dennehy, and Abigail Breslin. The President's Committee on Equal Opportunity selected Jim Stovall as the 1997 Entrepreneur of the Year. In June 2000, Jim Stovall joined notables such as President Jimmy Carter, Nancy Reagan, and Mother Teresa when he received the International Humanitarian Award.

Jim Stovall can be reached at 918-627-1000.

after words

... a little more ...

When a delightful concert comes to an end,
the orchestra might offer an encore.
When a fine meal comes to an end,
it's always nice to savor a bit of dessert.
When a great story comes to an end,
we think you may want to linger.
And so, we offer ...

AfterWords—just a little something more after you
have finished a David C. Cook novel.
We invite you to stay awhile in the story.
Thanks for reading!

Turn the page for ...

• An excerpt from *The King's Legacy,*
the new novel by Jim Stovall

A Story of Wisdom
for the Ages

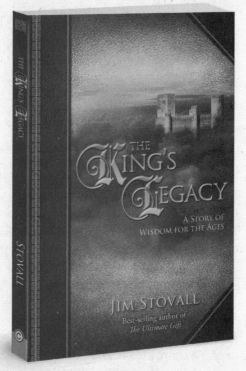

The new novel from Jim Stovall

Now available

800.323.7543 • DavidCCook.com

David C Cook
transforming lives together

CHAPTER ONE

THE TRIBUTE

Material possessions will all pass away, but
the Wisdom of the Ages will last forever.

ONCE UPON a time, there was an enchanted kingdom in a land far, far away. The kingdom was ruled by a benevolent and much-loved king. He had led his people through many difficult times, and they had finally reached a golden age of peace, prosperity, and happiness.

The king summoned all of his wise men together and said, "Now that our land is enjoying a season of prosperity and peace, I wish to leave a permanent legacy of my reign as your ruler."

The king went on to tell his wise men that he would like their best thoughts and ideas about what he could do to create a fitting tribute to all the people of the kingdom and his reign as their leader. Each of the wise men left the Throne Room determined to come up with the best idea to present to the king, as they all knew that the king's chosen action would be remembered for generations.

On the appointed day and hour, the wise men reconvened in the Throne Room.

The king said, "I want to hear your suggestions one at a time, so that I might determine what would be a fitting legacy for me to leave in honor of my reign as king."

The first wise man approached the steps leading to the throne, bowed with dignity, and began. "Your Highness, since the beginning of recorded history, great rulers have left magnificent feats of architecture as tributes to their greatness. One need only look to the east and think of the great pyramids that have stood for generations and will remain throughout time, paying homage to the pharaohs."

The wise man bowed again and backed away from the throne.

The king fell silent and was lost in deep thought, then said, "I am pleased with your suggestion as it has much merit. Indeed, a great edifice could stand for thousands of years to proclaim the greatness of our people and my reign as their king."

The second wise man approached the throne and bowed reverently. He said, "Oh great king, if I may humbly suggest that a gold coin be designed and minted bearing your image and in your honor. This coin could be distributed throughout the kingdom and, carried along the trade routes as if by friendly winds, it would be distributed around the world signifying your power and majesty."

The king nodded and smiled. He seemed pleased with this suggestion also. He then beckoned the next wise man to approach. The wise man dutifully bowed and said, "Your highness, may I suggest that a monument of heretofore unknown proportion be erected in your image. Great reflecting pools and immense gardens would surround the statue. People would travel from the four corners of the earth to marvel at its splendor and pay respect and tribute to your greatness."

The king smiled and stated, "Each of these suggestions has been well thought out and presented. Before I go to deliberate my final decision, are there any other suggestions?"

After a long pause, the eldest wise man stepped forward. The king smiled and said, "My great and wise adviser, you have been with me from the beginning of my reign to this day, and you have always served me well. What say you in this matter?"

The elderly wise man replied quietly, "Your Highness, may I suggest that each of my colleagues has proposed a fitting tribute to your greatness in the traditional sense; however, great buildings, gold coins, and monuments serve as tributes to other rulers from other days. May I humbly offer my suggestion? Something altogether different?"

The king nodded in assent.

"The one thing that could pay tribute to your greatness for thousands of years to come would be the proclamation of the Wisdom of the Ages. This would be an opportunity for you, oh great one, to communicate the greatest secret of the known world to benefit all humanity.

"Buildings and coins and statues will all pass away, but the Wisdom of the Ages would last forever. This would, indeed, be a fitting tribute to the king I humbly serve."

The king fell into deep thought. Finally, he told all of his servants and the wise men to leave him so that he might choose the tribute most fitting to his reign as their king.

CHAPTER FIVE

THE POET

*All poetry does not contain wisdom, but at the
heart of all wisdom, one will find poetry.*

THE THRONE ROOM became quiet as the king entered through his ornate door, climbed the steps of the dais, and settled himself upon his throne. Before he could signal the doorman to usher in the next citizen to set forth his version of the Wisdom of the Ages, a voice hailed from the gallery where the wise men were seated.

The king called out in annoyance, "Who spoke there? Step forward and be heard."

The youngest of the wise men separated himself from the gallery, walked into the carpeted aisle, and approached the king. He bowed respectfully, and the king beckoned him to speak.

"Your Royal Majesty, we have heard the wisdom of

the merchant and the wisdom of the soldier. It is very clear that many wise thoughts have been presented to us for consideration. If we continue to hear more each day, I fear we may confuse the issue at hand. Would it not be more prudent for your wise men to deliberate and establish your proclamation of the Wisdom of the Ages now? Certainly the Wisdom of the Ages must have been heard in this room within the last two days."

The king leaned back in his throne and contemplated. Then he addressed the rest of the wise men seated in the gallery.

"Does my council of wise men agree with their young colleague? Have we, indeed, heard enough?"

As the king awaited an answer, an uneasy silence fell over the room. Finally, the eldest and most trusted wise man approached the king. The king nodded to his old friend, who spoke.

"Your Highness, as always I welcome the opportunity to be heard by you and have you consider my thoughts. My young colleague is arguably the best educated among the wise men; however, at times he suffers from the delusion of many young, well-educated people, thinking that all there is to know is already known. I would submit to you that wisdom is boundless, immense, and eternal. If we are to distill the Wisdom of the Ages into one proclamation for all time, we must hear every bit of thought from as many sources as possible."

The king thanked his old friend and dismissed the youngest wise man with a wave. He rose and surveyed the assemblage.

"Once again, my old friend has served me well.

The undertaking of establishing and proclaiming the Wisdom of the Ages is a profound and awesome task. We must, therefore, hear from all our citizens who wish to speak."

The king resumed his place on his throne and signaled the doorman. A young man entered and slowly walked up the center aisle of the Throne Room. He was dressed in a somewhat casual and haphazard method, particularly for someone approaching the throne of the king. The young man bowed uneasily and began to speak.

"O King, I am a poet, a simple man of words, thoughts, feelings, and ideas. In your search for the Wisdom of the Ages, you must consider the fact that a profound and wise thought is accepted as such only when it can be delivered in a meaningful fashion. All poetry certainly does not contain wisdom, but I believe at the heart of all wisdom, one will find poetry. Throughout recorded history, the poets and artisans of the word have been those who have laid down the thoughts and feelings of their time.

"Wisdom must stir people's hearts and souls to action, because without action wisdom is nothing more than a theory. It becomes practical only when that wisdom is applied. Therefore, I say that the Wisdom of the Ages is a collection of words and phrases that will stir men's hearts to reach for and achieve their highest ideals. Wisdom is as wisdom does.

"We all have come to know people that we perceive to be wise, but they are wise because of the things they do, not simply because of what they say. While a wise man may share his ideas, they will only be accepted if he himself is known as one who acts upon them in his daily life."

The poet looked up at the king seeking approval. The king smiled at him and motioned for him to continue. The young poet reached into his tunic and withdrew a worn piece of parchment. He asked, "May I set forth these words for your consideration?"

The king nodded.

The poet glanced down at his parchment. He seemed to grow in stature, and his chest swelled with pride as he began to read.

If I am to dream, let me dream magnificently.
Let me dream grand and lofty thoughts and
 ideals
That are worthy of me and my best efforts.

If I am to strive, let me strive mightily.
Let me spend myself and my very being
In a quest for that magnificent dream.

And if I am to stumble, let me stumble but
 persevere.
Let me learn, grow, and expand myself to join
 the battle,
Renewed for another day and another day and
 another day.

If I am to win, as I must, let me do so with
 honor and gratitude—
Honor and gratitude for those people and things
 that

Made winning possible and so very sweet.

For each of us has been given life as an empty
    plot of ground,
But on that hallowed ground are the four
    cornerstones of a great life:
The ability to dream, to strive, to stumble but
    persevere, and to win.

The common man sees his plot of ground as little
    more
Than a place to sit and ponder the things that
    will never be.
But the uncommon man sees his plot of ground
    as a castle,
A cathedral, a place of learning and healing.

For the uncommon man understands that in
    these four cornerstones
The Almighty has given us anything—and
    everything.

The silence in the Throne Room was broken as the
king began to applaud. The assemblage joined in the
acclamation. The young man held the worn piece of
parchment up as a gift for the king. The king climbed
down the stairs of the dais and accepted the parchment.
He then gave the poet an immense jeweled box that
had adorned the table next to the throne.

The poet bowed humbly, held the box, and gazed

at it, saying, "Your Highness, it has value beyond compare."

The king was heard to say, "Yes, it does, and I shall treasure it always," as he placed the worn piece of parchment on the table beside the throne.